STORMY NIGHTS

STORMS OF BLACKWOOD BOOK TWO

USA TODAY BESTSELLING AUTHOR

ELLE MIDDAUGH

STORMY NIGHTS

STORMS OF BLACKWOOD BOOK TWO

Edited by: Hot Tree Editing
Published by: Moon Storm Publishing LLC
Cover Designed by: Cover Reveal Designs

To anyone out there
who's ever felt like you're not enough...
You are enough.
This is for you.

CHAPTER 1

A LEXIS

THERE WERE A MILLION SCENARIOS IN WHICH I'D IMAGINED Adam crashing back into my life.

Riding in like a knight in shining armor. Throwing rocks at my shack in the middle of the night. Randomly bumping into me on the street. To name just a few.

But I never once imagined he'd emerge from the ashes of my *dead pet sloth*.

"Do you have any idea how *fucking* long I've been trying to die?" he asked me.

Of course I didn't. How could I have possibly known that he was the same suicidal sloth that took baths with knives, fell headfirst out of trees, and drank cleaning supplies for fun?

But for some reason, I said none of those things. Instead, the first words that came out of my mouth were, "You shit on me!"

"Are you kidding me right now, Sweets?" Adam, or I guess *Asher*, argued in a heated tone. "Way back when you first arrived at Blackwood Palace? When you were ogling my brothers right in front of me? It was a sloth-like instinct."

"It was a shitty instinct."

Literally.

I glanced from face to handsome face, trying to find the family resemblance, and pretty much failing. Cal was tall, blond-haired, blue-eyed, and built like a mountain. Dan was slightly shorter than the others but still at least a whole head taller than me, with pale green eyes, light brown hair, and a near-constant cheeky smirk. Ben was richly tanned with dark brown hair, chocolatey brown eyes, and a sweet demeanor. Rob was burly and brooding, with black hair and dark stubble, stormy gray eyes, and tattoos covering most of his delicious body.

And then there was...*Asher*. Probably the leanest of the brothers, but still packing some stunning abs and biceps. His hair was light brown, like Dan's, but featherier. His eyes were a rich amber color, and his overall disposition was playful. Or at least, it used to be.

In fact, none of the brothers really looked related in the slightest, except for the fact that they were all freaking gorgeous. Maybe that sneaky servant was right; maybe they *were* immaculately conceived by the gods themselves?

Cal pulled the shirt off his back and handed it to Asher, who immediately covered the front of his nakedness. A shame, really. Though it was nice to have the Sky Prince shirtless too.

"What's *shitty*," Asher emphasized, "was watching my girl drool over my brothers."

"She's not *your* girl anymore," Rob spoke up, turning the conversation in a deadly direction. My stomach flip-flopped

2

as I glanced between them. "She's bonded to us, and we're all committed to each other."

Asher narrowed his amber eyes. "I heard. You said, and I quote, 'This bond is between Alexis and us Storms.' But the last time I checked, I was a Storm too."

"You're also an ex-boyfriend," Rob argued, crossing his burly, tattooed arms, "which was strictly forbidden."

"Technically, I never broke up with her. So, I was never really an *ex*. I was just... gone for a while, even though I never really left."

Rob shrugged. "It still counts."

"It does not," Ash argued.

"Does too."

"You really want to keep your own brother out of the group?" Asher demanded, staring at each of their faces in turn. "The Storm King damn near kills me, and when I return, you want to act like I'm not even welcome?"

Ben sighed and shook his head. "Fuck this."

He wrapped Ash in a fierce hug, latching on to him like he was scared he'd disappear again. I couldn't blame him; I feared the exact same thing.

"Why didn't you come back?" Ben asked, *pleaded*, as he clung to his brother. He'd told me once that Asher was his best friend and that he'd taken Ash's death the hardest. I could now see that was absolutely true.

"She wouldn't let me die!" he protested.

"Before that."

"You *know* why I couldn't come back," Ash said, his voice sounding raw and devastated rather than angry. "Our father tried to kill me, Ben. If I'd have come back, he would have made damn sure he succeeded the next time. It was safer to just... disappear."

He turned my way, and his amber eyes practically melted me.

3

"Then I found Alexis, and for the first time in my life, I thought I had a chance at genuine happiness. I fell in love with her—I'm sure you guys know how easy that is—and I wanted to stay with her always. I even had a ring picked out and was going to ask her to marry me."

My breath hitched, and my chin quivered. Emotions that I'd suppressed for years suddenly rose to the surface, killing me from the inside out.

"But then one of the magical prisoners found a way to escape the palace," Ash continued, "and I heard the guards were about to be passing through Blackleaf in pursuit of him. I knew I couldn't risk being seen, so I wracked my brain for something, *anything*, that I could turn into that would allow me to live long enough to avoid the king but short enough that I could return to human form as quickly as possible. A sloth seemed like a great idea—slow, defenseless, prey to just about anything. But then Alexis found me and..."

He sighed.

"You are the kindest girl ever, Sweets, you know that?" Ash asked me, shaking his head. "But I wished every single day that you'd been just a bit more of a bitch and let that damn sloth die an ugly, gory death a long time ago."

I laughed as a tear slid down my face.

There were so many things I wanted to say to him. So many touches and kisses I wanted to share. But I had no idea if that would ever be possible again.

I swallowed hard and turned to the remaining four guys. "What do you think about adding him to the group?"

Agony and confliction wrecked their gorgeous features. They looked torn in so many different directions—happy, angry, dubious, and uncertain all at once.

Cal shook his head. "I think we should give it some time. Test the group dynamic with him back in it and see how natural it feels."

"I vote no," Rob grumbled, glaring at his brother. "It's been too long, and if he comes back now, there will only be jealousy and resentment."

"Well, I vote yes," Ben countered, patting Asher on the back.

Dan sighed. "I need time to think too. I love my brother, but Rob's right. It's been a while. We need to make sure the dynamic is still the same. We made a commitment, a very serious commitment forged in blood and magic, and we can't disregard that so easily."

Ash's gaze dropped to the ground, and he nodded. "Fair enough."

"Regardless as to whether or not you let him in the group," I said, staring at him as he focused on the ground, "can I have a few moments with him?"

They did not look all that happy, especially Rob, but they reluctantly obliged.

"You have an hour until our meeting with the King and Queen of Timberlune," Cal said, shooting me a knowing look.

My spirits lifted. "Bria was able to get us an audience?"

"She was."

"Oh, thank the gods," I muttered, putting a hand over my heart. Something was finally... Actually, no, I wasn't even going to jinx it by saying "going right."

"Come on, guys," Cal said, gathering up his brothers and ushering them toward the castle.

"This is fucking bullshit," Rob spat, glaring at Ash before turning and leading the way.

Ben sighed heavily behind him. "Give it a rest, would you?"

Dan scoffed, his muscles clenching as he crossed his arms. "Well, I don't exactly like it either."

"You'll get over it—*both* of you," Cal said dryly, bringing up the rear.

Ash rolled his eyes and stood there silently, fists balled, jaw tensed, as their grumbling faded into the distance.

Then it was only him and me.

We said nothing for a long while, didn't even look each other in the eyes, but eventually the silence ate me alive.

"You have no idea how much I've missed you." The truth and the weight of those words practically crushed me.

His fingers relaxed then, and a sad smile crept onto his face. "I do, Sweets. I've felt that same pain every single day I was stuck as a sloth. But I was never really gone."

Heat burned in the back of my throat as tears started forming once more. "I'm so sorry," I said, allowing the scalding drops to fall. "I wish I would have known. I would have changed everything."

He took a step closer, hesitating as he waited to see what I would do, but I did him one better and bridged the rest of the gap myself. As I nestled into his warm chest, breathing in his familiar spicy scent, I couldn't help but feel complete.

He took a deep breath, and when he spoke, his voice was raw with emotion. "If I hadn't been stuck as a sloth, you never would have become magical in the first place. You never would have met my brothers or the king. You never would have suffered... or made that stupid blood bond."

I bit my lip and nodded. "I suppose you're right. And... if that's the case, then I suppose everything happened for a reason."

He pulled away from our embrace and looked me in the eye, his amber gaze filled with confusion and disbelief. "You wouldn't change the events that led us here? You wouldn't exchange the bond you made with *them* in order to live a peaceful life with *me* back in Blackleaf? Am I no longer enough?"

It broke my heart to have this conversation with him. It

wasn't what I'd always dreamed it would be. I still loved him, that was for damn sure, but he wasn't the only one I loved anymore. Things had become inexplicably complicated.

"You *are* enough," I promised him, taking his hands in mine. "All five of you, in and of yourselves, are enough... for any woman. But for me, I need *all* of you. To me, you're five pieces of one soul. I can't have one of you and not the rest—not even you, the one who inadvertently started it all."

He swallowed hard and released my hands. "Are you breaking up with me?"

I grasped his hands again and stepped in closer. "Adam—I mean, Asher—no. I don't want to lose you. All I'm saying is that, in order for us to be together again, you're going to have to join the group. It's not just you and me against the world. It's *us*. It's our group against the world, against the Storm King. And I want you to be a part of that, which means, I need you to convince the guys that you're here to stay. That you're back for good. That our dynamic is even stronger with you around, rather than hostile and fragile. That we're perfect as a team, rather than a misplaced bunch of lovers."

He licked his lips and sighed, glancing away as he pondered my words. "I spent the past six years of my life trying to get back in your arms, Sweets. And now that I'm finally here, it's going to take a hell of a lot more than *this* to drive me away. I'll do it. I'll reintegrate myself. I'll pull my own weight and do whatever it takes. I swear it."

My heart freaking leapt up into my throat and did a dance of joy. As I smiled, Ash leaned in, his lips mere inches from mine.

"Would it be okay if I kissed you?"

No. I knew the guys would be furious. It would make them jealous. But this was Ash we were talking about. My long-lost love. Their brother. He belonged with us, whether they wanted to admit it or not.

"One kiss," I told him. "After that, we have to wait and see what the group decides."

He bit his lip, drawing my gaze, making me long for the days when we kissed each other freely, whenever we wanted, without question or consequence.

Then his mouth was on mine—gentle, cautious, full of love and longing, but careful and constrained. My lips parted on instinct, and his tongue slowly slipped inside, brushing mine with a sweetness that was almost maddening. As our lips moved against each other, the force behind the kiss intensified.

Memories flooded my mind, taking me back to the time when we were caught in the rain. When he'd called me beautiful and we'd kissed in the barn while it poured outside. When we'd laid a blanket down in the hay and touched each other for the first time.

The same passion and affection from that day radiated through me now, filling me with the same fire I used to feel. That's when I knew I needed to back the hell up.

I gasped, breaking our kiss quickly and retreating a few steps.

His smile stoked a slow-burning smolder that lit my freaking soul on fire.

"We still have it, don't we?" It didn't sound like a question. And really, it didn't need to be. If he felt even half of what I was feeling—and he did, I could literally sense his emotions —then fuck yeah, we still had it.

"You need to get back in with your brothers," I said in response. "I don't want that to be our last kiss."

I spun on my heel, intending to hurry inside before I changed my mind and jumped him right there in the garden, but something made me pause. With all the conflicting emotions churning inside me, I wished beyond anything that I could talk to my stupid sloth again.

"Damn you, Speedy! Where are you when I need to talk?" I grumbled.

He chuckled. "I'm right here, babe. What do you want to talk about?"

I glowered at him over my shoulder but couldn't stop the smile that immediately followed. "You know damn well." I headed for the door, but he called out to me before I could take another step.

"Hey, Sweets?"

"Yeah?"

"I have to shift back into an animal or someone might see me. I'm going to pick a bird this time, I think. Can I hang out on your shoulder for a while?"

I smiled and shook my head. "Come on, then."

"Oh, and I might need you to kill me so that I can turn back into myself. Can you handle that?"

What the fuck kind of a question was that? I'd watched him die in sloth form less than an hour ago, and now he wanted me to kill him in bird form?

I took a shaky breath. "Why would you *ever* ask me to do that?"

Wait. Did he just say "so I can turn back into myself"?

I cocked my head in thought. "Is the price of your magic... death?"

Ben and I had chatted about the Shifter Prince a lot, but I couldn't recall if we'd touched on that particular subject or not. It wasn't ringing any bells, and yet it still felt... right.

"Yes, ma'am," Asher said with a handsome grin. "I can't shift out of animal form until the creature dies, hence my years as a suicidal sloth."

Oh hell. I scrunched my face up and rubbed it with both hands. What a fucking disaster this whole thing was.

I nodded. "Now that I know who you are and how your magic works, I suppose I could try, if I have to, I guess."

9

He grinned. "I love you, Sweets."

Before I could reply—not that I necessarily would have, considering that was *dangerous* territory—he spiraled into a swirling cyclone of magical gold dust. When the dust settled, all that was left was a little brown bird with a white belly and a single black spot near the throat. He flitted over to me and perched on my shoulder.

I raised a brow at him. "I'm still calling you Speedy, okay?"

He chirped, and I had no idea if it was a protest or not.

"Good. I'm glad we're in agreement."

Now that he was back to being my pet and not my old boyfriend, I was more than willing to open up and talk.

"You know how fucked up this whole situation is?" I asked, as we went inside to find Cal and the others. "I thought Adam had run off and left me behind for *years*. Turns out, he'd been with me this entire time. I'd been talking to him about his own brothers. I mean, no wonder he was pissed at me."

Was I talking to Asher the bird as if he *wasn't* Asher the man? Yes. Did I give any shits? No. If this was how we were going to survive our relationship for the time being, then that's just how it had to be.

"I should probably tell him that I'm sorry, huh, Speedy?" The little bird chirped once more, and I went ahead and presumed to know what the hell he was saying. "Yeah, I think he'll forgive me, too."

I'm pretty sure I saw the bird's black eyes roll.

Laughing, I knocked on Cal's door. He opened it a millisecond later, as if he was already on course to open it before I arrived.

"Oh, hey, Peach. How was your chat with...?" His blue eyes found the bird on my shoulder, and then he glanced back at me. "I take it this is him?"

I nodded. "We don't know who we can trust at the castle.

That servant guy, Frederick, already ratted me out to the king. Who knows who else is listening?"

As I said the words, I glanced discreetly down the hall.

Cal sighed. "Good point. You ready for the, uh, *wine tasting*?"

I grinned. *Way to be super inconspicuous, Cal.*

"As I'll ever be, I suppose."

He nodded, shooting one last glance at the bird on my shoulder. "Behave yourself, Ash."

"Call him Speedy," I cut in. "It's easier and much less obvious."

"Okay..." He raised both brows a bit sarcastically. "Behave yourself, *Speedy*. No actions that would prove you're anything other than a common, everyday bird. And certainly no dying and turning into a man right before the king and queen's eyes. You're supposed to be long dead. Let's make sure we keep it that way."

The bird rattled off a string of tweets that I assumed was Ash telling Cal off.

"Speedy!" I scolded him playfully. "Language!"

He turned to me then and directed his aggressive tweets my way.

"Okay, fine! I'm not one to talk. I cuss like a sailor." Then we both turned back to Cal, and I continued my half-assed translation. "I think what Speedy is trying to say is: he might be a birdbrain, but he's not stupid. He won't do any of that stuff. Right, Speedy?"

The bird's beady black eyes rolled again, but he let out one final curt tweet.

"See?" I asked Cal, who's eyes were wide as he took in the crazy scene.

"Yeah... let's just gather up the guys and get to it."

CHAPTER 2

*S*ince there were eyes watching and ears listening everywhere on behalf of the wicked king, we decided to host our meeting with the Timberlune royals in the castle's wine cellar—hence Cal's wine-tasting comment.

Honestly, after finding out Cal's betrothal to their daughter, Bria, had been called off, I'm surprised they agreed to meet with us at all, let alone in a *wine cellar*.

At least the cellar was vast. We weren't crammed into a tiny nook or anything, though it *was* damp and only dimly lit by a few torches mounted on the stone walls. I wasn't sure how eight high-back dining chairs had gotten down there and had been situated into a tight circle without drawing any unwanted attention from castle servants, but I kept my questions to myself. I was sure Cal had it figured out.

King Titus and Queen Bravia were already seated stick-straight in their chairs, along with Princess Bria on the left, who was slouched slightly and seemed quite small next to her domineering parents. As fae, their skin was a soft, semi-translucent periwinkle color, with freckles that were more like glowing stars. It was a bit startling at first but quite beautiful once you got used to it.

"I hear you've called off the betrothal, Prince Calvin," Queen Bravia said, staring down her bluish nose at us.

Apparently, we were cutting straight to the chase.

Cal took a deep breath and nodded. "I have."

"You realize this means war, son?" King Titus asked sternly.

As if playing the fierce father figure would have any effect on Cal. He had the worst father in existence.

"I don't believe it has to, Your Majesty." His voice was steady and confident, causing a sense of pride to rise up within me. He was damn good at this.

"Explain yourself," the queen snapped. "Bria said something about a promise the future princess made to her. What of it?"

At the mention of her name, Bria blushed and slumped a bit more in her seat.

"Alexis was referring to a blood bond, something we don't usually offer lightly." Cal glared at me as the two monarchs gasped. "She's unaccustomed to such things, so I pray you'll disregard her words."

The king and queen's faces were frozen in mild horror.

"Blood bonds are dark magic," Bravia insisted. "Why would she know of such evil?"

Rob rolled his eyes. "They're not dark *or* evil."

Cal cut him off. "Things get tossed around in conversation from time to time. The citizens of Southern Blackwood tend to engage in the dark arts more than the rest of us. Rob has told her all sorts of scary stories to keep her up at night."

Rob leaned over to me and whispered, "I'll keep you up at night, but I won't be telling you stories."

I shoved him away and fought off a laugh.

"The fact of the matter remains, though," Cal continued, "that we would still like another chance at peace, if possible."

"If you no longer wish to wed our daughter," King Titus said, "then we have nothing more to discuss." He rose from his chair and threw his royal robe about his shoulders.

"Sit, Titus," the queen insisted. "Let us at least hear them out."

"Your sympathy is going to be the death of me, you know this?"

Sympathy? Who was he kidding? Bravia was the farthest thing from a bleeding heart I could imagine.

"Nonsense," she replied to her husband.

Still, King Titus did not sit but rather crossed his arms and waited.

Pompous ass. I rolled my eyes, and Bria grinned.

"I heard you guys have a bit of a harpy problem," I said, interrupting the conversation before anyone could continue.

The queen glared at me with iron eyes. "And where did you hear such a thing?"

I half shrugged. "I've been to Timberlune once before. I heard a few things."

Neither of which were lies but were in fact only half-truths.

I could feel her anger radiating through the air between us. That's when I realized I needed to tread a bit softer, despite how much I hated the delicacy of politics.

I sighed. "What I'm trying to say is, whatever problem you have with the harpies, please allow us to help. As an act of good faith."

Queen Bravia cocked her head toward Cal. "Do you always allow her to speak on your behalf?"

Cal smirked and turned to Titus. "Do you always allow *her* to speak on your behalf?"

Titus put his blue hands on his hips and chuckled. Flinging his robe over his shoulder, he finally retook his seat and gestured for Cal to continue. "Carry on."

Cal bowed his head slightly. "What Alexis said is true. We cannot follow through on the betrothal, and for that, I am most apologetic, but we would still very much like to have you as allies. We can't have you as allies if you've been wiped off the map."

King Titus nodded his agreement. "What do you propose?"

Cal gestured to Ben. "My brother, here, is lord of the Obsidian Palace, which borders the harpy nation of Eristan. He has very good relations with them. I have no doubt we might be able to strike a deal."

Titus rubbed his blue bearded chin. "There was a treaty involving eastern Blackwood before, back when it was Essund, a nation of its own."

Ben nodded, smiling warmly. "The Treaty O' Ley. It would be my honor to invoke that agreement once more."

Queen Bravia still had her resting bitch face on, but there was a tiny line around both corners of her mouth that told me she was pleased.

"Very well," she decided. Then her icy gaze landed on me. "I assume the reason you've called off the betrothal is because of... *her?*"

Cal nodded once, a resigned sort of expression resting on his face. I could tell he didn't want to discuss any of this with them, but he didn't really have much choice.

"Then allow me to make you a deal. If you can solve our harpy problem before the inevitable marriage to the peasant, then we'll agree to this treaty."

Before Cal could say the word "deal," I quickly jumped into the middle of our circle.

"No, that won't work."

Cal looked confused. "Alexis, what do you mean? We already agreed that—"

I shook my head. "The terms have changed. Can I speak to you guys for a moment in private?"

Cal glanced remorsefully at the Timberlune royals.

Titus nodded and waved him away. "Take a moment."

"You have my gratitude, Your Majesty," Cal proclaimed before joining the rest of us in a shadowed corner. "What the hell is this about, Peach?"

"The Storm King," I whispered. "When he showed up and killed Speedy, he told me we had to be back at Blackwood Palace in three days for an official union between Cal and me."

"Fuck no." Rob pursed his plush lips. "You're not marrying any of us. We already decided."

"Or," I pressed, recalling the other end of that particular bargain, "I marry all four—or five?—of you... starting with Cal."

The Sky Prince swallowed hard and glanced away. "What did he threaten you with?"

"The life of my one-year-old cousin, Lilah." I worried my bottom lip. "Do you think he's bluffing?"

Dan scoffed. "The Storm King doesn't bluff, Lexi. Your cousin will be waiting for you at knifepoint by the time we get there, I can promise you that."

My skin immediately turned clammy, and my stomach dipped low in my core, threatening to make me sick.

Ben touched my shoulder and then gently rubbed my neck. "It's okay, Sailor. We'll figure out a way to get through this."

Cal shook his head. "What should our counteroffer be then?"

Dan shrugged. "Tell them the truth. Tell them you can't

make deals like that because the Storm King is volatile and unpredictable."

Cal shook his head, uncertain, but we all broke from our huddle and returned to the meeting anyway.

He took a deep breath and let it out slowly.

"Unfortunately, my father is... somewhat unpredictable. I cannot guarantee with any degree of accuracy the time or date that he'll require a wedding. That said, would you be willing to give us a month? One month to figure out what's going on with the harpies and see if we can reinstate the old Treaty O' Ley?"

Bria looked nervous and unsure as she glanced between her parents. King Titus looked unreadable and stoic. Queen Bravia's nose lifted even higher into the air.

Honestly, I had no idea how she was able to make eye contact from so high up there.

"One month?" she asked in a pissy huff.

"Sounds reasonable," King Titus finished sternly, as if trying his best to contain an impending fit from his wife. "But, considering you went back on your word once already, I'm afraid we're going to need a bit more proof before trusting you again."

"How so?" Cal asked. "Name your terms."

The fae king merely shrugged. "We have been dealing with a slight pollution problem."

"Pollution?" Cal asked in surprise, his brows furrowing.

The king nodded. "One of our cafes had an unfortunate... accident, and now the entire water basin is overflowing with luck, laughter, honesty, intelligence, bravery, and so on. It's causing a bit of a problem, as you can imagine."

Dan heaved an amused sigh and rolled his pale green eyes. "Water problems, huh? I think I might be able to help you out there."

King Titus smiled wide, feigning surprise. "Is that so?"

Dan grinned. "Mm, that it is. Suppose I offered you my services?"

The fae king pressed his fingertips together. "I'm listening."

Dan bit his lip and shook his head, as if the whole *playing pretend* thing was about to crack him the fuck up. "If I agreed to help clean your water supply, would you be willing to give us a month to reinstate the Treaty O' Ley?"

King Titus tapped his chin, as if contemplating Dan's proposal seriously. "Why, yes, I believe we would. Thank you kindly for offering, Prince Daniel." And before Bravia could protest, he added, "Now, let us discuss the terms of your failure. Seeing as how you've already canceled the betrothal and refused our first offer, if you should fail, it will, in no uncertain terms, mean war."

Cal nodded firmly. "I understand, Your Majesty. Meet us here, at Nightshade in the cellars, in exactly one month. And if the terms of our treaty have been fulfilled, we'll draw up an official document."

Cal held out his hand, and Titus stood and shook it.

"Deal, Prince Calvin. I hope you and your brother are as able as you seem."

He shot the king a half smile, one that *I* found sexy as hell. "Me too, Your Majesty."

And with that, all three Timberlune royals left, ascending the stairs and disappearing out of sight.

Speedy chirped, and I assumed that meant he was seeking permission to shift. Cal seemed to have come to the same conclusion. He nodded at the bird, and it shot into the air, soaring fast... straight into a stone wall. He fell with a thump and a puff of feathers, and a moment later, Ash stood in the bird's place.

"This is fucked up, you guys," he said, as soon as he had a human voice.

Dan seemed to agree. "I can't believe she has to marry Cal."

"Maybe she doesn't," Cal insisted, though he didn't sound very sure of himself.

"If it's *marry Cal* or *Lilah dies*," I told them, "then I'm sorry, but I'm going to marry Cal. And like we talked about, if I marry one of you, then I'll marry all of you. We have a commitment and a bond. A ceremony and a piece of parchment isn't going to change that."

"We need each other," Ben agreed, and we both glanced at Asher.

Rob just shook his head and turned away.

I wondered why he seemed so personally against Ash joining the group. Had something happened there? Some fight between them? Some hurt feelings or betrayal?

"You said we had three days to get back to Blackwood?" Cal asked, running a hand through his golden hair.

I nodded.

"I suppose we'd better get packing then."

"Wait," I said, halting everyone midstep. "We need to have a *chat*."

"Oh, don't even start," Rob complained. "It's bad enough when *Cal* forces us to talk. I don't need *you* starting this bullshit too."

"No, Alexis is right," Cal agreed. "We're already in the wine cellar. Let's pour some drinks and make ourselves comfortable. We're going to hash this thing out—whatever it is—before we even think about going face-to-face with the king. We need to make sure we're solid and strong before we expose ourselves to his toxicity."

Everyone grabbed glasses and mugs, except for Rob who grabbed a whole fucking barrel, and we all sat down around the circle.

Cal put his fingertips together and leaned his elbows on

his knees. "I'll go first. I'm so damn happy that Asher is alive after all these years. It feels like a boulder has been lifted off my chest. I didn't even realize it weighed so heavy on me."

Ben and Dan nodded their agreement. Rob didn't.

I couldn't stop the question from leaving my lips.

"Why aren't you happy?" I asked Rob.

He glared at me. "I go out of my way to protect my brothers, Jewels. I'd gladly take any punishment on their behalf just to keep them an ounce safer than me. Knowing my character and my method of operation, can you seriously not guess why it'd piss me off so much to hear Ash just scurried off like a coward?"

I sighed, finally realizing the root of the tension. "Bravery is your thing, Rob, and you're amazing at it. It's your extra power."

His eyes narrowed further as he shook his head. "So, I'm braver than everyone else, who cares? The other guys are still brave in their own right. What Ash did? That was spineless and weak."

"It wasn't weak," Asher insisted, staring at the ground. "It was the hardest thing I ever did in my life."

"Running away seems like a pretty easy way out, dickhead," Rob shot back, crossing his tattooed arms.

"I didn't run away as much as I just... started over. Try to put yourself in my shoes. If the Storm King thought he killed you, and everyone else thought you were dead... but you were alive, so you basically had a chance at a whole new life, what would you do? Come rushing back into the shitshow of gore and torture? Or take your second chance at life?"

It made sense to me, but I could tell it still wasn't enough for Rob. His lips were twisted in a sarcastic grin, and his eyes were swimming in scorn.

I quickly cut in between them. "Regardless of whether or

not what he did was brave or cowardly, how would you have him fix it?"

"He can't," Rob said, shrugging. "It is what it is, now."

"No," Ash disagreed. "To offset a 'cowardly act,' as you would call it, I should be able to do something brave in order to regain your favor. Anyone disagree?" He glanced around the room, looking into the eyes of each brother.

I thought back to the plethora of books I'd read over the course of my years. Any time anyone did something shitty, they had a chance at redemption. Ash deserved that redemption arc too—even though I didn't think what he did was actually all that shitty. Anyone who'd been subjected to that kind of violence would want to escape. Probably even Rob, if he could.

"What do you have in mind?" Rob asked, tone cocky.

"Whatever you want, bro. Think of the bravest, stupidest act you want, and I'll do it just to prove to you that I made a mistake and that I'm sorry. That I'm back, and that I'm committed."

Ben and I shared a hopeful smile.

Rob pursed his lips. "Dive off the cliffs at Ebony Chateau."

"That's suicide," Dan protested, and he would know— Ebony Chateau was his place of residence.

"It's too far out of the way," Cal argued. "We're heading from here to Blackwood Palace at the citadel then to Eristan. Western Blackwood is the opposite direction."

Rob sighed. "Fine. Dryroot Canyons."

Ash's jaw ticked. "You want me to commit suicide? How cleverly counterproductive of you."

Rob chuckled darkly. "You're part god, Ash. Suicide is only a daydream."

His leg bounced in annoyance as he contemplated Rob's suggestion. "Fine. If I jump from the canyon, will you stop being pissed at me? Can we drop this and pretend it never happened?"

Rob half shrugged. "Maybe. I'll probably still roast you about it, but it'll be for fun instead of actual hostility."

Ash leaned back in his chair, a look of steely determination set into his features. "Done."

"So..." I said slowly, unsure I'd followed that conversation right, "Asher has to jump from a canyon... and then he'll be a part of the group?"

"A part of your reverse harem of Storms, you mean?" Ben asked, grinning cheekily. "That's what I heard."

"If you *want* him to be," Dan added teasingly. "He *is* the tiniest, least impressive specimen of us all."

I turned back to Ash whose muscles were lean but not tiny in the slightest. And, considering we'd already had sex, I knew he wasn't tiny in *that* department either. My cheeks heated at the thought.

"He's your brother, and he's a Storm," I said decisively. "I want him in the group."

"Okay. Then it's settled," Rob said, grinning darkly. "As soon as you jump from the canyon, you're back in."

"Good." Ash's eyes were narrowed, but I could tell he was actually relieved. "Let's get this show on the road. The sooner we get to Blackwood citadel, the sooner we get to Eristan. And the sooner we get to Eristan, the sooner I can jump off that cliff."

"All right, now that that's settled..." Cal said, trying to get the conversation back on track, "Ash, let's make a deal. To avoid ever replaying the sloth incident again, how about every time you turn into an animal, you pick a definitive marking so that we'll know it's you?"

"Like that black dot you had on your bird form," I said, recalling the mark. "You could put a spot on your chest, no matter what type of animal you are, and then we'll know it's you."

"I can do that," he agreed. "And if I ever want to be a human again, and I need one of you guys to kill me. I'm going to want a signal for that too. How about I hum a tune or something?"

"What if you're a snake and can't hum?" Rob asked, probably just to be a dick. "Or a bear? Or a fish?"

"Then I'll hiss, growl, or bubble the tune," Ash replied through gritted teeth.

"Why don't you just attack us?" Rob suggested, spreading his arms out wide. "That's a surefire way to make me kill just about anything."

"Maybe I will."

Cal waved his hands and shook his head. "Whoa, no. Let's just calm down. For the good of the entire group, you two need to put your differences aside. I want to see you actively trying to get along again. Can we agree on that?"

"I agree," I said, raising my hand first. Ben and Dan agreed too.

Rob merely shrugged. "I don't have to do jack-shit until he dives headfirst off a cliff."

"Rob," I said softly, walking over to him and taking his hand in mine. "I get why you're mad. I get why *everyone's* mad. I'm still a little pissed at him too, because it's hard to just up and forget all those years I thought he was gone. But please. For me, can you try to keep the fighting to a minimum? Not because he doesn't deserve it, but because we're already drowning with stress, and I really don't know if I can handle any extra right now."

He looked up at me, stormy gray eyes swirling like a hurricane of unreadable emotions. "All right, Jewels."

It wasn't exactly a promise, but I'd take it. I had a feeling it was the best I was going to get for now.

"Okay, guys." Cal stood, and the rest of us followed his lead. "Let get to packing. Why the Storm King ever gave us three whole days to return home, I have no idea, but I can guarantee you, the faster we get there, the less damage will be done in our absence."

Asher walked over to me and took my hand, bringing it up to his lips for a kiss. "I'll be by your side the whole time, just like always."

As his magic kicked in and he shifted back into a bird, my stomach tied itself into knots. I had a very bad feeling that his brothers were not going to be happy with any PDA between us. At least not until he was officially part of the group, and even then, maybe not for a while.

Speedy lit on my shoulder, but before we even reached the stairs, Cal stopped us.

"Ash. Shit, I mean, *Speedy*." He waited for me to spin around so both of us were facing him. "You can come with us guys. You don't need any more alone time with Alexis than you've already had."

I held my breath. Damn it, I knew something like this would happen.

Asher must've known too, because he didn't even put up a fight. He simply flew from my shoulder and perched on Ben's.

The Sand Prince's lips tugged back into a grimace as he glanced at the bird. "So help me gods, if you shit on me, this is never happening again. Swamp-ass Fever is legit, bro."

Dan sighed to keep from chuckling. "You've never had Swamp-ass Fever, Ben. You've never even seen it infect anyone in real life."

"So?" he argued. "I've read about it plenty, and I have no desire to shit out my mouth, puke out my ass, or develop a blistering, itchy rash that makes it impossible to sit for a week." He shivered at the thought.

Shaking my head, I reluctantly left to pack my bags.

I doubted if Swamp-ass Fever even existed. It sounded completely made up. Still, even if it *was* real, I'd rather contract that than have to face the Storm King in a day or so.

CHAPTER 3

By the following evening, we arrived at the citadel.

We'd traveled all night and all morning. My wine-colored riding gown was officially dirty, I was mildly smelly, and I was dead-ass tired.

"Whoa," Cal called out to his dark brown, braided-haired stallion, who clomped to a stop at the crest of a hill looking down on the palace below. I pulled on my own horse's reins, a pretty palomino mare named Caramel, and we stopped on Cal's right.

I glanced down, surprised to find a massive crowd of people gathered at the gates.

"What the hell is this about?" I asked, leaning forward to get a better look.

Speedy chirped from my shoulder, seeming just as clueless as I was.

Was it a riot? A protest? Was there even a glimmer of hope that the Storm King's rule might be cracking or coming to an end?

"I think you know *exactly* what this is about," Cal muttered, shooting me a grim glance.

And then I knew.

Fear crackled through my veins like ice, making it hard for me to breathe. "You think this is our wedding?"

He nodded. "I do."

Well, if that was the case, he'd be saying that tiny phrase again in just a few moments...

It didn't matter that we'd technically arrived early. The Storm King had eyes and ears all over Blackwood. He'd no doubt gotten word of our approach with plenty of time to orchestrate an official ceremony.

My stomach sank like a rock, filling me with dread. It wasn't that I didn't want Cal, or any of the brothers, because obviously I did. It was the fact that I wasn't ready for marriage. And more than that, it was the fact that someone else was telling me how to live my life—no, *forcing* me to live a life that wasn't even really my own.

Dan and his horse trotted up beside me, and he kissed my cheek. "It's okay, Lexi. We all know we're committed. The marriage will mean nothing more than salvation for your family's lives."

I nodded, but I still felt hollow.

Cal leaned forward and made eye contact with Speedy. "Time for you to disappear. Keep a close eye, though; you never know when we'll need to make a fast escape."

Speedy chirped and flew up ahead, disappearing into the slowly setting sun. The sky was a deep red, and while "red at night" was supposed to be a "sailor's delight," I could say with absolute certainty that it filled *this* Sailor with "distress" instead.

"Come on." Cal sighed. "Let's get this over with."

When we reached the gates, we dismounted, and a handful of servants escorted our horses to the stables. Two armored guards granted us passage through the gateway, and the crowd beyond parted like a breezy curtain. A beautiful scene came into view: a pure white dais, decorated with flowing silks and laces, covered in bouquets of beautiful flowers, complete with an orchestra playing romantic tunes on the same stringed instruments I'd seen back at Nightshade.

Every face was genuinely smiling...

And that's when it hit me. These people had no idea who the Storm King really was. What he did behind closed doors. What he forced his own children and his own wives to endure. They thought this wedding was perfect, a gift to the peasants that he allowed one of *them* to marry one of his precious sons. Their tickled features made me want to scream at the top of my lungs, but for the sake of their very lives, I stayed silent.

Cal and I were immediately whisked away—separately— into little sitting rooms just inside the palace doors. I was quickly stripped and scrubbed down with damp cloths that smelled of sweet rose and lush lily. One of the servants pinned up my hair, while another coaxed me into a beautiful white gown. The sleeves were long and made of mostly transparent lace, and they sat low on my shoulders, exposing my collarbones. The train of the garment stretched out behind me for nearly ten feet. It was overkill like I'd never seen, but then again, I'd *never seen* a royal wedding, let alone participated in one.

Everything happened so fast, I could barely process it. I blinked, and suddenly we were back outside in front of the awaiting crowd.

A herald stood off to the side, bellowing our entrance. "Prince Calvin of Northern Blackwood, and his bride-to-be, Lady Alexis Ravenel of Blackleaf!"

The masses cheered wildly, their voices deafening my ears. They had no idea what they were cheering for. No idea whatsoever.

I glanced at Cal, who looked handsome as ever in his white pants and royal purple uniform. Silver emblems and tassels lined the front of the suit as if he were an accomplished war hero, rather than a repressed prince. His blond hair had been slicked off to the side, and his blue eyes sparkled despite his saddened features. If this whole thing hadn't been so tragic, it would've been utterly beautiful.

At the foot of the aisle stood the Storm King, smiling proudly, as if this were one of the happiest moments of his life. He was dressed in a suit almost exactly like Cal's, except his was even fancier, full of silver fringes, insignia, and crests. He also wore an elegant purple robe with white fur lining the edges and black spots covering the middle. It was as if someone had skinned a snow leopard and dyed its coat plum.

It was clear we were meant to approach him, so we made our way over and bowed deeply. Even in my supposed submission, I couldn't stand the thought of taking my eyes off the snake, so I stared cautiously into his dark blue eyes the whole time. He laughed as if our reverence was unnecessary, as if he were an inherently jovial man, rather than a maniacal tyrant, and told us to rise.

He handed Cal the rings, then removed the cloak he was wearing and placed it around his son's shoulders. He turned to me, attaching a long white veil around my head like a halo, gently tracing the lines of my face as he did so. It took every ounce of restraint I had not to spit at him or jerk away from his touch.

"As beautiful as your mother," he muttered, and a few nearby women sighed with envy.

I swallowed and forced a smile. "Thank you, Your Majesty."

He gestured to the aisle before us, and Cal held out his elbow.

I slipped my hand in, and every muscle in my body trembled as my heart hammered wildly.

"I thought we were going to have more time than this," I whispered as I clung to his arm for support.

"So did I, Peach, but it's going to be okay. We'll get through it."

"I don't even see my mother or Gemma."

Cal shook his head. "My mother's not here either; none of the queens are."

Were they okay? Were they being tortured at this very moment? It made me absolutely sick to think about it, so I tried not to.

The Storm King followed us down the aisle, and when we stepped onto the dais at the end, he took the podium and officiated the service himself. My mouth nearly fell open. Didn't he have an official priest or something for shit like that?

"Ladies and gentlemen, welcome to the royal wedding ceremony of Prince Calvin Storm and your very own Alexis Ravenel."

The crowd went wild, dulling my senses just enough to allow me to breathe.

"I'm sure these two are anxious to begin their lives together, so without further ado, let us have them take the sacred vows."

He cleared his throat and shot me a smug smirk. I probably looked even more toad-like than usual, all wide-eyed with my throat sucked in.

"Do you, Alexis, take this prince to be your lawfully wedded husband, for better or worse, come hell or high water, as long as you both shall live?"

It hadn't escaped me that he'd basically cut any of the lovey-dovey stuff right out.

I opened my mouth, afraid no sound would come out. "I do."

Cal slipped the ring onto my finger—a massive diamond the size of my thumbnail—and once more the crowd erupted into a frenzy of cheers.

"And do you, Calvin," the king shouted over the crowd, "take this woman to be your lawfully wedded wife, for better or worse, come hell or high water, as long as you both shall live?"

Cal stared at me, blue eyes delving so deep it felt like they touched my very soul. And to my utter surprise, my soul responded with longing. His lips parted, drawing me in as he took a deep breath. "I do."

He slid his own ring on, and the cheers escalated in anticipation for the climactic moment ahead.

"Then, by the gods as my witnesses, I now proclaim you—officially—husband and wife, Prince and Princess of Blackwood, Lord and Lady of Nightshade. You may now seal these vows with a kiss."

I blinked lethargically, watching the scene unfold in slow motion. Cal leaned in... lifted my veil... then planted a chaste kiss on my mouth, our lips barely brushing. As the cheers of the crowd somehow rose even louder, he moved to my ear and said, "I really do love you. I'm so sorry it had to happen like this."

His words were like a flickering candle in the dark, a tiny source of warmth in a cold room, and I clung to them. If nothing else came from this gods-awful experience, then at least there was that.

"I love you too, Cal."

I loved *all* my princes, even if I hadn't been brave enough to admit it until now.

"Food and drink for everyone!" the king shouted, electrifying the crowd to an unbelievable level of energy and noise.

At his command, a long line of servants rushed out offering up trays of meat and bread, fruit and vegetables, wine, ale, cake, and gods knew what else.

As the Storm King led us off the dais, the anxious crowd parted once more, allowing the three of us safe passage into the palace. We took several twists and turns down the hallways and corridors before the sound of the party disappeared. But as soon as it did, the king stopped walking and turned to us.

"Congratulations, you two. And nice choice, Alexis," he said with a sickening wink.

He knew damn well I didn't *choose* to marry Cal. He'd made the choice for me.

"Now, let's get down to business. This marriage will signify the end of peace between Blackwood and Timberlune. But I'm not stupid. I know you'll try to salvage relations, and I know you'll focus on the harpies, because that's Timberlune's biggest weakness. When you're in Eristan, which I'm *certain* is where you're headed next, I want you to find and bring back a chimera egg."

Cal's brows furrowed as he glanced between his father and me. "A *what?*"

"You heard me," the Storm King threatened, tone dark and deadly. "You have one month. I'm sure you understand the consequences of your failure."

I scoffed on the inside. Of course we did—torture, pain, and death. Unending guilt and sorrow.

With that, the king straightened his posture and spun back around, strolling once more through the hallway.

"If you'll just follow me," he said, sounding far more cheerful than I'd like, "I have one last item on the agenda."

I couldn't breathe all of a sudden. I didn't know what the bastard had in mind, but after a forced wedding and the mandate of an impossible task, I knew damn well it couldn't be anything good.

He turned and led us into a long hallway on a wing of the palace I hadn't seen before. It was decorated in all sorts of random things—animal heads, coats of armor, shields with crests, banners, paintings. Each looked ancient, and, seeing as there was exposed stone and gritty dirt all over the place, I had a feeling this particular area actually *was* quite old.

At the end of the hall, he opened a set of thick double doors made of roughhewn wood. Beyond the entrance sat a massive four-poster bed, dressed in red silk linens and covered in rose petals. Surrounding the bed stood the other Storm Princes, the queens, my mom, Gemma, and little Lilah, clutched tightly in her mother Janna's arms—all of them held at knifepoint by a group of the king's guards.

I spun around, adrenaline pumping ravenously through my veins. "What the fuck is this?"

Cal tried to hold me back by tightening his grip on my arm, but I was livid.

"This is your marriage bed," the king said unquestionably. "Recall when I said that I wanted you to produce an heir, strengthening the Storm family line?"

Of course, I did. How could I forget?

I nodded, and he shrugged.

"This is me making sure that happens. You see, if you do not produce an heir—another child with magical abilities—then there really is no use for you at all, is there?"

I glanced at the queens, from face to hopeless face. How much time had he given them when they were expected to produce a Storm heir? And how much time would he give me?

"You want me to fuck your son?" I boldly asked him. "Fine. I'll fuck him. You want a magical heir for the Storm family line? Fine. Leave us, and we'll seal the deal right now."

Zacharias laughed, the echoes of his booming guffaws rattling off the stone walls.

"You ridiculous girl. Do you actually think I trust you? I don't. I want to see for myself that the deed is getting done."

I cocked my head, glancing at Cal to make sure I'd heard his father right. He wanted to... *watch* us have sex?

"Why is everyone else here?" Cal asked, looking around the room.

The king smiled malevolently. "They're here as incentive, in the event that you might refuse. Fail to do as ordered, and I'll start slitting throats—starting with Lilah."

Janna's screams flooded my blood like acid, and she squeezed her baby tightly to her breast. "Please, Alexis! Do as he says! Please!"

I stole a quick glance at Mom, who was already crying, before closing my eyes. Janna was her sister; Lilah, her niece. My failure would probably be just as difficult for *her* to endure as my success would be for *me*.

I took a deep breath, willing the world to slow down, willing time to freeze, willing this to be nothing more than a dream I'd soon wake up from.

I'd had sex before. I'd had sex *with Cal* before. It wasn't going to traumatize me; I was already in love with him. But having to do it in front of all these people, and his disgusting father... knowing that we couldn't refuse or there would be blood spilled... it was abhorrent. I hated that snake so fucking much.

When I opened my eyes, I was unsurprised to find the nightmare wasn't over.

"I can't do this," I whispered to Cal, shaking my head, trembling all over.

"Shh," he cooed as gently as I'd ever heard him. His warm palms reached up to cup my face in a tender embrace. "It's okay, Peach. Look at me. It's going to be okay."

I shook my head again, cringing as the salty tears washed down my face in waves. "I can't, Cal." My voice quivered as another wave of tears overwhelmed me. "This is the most fucked-up thing that's ever happened to me. And I know you're scared too."

He nodded. "I know, but we have to... for the sake of our mothers and your family. Close your eyes, Peach. Pretend it's just you and me."

His lips trailed gentle kisses over to my ear, and he whispered softly, just loud enough for me and no one else to hear, reiterating the words like a spell.

"Pretend it's just you and me..."

CHAPTER 4

$\mathcal{G}$EMMA

I watched from a tower window as Alexis and the four princes left Blackwood palace in the dead of night. I had no idea where they were going, but it broke my heart to see her leave... *again*.

She hadn't spoken to me or her mother, but I didn't begrudge her for it, not after what she'd just gone through... what I'd just been forced to *watch*.

I could still see the dead look in their eyes when it was finally over and the Storm King granted them permission to leave. How Alexis cried into Cal's chest as he tenderly scooped her up and walked them toward the door. How the sharp pain of the Storm King's final promise had sliced through everyone's ears and into our very skulls: that we'd be doing this every single month until Alexis fell pregnant... or she would be killed.

I touched my throat, feeling the scabs and the sting from the blade's edge at my skin. The godsdamned Storm King was a monster. I'd been wrong when I said we were lucky to be living in the palace. Dead wrong.

Still, it wasn't in my nature to stew in the darkness and evil around me. I needed to look for a bright side, a silver lining against the blackened clouds our lives had become, and find a way to rise above. This wasn't the life we were destined to live. I couldn't allow myself to think like that. Negativity would only crack my spirit, and I prided myself on my tenacity.

I silently slinked down the stairs and entered the servants' quarters, following the narrow corridor until it ended at a door to the outside. Many of the servants worked in the stables, including my new boyfriend, Tristan, so I knew this was the fastest way to the barns.

I crept through the door and tiptoed across the lawn, the light of the moon shining brightly on my emerald green robe. I pulled the hood even further over my golden blonde hair, hoping it would help conceal my identity. Technically, since I didn't work in the stables, I wasn't supposed to be out there, but after the day I'd just had, I needed Tristan's warmth, his kind smile, the strength of his arms holding me together so I didn't fall apart.

As I scurried across the lawn, a bird swooped by and darted toward the path Alexis had taken. I wondered what had startled it, and just as my eyes scanned the trees, movement caught my eye, along with another robed figure hurrying through the woods.

I paused, scrunching my nose. I really wanted to see Tristan, but an even bigger part of me wanted to follow the person and find out what they were up to. One thing I'd learned during my time here at Blackwood? The palace was full of secrets, and I *loved* finding them out.

With a sigh, I ran to the tree line and followed the person toward the eastern side of the grounds. The closer I got, the more I was sure it was a woman. Based off the purple color of her robes, I'd guess it was a royal, and the only royal women around here at the moment were the harem ladies. It almost had to be one of them.

I decided to guess which one it was and whisper her name. Even if I was wrong, it would make her pause.

"Psst! Caroline!" I whispered as loudly as I dared, and just as I'd hoped, her steps faltered. "It's me, Gemma."

Her shoulders visibly relaxed when she heard who I was and she turned around to meet me in the trees. The woman was breathless and shaking by the time I got close enough to realize it was Ashlynn, not Caroline.

I smiled kindly as I always did, a stark contrast to the general dismal atmosphere of this place. "What are you doing out here?"

She put a hand up to her throat where her pulse jumped madly. "I should ask you the same question. If we're caught, you know we'll be tortured."

I rolled my eyes. "If we breathe wrong, we'll get tortured, so what's the difference?"

She nodded her agreement, then glanced around, making sure we were alone. She ducked down into the weeds and pulled me along with her. "I was meeting up with someone."

I smiled brightly. "Me too! I was just about to meet Tristan in the barn. Maybe go for a little roll in the hay, if you know what I mean." I nudged her shoulder, and she pressed her palms together as if sending a silent prayer to the gods.

"The person I met was not someone I ever want to roll around in the hay with," she said. "Although it *was* a man and I *do* love him with all my heart."

I raised a curious brow. "Your love life needs a lot of

work, Ashlynn, you know that? I could probably help you in that department. Get you hooked up with a hot, muscled stable boy like me. You know how ripped they are? They could lift you into the air and shove your—"

She put a hand up to silence me. "Enough with your vulgarity, adorable girl; you might make me vomit."

"Oral sex is not vomit-inducing," I protested, crossing my arms. "It's actually orgasm-induc—"

But she cut me off again. "I was meeting up with Asher. *My son*. Please don't say another word about sex in this context."

Oh, now it made more sense. Someone she loved but wouldn't want to fuck around with... her kid. Got it. Gross.

"Sorry," I muttered, feeling a little sheepish. "Hey, wait, I thought Asher was dead? I thought the Storm King brutally murdered him in cold blood?"

She cocked her head, and her mouth fell open. "Have you no filter whatsoever?"

I tightened my jaw, and my lips stretched in an apologetic smile. "Not really, no."

Her brows furrowed almost sympathetically. "I'm surprised Zacharias has allowed you to keep your tongue this long."

"Me too, to be honest. But, anyway, about Asher..."

She smiled wide as tears suddenly filled her eyes. "He's alive, Gemma. He just met with me. He's with his brothers and Alexis, and he's safe and well, and oh my gods, I've never been so happy in my life."

She latched on to me, sobbing happy tears into my robes, and I hugged her right back. I loved connecting with people on such a real level, and I was honored that she trusted me enough to share in this moment with her.

It was times like these that I needed to keep in the forefront of my mind when the Storm King threatened to steal away my light.

"I'm so happy for you, Ashlynn. I know how much you've missed him."

The harem ladies and I had gotten close over these past few weeks. We shared a lot of similar experiences—beatings, lashings, cuttings—and as such, it was pretty easy to open up to one another. I might have been the youngest woman of the group and not technically one of them because, thank the gods, the Storm King hadn't taken me into his harem, but still they treated me as one of their own, and I appreciated the sentiment so very much.

"Please, don't tell anyone."

"I won't." I crossed my heart with my pointer finger. "I swear it."

"Not even during torture." She clung to my robe as if her life depended on it. "*Especially* not then."

I smiled and removed her hands, squeezing them gently. "You know I'd never do that to you."

She squeezed back almost painfully tight, and I knew it was a subconscious reaction to her fear.

"Breathe, Ashlynn," I guided her smoothly.

She took a deep breath and let it out slowly.

"That's right. In and out. Nice and slow. *I'm* not going to tell a soul. *You're* not going to tell a soul. And everything is going to be okay."

She smiled, finally, and let go of my hands. "I have to get back before Zacharias notices I'm gone. You should make your visit with Tristan a short one. I don't trust the king to be in a good mood."

I scoffed. "I never do."

She grinned back at me before disappearing across the lawn and into the shadows at the base of the palace. I went the opposite direction, finally reaching the stables like I'd originally intended.

The ripe stench of manure filled my nose and laid heavy in my lungs, but I did my best to ignore it. It was a scent I'd almost gotten used to by now but not entirely. A single lantern was lit in the middle of the giant structure, and despite the late hour, several servants still bustled about tending to the horses and the hygiene of the barn.

I found Tristan shoveling hay in Caramel's empty stall— Alexis's horse. It didn't surprise me to find him there. After all, the five Storms had just left on horseback. Someone had to clean up the mess their horses had left behind, and my sweet boyfriend was just the man for the job. I watched as his muscles stretched and flexed beneath his tight black pants and the rolled-up sleeves of his baby blue shirt. I could watch him work for hours, but unfortunately, we didn't have that kind of time.

I tapped his left shoulder but quickly hopped to the right, tricking him as I often did. As he spun left, I jumped in front of him, and when he turned back around, I planted a quick kiss on his lips.

He grinned and wrapped me in his giant arms, enveloping me with warmth. "Hey, Gem. What are you doing out here tonight?"

"You?" I asked, mostly in jest. He had a job to do, and I refused to be the reason he got a thrashing. "Actually, I just wanted to see you a bit before bed. I missed you."

He kissed the top of my head and chuckled, the sound reverberating into my skin like a salve for my aching soul. Gods, this man was... everything. If nothing else good ever came from my time at Blackwood Palace, then he would be enough.

"I missed you too. I could probably take a quick break, but it wouldn't be very long. Maybe five, ten minutes tops."

"Can you even get off that fast? It usually takes you hours."

He bit his bottom lip and hefted me into his arms. "I could try."

I giggled and squirmed out of his grasp. Like I said, I had no intentions of getting him hurt. Now that I knew what true pain felt like, I never wanted anyone else to experience it—ever. And least of all *because of me*.

"Did you have a good day?" he asked me as he got back to shoveling soiled hay into a cart.

I swallowed hard, my smile finally faltering. "Not exactly."

"Worse than usual?" he asked, knowing full well my *usual* was absolutely terrible.

I nodded, and my *yes* came out as a whisper.

He stopped shoveling, jabbing the forked end of his tool into the ground at his feet, and wrapped me in another tight hug. "I'm so sorry, baby."

I tittered, trying my damnedest to hold back the ridiculous tears flooding my vision. "It's so stupid, because I wasn't even hurt this time. Not really."

He pulled back, his charcoal-colored eyes dropping to my throat, and he raised a knowing brow. "Oh?"

"This is just a scratch," I told him, tracing the scab with my thumb.

"No," he protested, shaking his head slowly. "No, this is bullshit. He's going to take it too far one day, and then I don't even know what I'll do."

I smiled and smacked his chest. "You'll mourn my death like the good boyfriend you are."

"Gods, Gemma," he muttered, pulling away before leaning on his pitchfork for support. "You can't talk about your life like it's so meaningless. It matters to me. *You* matter to me."

I grinned and tapped his nose. "Good. Which is why I

expect you to mourn my loss properly. I want you to wear black for as many days as the Storm King will allow and to wait at least a month before hopping into bed with a new woman. I know it'll be lonely, but I swear to the gods, I'll come back and haunt your ass if you don't."

"Run away with me," he whispered, not for the first time since we'd gotten close.

"Never," I teased, shoving down the hope that surged up inside of me at his words.

"This place is terrible," he insisted.

"Not for you."

"If it's terrible for you, then it's terrible for me."

I swallowed hard and forced my lips to curl. "It's not all that bad. Nothing I can't make it through."

He shook his head, pure and raw emotion burning in his dark eyes. "Please, Gemma. Don't wait until it's too late. Run away with me. We can make a good life for ourselves; I know it. We'll change our names, change our appearances. Hell, we can get a boat and paddle across the sea to a new kingdom and start all over again. Just... please. Don't let me lose you."

It was the single most gut-wrenching experience of my life—and I'd thought Alexis's defiling had been bad.

"You won't lose me," I promised in a whisper. I had no idea how I kept the tears from falling. "Everything is going to be okay."

He shook his head, and as he stared at me, I noticed his lids were rimmed in red. He grabbed my chin and kissed me hard, then let me go.

"You better get back inside," he said. "You'll be punished if you're caught."

I sighed, knowing he was right but also knowing that he was upset with me. I didn't want to leave on those terms, but unfortunately, there was nothing I could do. At least, not yet.

"Good night, Tristan," I said as I slowly backed out of the barn.

He sighed and smiled slightly. "Good night, Gem."

But he didn't get back to shoveling. He just stood there hopelessly, watching me disappear into the night.

CHAPTER 5

$\mathcal{A}$LEXIS

A WEEK LATER, AFTER A BRIEF LAYOVER IN BEN'S KINGDOM, WE found ourselves approaching the first town on the other side of the brutal Obsidian Desert.

The days had been blistering hot and the nights freezing cold. There was simply no in-between. During the day, counterintuitive as it might've seemed, we actually stayed cooler by covering our bodies in a layer of thin clothing from head to toe. It did wonders to prevent our skin from burning, while simultaneously allowing in a bit of a breeze—not that the wind blew all that much across the sands. And during the night, we huddled together for warmth. If nothing else, it was a group bonding experience I wouldn't soon forget.

In fact, I wouldn't soon forget *anything* I'd experienced over the course of these past few months. Every minute detail would remain permanently burned into my brain for eternity. Good or bad.

I fingered the wedding ring that was looped through a thin chain about my neck. The massive stone was just another reminder that the king gave zero fucks about what I thought. Everyone knew I hated jewels. He probably picked the biggest one that would fit on a ring just to spite me. The bastard.

I'd remained unusually silent since the night the Storm King ruined my world, and my Storm Princes had been kind enough to give me my space. It was hard to categorize my feelings about the whole thing. It was Cal who I'd been with —a man I knew and loved—not the Storm King. It wasn't exactly rape, though neither party was all that willing.

I didn't hold it against Cal, and none of the other brothers held it against either of us. We were all smart enough to know exactly who to place the blame on. Still, there was a part of me that was raw and irritated, closed off and caved in.

But there was another part of me that was ready to heal. I didn't tend to dwell on negative things for very long. So much of my life had been scraping the bottom anyway, that I'd learned a long time ago to keep moving forward without looking back.

I made a promise to myself, though. I might be talking and laughing and loving again soon, but I would *never* forget what he made us do, and I would *never* let him do that to us again.

The only problem being, he'd already promised that the sex-watching escapades were going to be a monthly occurrence. If I failed to fall pregnant by the end of the sixth month, he was going to kill me. How he planned on doing that, exactly—considering he hadn't even truly killed Ash— was anyone's guess. Personally, I didn't want to find out. Ash's gift involved dying in order for his magic to work; mine didn't. Maybe he'd be able to kill me much easier because of that?

"Ravibad," Ben said, gesturing to the town before us. "It's the second largest city in Eristan. Full of gangs, lawlessness, and irresponsibility but also a very chill group of people."

I wasn't exactly sure how "gangs" and "chill" related much, but I had no doubt I was about to find out.

Drums and *rockas* sounded in the street as random people danced around unattended fires. Clotheslines hung from window to window like some intricate spiderweb, soaking up the smoke. I bet they'd smell awful in the morning.

The skin of the Eristani people appeared at least three shades darker than mine, which, given my all-too-recent status as an ex-miner, I supposed it wasn't all that difficult to achieve. Still, these people were a similar shade to Ben, all tanned and beautiful with perfect complexions. Some of them even had wings protruding from their backs, dark like charcoal, with orange silhouettes due to the fire.

Ben waved us ahead, weaving through the streets of endless people. It was late, the swollen yellow moon hung heavy in the star-speckled sky, but there were just as many people out as I would expect to see in the day. Were they nocturnal? I had no idea. It might make sense because of the extreme heat, but I knew so little about the world we lived in that it was impossible to really guess.

Crammed between Dan and Ben, with Speedy on my shoulder, I shuffled along until we came across a building with a sign that read "Inn." The establishment looked nothing like any inn I'd ever seen. Blackwood inns were sturdy and cozy, while this was a shitty, green, two-story structure that looked like it'd seen better days *decades* ago.

Ben turned around and smiled sympathetically. "We can rent a room for tonight, and then tomorrow morning we'll finish the journey to the capital of Eristan—Erishwar."

Inside the inn, a woman with a floral turban sat with her bare feet propped up on a desk. She had a cigarette of some sort loosely grasped between her thumb and index finger, except it was greenish and sweet smelling rather than harsh. I didn't see any wings on her.

"What coin you got?" she asked us in a bored tone that suggested she asked that exact same question *a lot.*

Ben dropped a bag of jewels on the counter. "Blackwood jewels."

The woman pursed her lips. "Blackwood currency is worth almost nothing here. You better have at least another bag if you're hoping to accommodate all five of you."

"Oh, and the bird," I added, pointing to my shoulder.

What a stupid fucking thing to say. I mean, it was the truth, but it was probably going to cost us *three* bags of jewels now.

To my surprise, the woman smiled and shook her head. "Animals always stay free in Eristan."

Interesting... Animal lovers? Who would have guessed? Although, as a nation of part animals, I suppose it made sense.

Ben plopped a second bag of jewels on the counter, and the woman at the desk scooped them up and handed us a key. "Second floor. Third room on the left. Be out by dawn."

Ben nodded and took the key, leading us up a wide set of sandstone stairs.

"Well, she seemed... pleasant," Dan muttered, glancing over his shoulder.

Ben chuckled. "Eristani people aren't really well known for their hospitality. More like their hostility. It's a good thing it's after dusk or we probably would have been in a fight by now."

"Wait a second." I shook my head. "I thought you just said they were chill?"

"I also said they were violent and lawless... *during the day.* After dusk, though, everyone drinks and smokes and puts their differences behind them to have a nice, relaxing evening."

That was... *so weird*. I couldn't imagine drinking with someone I'd just been fighting with earlier in the day.

Ben grinned. "Obviously the smoke and drink help to keep things peaceful."

When we reached the top of the stairs and found our room, I groaned. It might've been the third on the left, but it was still an even number—fourteen. *Yuck*. I hated even numbers. There was something so disgustingly perfect about them, it made my skin crawl. Ben once said I had some impossible-to-pronounce phobia, and I was pretty sure he was right.

The Sand Prince sighed amusedly and tossed the key into the air, catching it quickly before turning around and heading back downstairs. "I'll go request a different room."

Gods, he was so freaking sweet. I didn't even have to say a word. He just knew.

Cal raised a brow. "What the hell was that about? We didn't even open the door. How could he possibly know that this room isn't in acceptable condition?"

I grinned. "He's Benson Storm. He pretty much knows everything."

Cal tipped his head in my direction, conceding that I was right. There was no denying it; Ben really was incredibly knowledgeable.

"Plus, I kind of hate even numbers."

"Oh, Jewels," Rob said, shaking his head. "How quickly you've gone from deprived peasant to spoiled princess."

I stuck my tongue out at him. "I'll have you know, I hated even numbers long before I ever became a princess. I could barely stand to work in the even-numbered mine shafts."

As they chuckled at my ridiculousness, Ben jaunted back

up the stairs, wiggling a new key out in front of him. "How does room *fifteen* sound, Sailor?"

I sighed, and the resonance seemed to come straight from my heart. "It sounds wonderful. Thank you."

Ben opened the door and ushered us inside, locking the rattly knob behind us. There were no beds, no furniture, no lanterns, just a pile of silken pillows of various shapes, sizes, and colors scattered about the floor. It reminded me of the massage parlor Dan had taken me to, only a hundred times dirtier.

Rob flopped down and put his hands behind his head, getting comfortable as if the filth didn't bother him at all.

Speedy started whistling an old mining tune I used to know, so Cal grabbed him—his body in one hand, his head in the other—and twisted. A sickening crack filled the air, instantly turning my stomach, and soon the golden dust appeared, transforming the little bird into my precious Adam. *Asher*. Fuck.

"So, what's the plan?" Ash asked, grabbing a pair of boxers from a rucksack and slipping them on. "Tomorrow we just waltz up and request an audience with the king?"

Ben sighed. "Sort of. I mean, we're going about this visit all sorts of wrong. Usually when a royal comes to visit, there's pomp and circumstance, weeks' worth of planning, an official entourage, and so on."

"*Right*," Ash said, as if urging his brother to continue faster. He lifted a shirt and a pair of pants from his bag and continued dressing.

I didn't know why his magic made his clothes disappear every time he used it, but I was secretly thanking the gods for their little quirks. A naked Storm Prince was a delicious sight any time of day.

Ben took a deep breath. "They might be a little offended that we didn't formally announce our presence prior to our arrival, but we just didn't have time. We have less than a month to solve the harpy problem and return with a chimera egg, and I have no idea how to go about doing any of that."

"What are we hoping the king will even say?" I asked, lying down beside Rob and resting my head on his chest. He shot a decidedly smug grin at Asher before putting his arm around my shoulder.

Cal moved to stand between them, breaking up the stare down they had going on. "We're ultimately hoping he'll reinstate the old treaty they once had with Essund—Ben's family's kingdom before the Storm King took over. But I'm not necessarily expecting cooperation."

Ben shook his head. "No. Not without something in return."

I sighed. "So, we have to do a favor for Timberlune by doing a favor for Eristan. Probably *that* favor will involve doing something for Hydratica..."

It all seemed like a hopeless, tangled mess of dead ends.

Dan lay down on the other side of me and curled into my back, cocooning me in heat and safety. I loved being close to my guys. It had been so long since we'd had a moment just for *us*... and now we were on this hairbrained mission to save Timberlune from extinction and to find some elusive chimera egg, which, what the fuck even was a chimera? The guys didn't seem to know either. Maybe that was something else we'd learn from the king.

"We'll figure it out," Dan promised me. "And we'll get it done, even if it *is* another wild goose chase on behalf of another kingdom."

I shook my head and sighed once more. This whole thing was a shitshow, an epic disaster just waiting to happen, and we had no choice but to follow through with it.

"Rest up, guys," Ben suggested. "Tomorrow's going to be a long and interesting day."

~

THE NEXT MORNING, I AWOKE BEFORE ANYONE ELSE AND immediately grabbed some ink and a parchment from my sack. There was a sadness clinging to my gut, residue from a terrible dream I couldn't quite remember. All I knew for sure was that Mom and Gemma were in it and that now I missed them terribly.

I wished more than anything that I hadn't unknowingly dragged them into this fucked-up world. That I hadn't written that letter to Gem. But none of that mattered now. I couldn't change it, so I may as well embrace it.

I decided to write them each a letter. It wasn't like things could feasibly get any worse. But just in case, I vowed to keep them short.

DEAR GEMMA,

How are you doing? I don't know if I even want to know the answer to that question...

I miss you so much. I think about you often, hoping and praying that you're happy and well—but I don't even know who I'm praying to anymore. The gods are clearly not listening.

Stay strong. *Please*. I love you.

—Alexis

SINCE I WAS THE ONLY ONE AWAKE, I ALLOWED A HOT TEAR TO burn down my cheek, succumbing silently to my sorrow. I took a shaky breath and put her letter off to the side, immediately beginning on Mom's.

· · ·

DEAR MOM,

I love you.

I feel like it's been forever since we last spoke...

I hope you're not worrying about me. I'm fine. The princes are amazing, and they treat me like... well, a princess. I'm doing my best to *serve the king* while still honoring and protecting *you*, but I'm terrified it won't be enough. Please know that whatever happens, I gave it my all. And I will continue to give my all until the day I die... if that ever happens.

Stay strong, Mom. For me.

Love,

Alexis

I NO MORE THAN WIPED MY TEARS AND TUCKED MY LETTERS into my pack when I startled at the sound of our freaking door breaking down.

Five or six people rushed into the room brandishing curved weapons and shouting at us in another language. They wore torn clothing with red kerchiefs tied to their arms and sported badass expressions that had my blood running cold. They didn't look like royal guards, so it was a pretty fair guess to assume they were gang members looking for some easy coin.

I couldn't help it, my magic flared up on instinct to save my life, coating me in a layer of curly peach flames that seemed to be dancing rather than raging.

That was how it worked. If I was in danger, it came to my aid no matter what; but if I wanted to control it any other time, I had to actually speak the word "fire" in order for it to comply. Fickle fire, anyway.

Suddenly, the guys were up, charging the air with an energy and power I couldn't yet see. It must've been simmering underneath their skin, just waiting to come out, unlike mine, which was on display for the world to witness.

There was no water nearby, so Dan couldn't do much. And unless the intruders jumped into the air, Cal couldn't do much either. Ben had no plants to manipulate. But Rob could be brave, which he was already doing, muscling his way to the front of the line; and Asher could shift, which he did, into the shape of a fearsome jaguar.

At the sight of a girl who was on fire but unburnt by the flames, a man who was now a ferocious animal, and another man covered in tattoos with his teeth bared and a look of death in his eye, the thugs backed away in terror. Ash snarled, pushing them closer and closer to the door until they finally ran, leaving us and our jewels far behind.

Next thing I knew, Rob had a blade sunk deep into the jaguar's chest.

The poor thing howled and whimpered as it bled out on the pillows, and before I knew it, Ash was back.

"Fucking *hades*, Rob. Next time at least make it a clean kill."

He chuckled darkly. "Sorry, I didn't realize I had to cater to your delicate shifter sensibilities."

Ash didn't say a single word, just hauled off and punched his brother square in the face. Rob, of course, retaliated, and soon they were an angry mess of limbs on the floor.

I was in shock, standing there with my mouth gaping wide, arms hanging dead at my sides, mind absolutely numb aside from a few incoherent thoughts. Like: *gods, they're hot when they were fighting*. Especially since Ash was totally freaking naked thanks to the shift.

What? I shook my head. They were brothers; they weren't supposed to get into fist fights, and I certainly wasn't supposed to *enjoy* watching it.

I glanced down, realizing I was still covered in dancing,

curly flames, and I cursed under my breath. I quickly extinguished my magic to help slow the burn, but it was already too late to stop the effects. Because... all magic had a price, and the price of using my fire was uncontrollable lust.

It usually affected at least one other person too, so that we could have sex, effectively cooling the desire raging inside of us. But then, the other part of my magic involved marriage proposals, which tended to make the whole thing just a teeny bit awkward. Aside from having sex, my only other options were being exposed to the freezing cold or waiting the torturous desire out until it faded on its own... and who knew how long that might take or if it was even truly possible?

I took a step toward them as they fought, drawn to the wildness in their eyes, the tension in their muscles, the testosterone they were emitting in violent waves. I could practically feel my pupils dilating.

But Ben held out an arm and stopped me. "I think we better let them get this out of their system. I don't know exactly what's going on here, but they clearly need to let out a little aggression."

I pursed my lips, trying to ignore the lust tugging me in the direction of the fight.

"Is this some sort of 'boys will be boys' bullshit?" I asked sternly. "Because I don't believe in that kind of mentality. Boys should be responsible for their actions too."

Even if they *were* two incredibly sexy boys who were absolutely wrecking each other and turning me on more by the second.

Ben shook his head. "Nope. If you wanted to blow off a little steam and fight with one of us... okay, fine, yeah. That wouldn't happen. You're our lover; fist fighting with you isn't even remotely an option. But the five of us... we're brothers. Sometimes shit just builds up. If there was another girl or guy—outside of our group—who you wanted to fight, no way in hades would we interfere."

Dan leaned forward and grinned at me. "For the record, I think it'd be hot as hell to watch you kick someone's ass."

I huffed out a breathy laugh, watching in heated torment as the guys landed blow after blow, tumbling to the floor and then launching back into one another. Gods, I wanted to be the meat in the middle of that violent sandwich.

I forced my gaze onto Dan. "If only I knew how to fight."

Cal pursed his lips from where he stood at Dan's other side. "We really do need to get you back in with Taron and Tamara."

They were the twin vampires who'd been training me thus far. I would have preferred them to tag along with us on this journey so that I could continue running drills and shit, but they were *vampires* and therefore restricted by the sun. We didn't have enough time to only travel at night, and so, we'd ultimately decided to continue my training once we returned—assuming we *did* return.

The guys might not have known it yet, but I had every intention of learning how to kick ass and take names so that one day I could complete Rory's quest—the magical guy who'd given me his powers upon death—and kill the fucking Storm King once and for all.

I kept that shit to myself, of course. No need to worry them unnecessarily.

Eventually, one last punch was thrown—Rob's fist splitting the skin of Ash's cheek. But instead of retaliating, Ash just stood there taking deep breaths and stretching out his neck with a glare—a sexy as fucking sin glare.

My desire was soaring to unimaginable heights now, making it hard for me to even breathe. The scorching ache in the pit of my core had quickly turned maddening, clawing at me as it demanded release. I couldn't put it off any longer.

"Are you two done yet?" I asked, a little too breathlessly, but they didn't seem to notice.

They each nodded.

"Good. Because now it's *my* turn to wreck your world."

I grabbed both of their necks, pulling them in and alternating deep, passionate kisses between them. They didn't even resist; I don't know if it was because they were too tired from fighting or if my magic was simply too strong, but I was thrilled nonetheless. Each of their hands found one of my breasts and squeezed, while Rob's other hand roamed across my ass, and Ash's other hand knotted in my hair.

"Gods, Sweets," Asher groaned against my mouth, "you're so fucking perfect. Tell me you'll marry me?"

Rob pulled my lips over to his, consuming me from the inside out. "No, Jewels, marry *me*."

This was all very ironic, considering I was already technically married to Cal.

"How about we skip the proposals and head straight to the honeymoons?" I suggested, unbuttoning Rob's pants and sliding them down his legs to make him as naked as Asher already was. As his cock sprang free, I noticed Rob's tattoo hiding between his hip bone and his groin. It was a jewel. I'd picked it out—a representation of *me* forever marked on his body. I didn't realize how aroused it'd make me to see it.

Our eyes met as Rob stepped the rest of the way out, kicking his clothing off to the side. The two Storms approached me then, so in sync it was hard to believe they'd just been beating the shit out of each other.

Lust flared hotter within me, stoking my need for sex like a bonfire.

Dropping to my knees, I grabbed both of their dicks, pumping them slowly as I took Rob's head into my mouth. He groaned instantly, imbuing me with confidence and carnality. A moment later, I switched over to Ash, sucking him like I always wanted to back in Blackleaf. He gasped, and his fist clamped down harder in my hair, pulling the roots tightly.

Fucking gods, I loved this. Knowing it was *me* who did this to them; *me* who had absolute control over their pleasure and their bodies. *Me* who would give them everything they craved.

When I popped my lips off them, I stood up and stripped out of my gown. "I want you to fuck me. *Right now.*"

"Think you can handle us both?" Rob asked, spinning me around and shoving his erection into my butt cheek.

I shook my head, overwhelmed with lust. "I don't know, but I sure as fuck want to *try.*"

"Good," Ash groaned, dropping to the floor on his back and pulling me down on top of him. His dick was already slick from my mouth, so he had no trouble easing into me. Then he pulled me down to his chest, exposing my ass.

"We're going to do this slow, Jewels," Rob promised. "Roll your hips and see how this feels."

I did, and as Asher filled one part of me, Rob started to fill the other.

"Relax, babe," Rob coaxed me as he slid in a bit deeper. "Don't squeeze."

Taking a deep breath, I tried my best to remain calm and malleable. It didn't take long for that calm to morph into intense pleasure though, as they both started moving inside of me.

"Oh, gods," I moaned, panting like a bitch in heat. The sensations were so powerful, they were almost too much to handle.

"Slow breaths, Sweets," Ash whispered, staring deep into my eyes as he fucked me. "No hyperventilating and passing out on us."

I wanted to chuckle, but my body wouldn't allow it. It was

strung too tight, filled to the brim by two of the hottest guys I'd ever seen. Two guys I fucking loved unconditionally.

I moaned again, feeling my body tense, knowing I was about to explode from the pressure and the pleasure. My magic heightened every sensual stroke, every silken touch, every thrust and every plunge and...

Then I was coming, crying out as my muscles pulsed from *both* places, heightening the force of my orgasm that much more. At the carnal sound of my release, both guys growled and groaned as they too let go and came undone.

The heat of my magic finally died down, and all three of us collapsed into the pillows, panting like crazy.

"Do you feel better now, Sexy Lexi?" Dan asked with a wicked grin as he tucked his spent dick back into his pants. Cal and Ben did the same. Apparently, they hadn't let our little show go to waste.

"Quite," I muttered, practically purring in contentment.

"Good," Cal grumbled, "because that better be the last damn time Ash touches you before he completes his deal."

My mouth hung open as I finally realized our error.

Rob sat up in the pillows and glared across my naked body at Ash. "You little fucker. I can't believe you cheated like that."

"It's not like I meant to!" he shouted back defensively. "She just like..." He shook his head dazedly.

"Hit you with an undeniable tidal wave of lust and attraction?" Dan filled in.

Ash pointed at him. "Exactly what he said. How the fuck did that even happen?"

"It's the price of her magic," Ben informed him with a smirk. "If she uses her fire, she ends up insatiably horny. The magic spreads out and effects at least one other person, sometimes more. It's a bit random with its victims, though."

I snorted. "*Victims*? As if any of you are in any way, shape, or form *unwilling*."

"Willing or not," Rob cut in, "this doesn't happen again, and it doesn't mean you're in either, *Shifter Prince*. You still have to jump in order to prove yourself."

"No worries, dickhead," Ash spat with a glare. "I'll jump, and I'll flip your dumbass off the whole way down."

"I'd like to see that happen," Rob growled with a sharp smile.

"*Okay*! Now that we've got *that* cleared up..." Ben interjected with an exaggerated roll of his chocolatey brown eyes, "let's get the fuck out of here before another gang decides to descend and we *all* get caught up in an orgy. We can't plan a meeting with the king if we're fighting and fucking all morning."

He tossed me my dress before opening a rucksack and passing out swords. Most of the guys already had knives that they kept on their person at all times, but I had no doubt these longer, more lethal weapons would come in handy.

"I should have done this last night," the Sand Prince muttered as he shook his head in disappointment. He saved me for last, tossing me a small sheathed blade attached to a strap. "Hook that around one of your thighs. You can hide the dagger under your dress—just in case things get... *ugly* on our way to, or even once we arrive at, the palace."

I wriggled back into my gown and attached the blade to my thigh. If Ben was expecting enough resistance to merit *me* wielding a blade, then we were heading into dangerous territory indeed.

I took a deep breath and squared my shoulders. "I want a sword too."

Ben glanced at Cal, who glanced at Rob, who glanced at Dan, and so on until they all exchanged the same stupid look.

I rolled my eyes and sighed dramatically, holding out my

hand, palm facing up. "I am not a damsel in distress, assholes. You're sure as fuck not giving me a tiny little knife just because I'm a woman. I want a damned sword too."

"I had a feeling you'd say that," Ben muttered, reaching back into the bag and withdrawing a final long sword.

Like the blade before it, this one also had a sheathe attached to a strap, but this belt was wide enough to fit a pair of hips rather than a single leg. I cinched it tightly around my waist and nodded, a shit-eating grin smeared across my face.

"Happy now?" Rob asked. His tone sounded half amused, half annoyed.

"I am," I bit back smugly.

He shook his head and pushed through the empty inn doorway. "Such a spoiled princess."

"Such an arrogant dick."

"An arrogant dick you like to fuck," he retorted.

The other guys chuckled at our banter as we all filed out of the room, finally on our way to the Eristani palace, at last.

CHAPTER 6

The sooner we left Ravibad, the better.

We had another jaunt through the desert, but only for a few hours this time, before we came upon the capital city of Erishwar. The closer we got to our destination, the more beautiful things became, and not just because I was *totally fucking done* with traveling. I mean, it was ten times more beautiful than the rest of the kingdom. It was almost as if the beauty had been transplanted there. There was no way it could have been natural.

The people were gorgeous and dressed stunningly in shimmering gowns and suits; the buildings were pristine, structural marvels made of the finest white sandstone. The streets were also made of sandstone, and they hadn't a single crack or stain on them. The environment was lush, and the flora was in bloom—boasting warm shades of pink, scarlet, orange, and gold—thriving as if it somehow received water every day, though I had no idea where it would've come from considering we were in a *desert*. It was seriously just... amazing.

I figured Blackwood—with their plethora of jewels—

would at least have something *similar* to this, but no. This place was like nothing I'd ever seen.

In the center of it all stood the palace, surrounded by a ring of water wide enough to hold docks and boats, and beyond that, another ring of buildings that branched out and formed the rest of the city.

I couldn't stop gaping. Everywhere I looked I saw something even more amazing or beautiful than before.

Dan leaned over and slipped his hand around my waist. "I can give you something to fill that mouth if you want."

I pinched his side, and he chuckled, pulling me even closer.

Cal and Ben were in the lead, strolling through the fancy streets as if they were right at home.

"Don't let the beauty fool you," Ben warned. "It's deceiving. These people may be richer and prettier than the others, but they are just as lethal. I wouldn't trust 95 percent of them before dusk."

Great. Just freaking great. I was bound to say or do something stupid, offensive, or just plain annoying, and we were all going to die. Or, on the off chance that we really were immortal, we would at least get into a fight with Eristan, starting yet another war. Maybe they should have just come without me.

By the time we reached the water's edge, we suddenly found ourselves surrounded by a hoard of winged guards. Their chest plates were black, and the metal was brushed so they didn't reflect the sun and blind someone, and there were slits at the back that allowed their ebony wings to protrude safely. That was the extent of their armor, though. They didn't appear to be wearing any clothing beneath the chest plates—unless they wore black muscle shirts or something— and all they wore on their legs were baggy black harem pants.

Either these guys didn't do battle very often, or they were so skilled they didn't need much protection. I was scared it might've been the latter.

Holding our hands up, we let Ben speak on our behalf.

"We come in peace," the Sand Prince assured them calmly. "We simply wish to have an audience with the King of Eristan."

The lead guard's dark chin jutted out. "No one simply walks up to the palace and receives an audience with our royals. Who do you think you are?"

"The Blackwood Princes and Princess," Ben said confidently.

The guards looked us over, but we were rough and untidy due to the nonstop traveling we'd done the past couple of weeks. I was sure we looked like *nothing* of the sort.

"I do not believe you," the guard growled, jabbing a spear in our general direction. "Leave the city now or pay the price."

Ben sighed. "What is the price? Jewels? We have jewels."

The guard spit on the ground at our feet. "Blackwood jewels—"

"Mean nothing here, yeah, we heard," Rob said sarcastically, waving his hand in the air.

Ben's body tensed, as if he were trying damn hard to ignore his brother's blatant disrespect. "Since when have relations gotten so bad? I thought we were allies?"

"We were allies when the Storm King wasn't overtaxing our trade routes to the east," he said mockingly. "He has worn out his welcome in these lands, and so have his jewels."

Ben cocked his head and raised his brows. "Fair enough. But still, I must insist upon seeing the king. It's urgent. Please tell them we're here and that we apologize for not having a formal meeting planned, but we just ran out of time."

"Save it," the guard snapped, raising his spear in preparation for launching it at us. "The price is death, not jewels. Leave now or meet your demise."

Dan sucked in a deep breath and lifted his hands, the water from the ring beside us rose into the air like a giant tentacled limb.

The guards watched in wide-eyed terror and disbelief as the massive wave undulated in the air. "What the gods?"

Ash used their moment of distraction to morph into a jaguar once more, stalking protectively between them and me.

Ben smirked as he looked from his brothers over to the guards. "You want to play this game? We'll play. This is your last warning, though. Take us to see the king."

The guard's mouth snapped shut, and he once again jabbed the spear in our direction. "We protect our royals to the death."

"We're not here to harm anyone."

"*Attack!*" he shouted, waving his men forward.

As they charged at us, Dan let the wave crash down. Some of them were quick enough to fly out of the way, others were hammered flat into the ground. I wasn't sure if I could have survived a hit like that and stood back up, but the Eristani guards were apparently quite tough. Less than half of them stayed down, while the rest rose up and rushed at us.

Panicked, I decided to call on my magic.

"Fi—" I shouted, but Cal came up behind me and grabbed my mouth, cutting off the word.

"Please don't do that." His voice was calm but pleading. "It'll be so much easier to fight these guys without stopping to have sex in the middle."

I pried his fingers from my lips and glared. "Fine."

Reaching down, I tried to unsheathe the sword from my waist, but he halted me again.

"Don't do that either."

65

I snarled at him and pulled my arm away. "So, what do you want me to do? Just *watch*, like some princess stuck in a tall tower? I can do shit for myself, Calvin."

"Don't think of it like that, Peach," he said as he caught a spear midair with his sky powers and sent it hurtling back at the Eristani guards. "It's merely a precaution. Save your power and your blades as a last resort. It's not because you're incapable of helping; we just shouldn't go there if we don't have to."

Like an indignant child, I plopped onto the ground, spread out my skirts, and crossed my arms and legs. Cal shot me one last apologetic smile before returning to the fight.

"Whatever," I muttered to myself. "I'll sit here and stay out of the way. No problem. It doesn't bother me in the slightest that I'm essentially just a shiny little trophy sitting on their mantle. A trinket they won in the 'get fucked' tournament."

I hated feeling so bratty, but sometimes these powers of mine made shit incredibly difficult. I grabbed a pebble and threw it into the water, huffing. I suppose I could at least count the guards.

One, two, three, four, five, and *six* on the ground after the wave. *Seven* with a spear in his chest. *Eight* hanging from a statue of a horse. *Nine* with jaguar teeth in his throat. Plus, *ten, eleven, twelve, thirteen,* and *fourteen* still standing—or flying—and battling it out.

I threw another rock into the water, sighing as the ripples slowly spread further and further outward. But in the water's reflection, I saw a boat coming at us—not an armored ship on the verge of attack but a fancy cruiser carrying what looked to be a royal entourage.

I glanced up and saw them sailing closer with my own eyes. At the helm was a shirtless man with black harem pants and washboard abs, a golden crown sitting crooked on his head. Directly behind him was a woman dressed in similar attire: black baggy pants and a bikini top with sashes attached to her elbows, wrists, knees, and ankles. Beyond her, an entire crowd of "jewel diggers," as Rob would call them, stood biting at the bit, waiting anxiously to get acknowledged by one of the royals.

"Enough!" the man shouted from the boat—the one who I presumed to be the King of Eristan. He lifted his arms high in the air. "What is this nonsense about?"

Everyone paused midpunch, except Ash, who intentionally launched onto an upturned spear. I stood and dusted off my gown, subtly moving in front of him so he could shift back unseen.

"King Solomon," Ben said, bowing deeply. "It has been too long."

"Prince Benson?" he asked curiously. His black wings spread out wide, and he glided from the boat onto dry land.

Their entrance was a little excessive. I mean, what was the point in the fancy boat if they could all fly?

King Solomon strolled closer, looking suspicious. "Why in the gods are you here? And without a formal declaration or invitation."

Ben sighed, still a bit breathless from fighting. "I told them to tell you, but they wouldn't listen; they insisted on getting their asses kicked first. We have urgent business to discuss."

King Solomon looked around, assessing the number of guards he'd just lost, then shook his head. "You owe me big-time now, Storm Prince. That's a bad position to be in, considering I'm already angry at your rudeness for showing up unannounced."

"Our deepest and sincerest apologies, Your Majesty," Ben repeated once more.

Solomon pursed his lips and waved a hand over his head. "Come on. We'll chat inside over a smoke and a drink."

I glanced at the princes, wondering where Ash had disappeared to, when a cute little brown bird perched on my shoulder. It cocked its head, showcasing a tiny red dot on its throat, and chirped pleasantly.

"Well, if it isn't my little Speedy bird," I said, smiling as I boarded the king's vessel after the others.

It only took a few minutes to cross the ringed lake and moor on the other side, and that's when it hit me: the boat must have been for *us*. I kind of felt like an idiot.

Inside the palace, there were all sorts of interesting things —statues of wild animals and oversized plants cut from marble, gold, and crystal. But also, *real-life* animals strolling through the halls—white tigers, leopards, lemurs, sloths, and birds—and *real-life* plants and vegetation weaving themselves into the very essence of the sandstone walls.

I glanced at Speedy on my shoulder and shook my head. "This place is pretty incredible, huh?"

He chirped flatly, and I had a feeling he was unimpressed with the excessive grandiose.

The king took his throne, sitting with his legs spread wide, hand on a scepter that must've been sitting there waiting for him. "What urgent business are we talking about, little prince?"

I quirked a brow. Little prince? If it weren't for the few strands of silver in the king's black hair, I would have guessed he and Ben were close to the same age.

A handful of scantily dressed servants sauntered in, delivering trays of drinks and tins of rolled-up weeds for smoking. They sort of reminded me of djinn, creatures I'd sometimes read about in fantasy romance novels, and I half-assed wondered if they were attached to a lamp somewhere.

"I want to discuss the old Treaty O' Ley," Ben said as he took a rolled-up tube of weed and lit it on a flaming bowl of liquid that one of the servant girls was bringing around.

"Out of the question," the king said easily, blowing smoke into the air. "Those lands are sacred to us. The last time we made that arrangement, we didn't know what it would mean. In that amount of time, almost all of our chimeras have become extinct."

"Chimeras?" I accidentally blurted out as I carefully picked up one of the rolls of weed. As in, the same creature that the Storm King wanted us to acquire an egg from?

The king turned to me. "Yes, rude girl. Chimeras. Eristan's sacred animal and idol."

"Can I see one?" I asked, because I guess if I was already being called rude, I may as well actually earn the title.

I lit the end of my roll on the flaming bowl and tried my damnedest to keep from coughing. I'd never done this before, but obviously I didn't want to look like a total fucking dumbass, so I exhaled quickly and took a few deep gulps of oxygen before trying again.

He sighed and rubbed a hand across his face. "What part of nearly extinct do you not understand?"

I shrugged, taking in a slightly deeper breath of the weed this time. I could practically feel the smoke swirling around in my lungs. Oddly enough, it was almost relaxing.

"We don't have any," he continued. "We've seen glimpses of them in the wild. But *only* glimpses. We estimate that there are only ten or less left on the planet."

"And you think this has something to do with the Lunaley?" Ben asked, piecing the puzzle together.

I knew the fae and harpies were fighting over that damned place for *some* reason, I just always assumed it was over *magic*, not *animals*.

"Of course it does," the king said, as if Ben were stupid. "What other reason is there? And those godsdamned Fae won't leave it alone. We're this close to wiping them off the map."

He pinched his thumb and forefinger together for emphasis. Then his keen eyes darted back over to Ben.

"Which is, of course, why you're here. Doing business on behalf of my enemies?"

"No, Your Majesty," Cal said, stepping forward and changing the direction of the conversation. "That's not at all why we're here. We don't want either of you as enemies, which is why we're here to help you get your land back."

The king's suspicious expression changed into that of surprise. So did mine. I thought that was *exactly* why we were there.

"We don't want the chimeras to disappear," Ben said, taking over once more. "They're beautiful and majestic creatures. We'd like to do what we can to help."

The king smiled. The warmth that touched his dark eyes surprised me. "Part lion, part eagle, part dragon—that's what our idols are made of. There are no more dragons in existence, so if chimeras die, dragons die for good."

"Part eagle," I whispered to Speedy. "That must be how they lay eggs."

He chirped in return.

"Yeah, or the dragon part," I admitted, is if Speedy had called me out.

My not-so-internal monologue drew the king's attention over to me once more. "You have a pet bird, I see."

I nodded and took a nervous drag on my weed. "Yes, Your Majesty. I used to have a pet sloth before the bird. But he..." I exhaled slowly and smoke gusted from my lips. "He died."

The king put a hand on his chest, covering his heart. "My sympathies. It is not easy to lose an animal you love."

"No, it certainly isn't. It was one of the hardest things that ever happened to me—and I've been through quite a bit."

He smiled softly and turned back to Ben. "And what would you want in return for helping us save our chimeras?

Money? A new treaty? My daughter Camilla's hand in marriage?"

His daughter? What was she, like a baby?

At the mention of her name, a woman—not a *baby*, but a *woman*—stepped forward and curtseyed low at Ben's feet. She had dark, shimmering hair, and even darker skin than the Sand Prince. Her eyes were dusky, exotic, and seductive, and her lips were almost ten times too plush for her face. The plum-colored attire she wore left little to the imagination—a belly shirt with short sleeves that slipped off her shoulders and taffeta harem pants that easily revealed bikini bottoms beneath.

In other words, she was fucking perfect, and I was jealous as hell. I took my deepest puff yet on the weed and ended up coughing a few times, looking like the amateur I was.

"Prince Benson," she said, her voice sultry and low, spoken in that sexy foreign accent. "It has been so many years since we last saw one another. You have aged like a fine wine."

He smiled and bowed to her in return. "And you, like a desert flower."

And me like an ex-miner about to become an ax murderer. Who the hell did she think she was, moving in on my prince? And why the hell was he flirting back? I was going to have to assert my dominance over my Storm territory somehow.

"Your Majesty," Ben began with slightly flushed cheeks, "as lovely as your daughter would be as a gift, I actually had something else in mind."

"Pray tell." He took a long drag of his weed and gestured for Ben to continue.

Yes, Ben, pray tell. As much as I'd simply *love* to hear about how perfect Camilla was, I'd rather hear the other thing. Whatever the hell it was.

"If we manage to help you save the chimeras, and they're no longer on the verge of extinction, then you will allow us to leave Eristan with a single egg."

King Solomon stared hard at us all for a long while, then out of the blue, he started laughing hysterically. I glanced at Cal, wondering if the desert king had lost his mind.

"Chimeras are deadly protective of their eggs," the king said, sobering up. "It would be suicide to take one. But I'll tell you what, if you *can* somehow manage to get one, then I shall allow you to have it. But you still owe me big-time for killing my soldiers and for showing up unannounced. How do you propose to deal with *that*?"

The guys glanced at each other, trying to silently come up with something suitable to offer the jilted king.

Eventually, Rob stepped forward and cocked his head. "How about I offer you something... *invaluable* in return?"

King Solomon's brows rose, and he flashed us a pearly white smile. "Whatever might that be, little prince?"

Rob brushed his bottom lip and chuckled. "Don't ever call me little prince."

At the subtle threat, the smile fell right off the desert king's face, but before he could get too pissed, Rob spoke back up.

"They don't call me the Spirit Prince for nothing. I know your wife passed suddenly a number of years ago." Rob quickly threw his hands up at King Solomon's sudden scowl. "Just hear me out. I can locate her spirit on the astral plane, and you can finally talk to her for some much-needed closure."

Camilla gasped in the background. "Mama? Can I speak to her too?"

Rob smiled, though it looked a bit like a grimace. "You can, but it'll cut your available time in half."

"How much time are talking about?" King Solomon

asked. His features looked stoic, but if his jittering fingers were anything to go by, he was actually quite nervous.

"However long I can handle the pain," Rob said with a cocky smile. "For both of you, maybe fifteen or twenty minutes?"

The king's eyebrows rose, and he nodded, slowly increasing in enthusiasm. "All right, littl—ah!" He chuckled and waggled his finger, catching himself before calling Rob a little prince. "*Spirit* Prince. Save the chimeras and let me talk to my late wife. If you do these things, it's a deal."

"Sounds good, Your Majesty," Rob said with a small bow.

He pointed at Rob once more. "Do not make me regret this."

Rob chuckled. "We won't, Majesty."

One of those djinn-like servants came back around with an empty gold tray, and following everyone else's leads, I crushed the end of my half-smoked roll of weed and deposited the remainder on the platter.

Ben, Rob, and the rest of us bowed—and curtseyed—preparing to take our leave, but when we stood back up, King Solomon was staring at us intently once more.

"Oh, and Storms?" he said in a dangerous tone. "No more using magic in my kingdom, least of all to kill my people with. Next time, I won't be so lenient."

Ben nodded and bowed his head. "Yes, Your Majesty."

CHAPTER 7

s far as I was concerned, the meeting had gone pretty well.

We were sort of on course for saving Timberlune, and definitely on course for saving the chimeras and securing an elusive chimera egg—which ultimately meant, we were also on track for saving our loved ones from the vicious Storm King. That was a hell of a lot better than being turned away or killed on sight.

Speedy flitted from my shoulder and swan dove straight into the sandstone at our feet. His neck broke with a cringe-worthy crunch, and soon a deliciously naked Asher was standing in his place.

"Why didn't you reinvoke the Treaty O' Ley?" Ash asked, covering his junk with both hands.

"I thought that was the whole point in being here?" Rob added, crossing his burly arms.

So did I, actually. Instead of vocalizing that, I concentrated on *not* staring at Ash's nakedness.

"Aww!" Dan teased them with a grin. "Are you two getting along, now?"

Rob punched Dan in the arm without even looking, and the Sea Prince broke out into a round of laughter.

Cal turned to glare at Asher, his blue eyes practically glowing with fury. "Why in the name of the gods would you turn back into a man *now*? Right in the middle of the fucking street? Do you want to get caught?"

Ash glared right back. "I had questions."

Ben pinched the bridge of his nose and shook his head in thought. "To answer said question, I just think there's more to the Lunaley situation. Plus, I didn't think I should barter too strongly until he was pacified; once the chimeras are safe again, then I'll mention a fresh treaty."

"What more do you think there is?" I asked as we skipped down the palace stairs and entered the creamy sandstone streets.

"Well, there are a number of reasons for animals to migrate," Ben replied thoughtfully. "Favorable climates, ample resources—mainly food—and yes, even to find suitable breeding and nesting grounds. But... I don't know. I guess I just need to see the Lunaley for myself before I can know for sure what's really going on with the chimeras."

"You've never seen it?" I asked, surprised. "I was under the impression that the Storm King had dragged you guys along on every foreign visit in order to show you the ropes."

Dan shook his head. "Nope. It's always been a hot zone for fighting. We were never allowed anywhere near it."

Ah, I supposed that made sense. No one could hurt the Storm King's pawns but him.

Suddenly, Ash's nose lifted into the air and he took a few quick sniffs. "Do you smell that?"

"Smell *what*?" Rob grumbled, shooting him a glare.

Ash sniffed again. "It's like... lavender and chamomile." Then his eyes went wide. "The princess."

He quickly shifted out of his human form, taking on the shape of the jaguar again, rather than the bird.

A moment later, Camilla sashayed from the shadows of a nearby alleyway.

"Prince Benson," she cooed, curtseying leisurely. "What a pleasant surprise to find you here."

Ben smirked but bowed in return. "I'm sure there was no element of surprise about it, Princess Camilla. To what do we owe the pleasure of your company?"

Pleasure? I wanted to smack him upside the head with a pleasure-*stick*. Even though... *ugh*. I knew he was just being polite in order to keep relations friendly. It was his royal duty, and it was probably saving our asses over here.

Besides, I trusted him. I thought. It was *her* I didn't trust.

She turned to Rob, staring uncertainly. "Can you actually help me speak to my mother?"

Rob's brows furrowed, his plush lips pursed, and he nodded.

Fuck, he was sexy. All dark and stoic and tattooed.

She smiled and turned back to Ben. "All right, then. Follow me." Then she glanced at the rest of us. "All of you. I have something you need to see."

Well, at least I'd been invited to tag along. But so help me gods, if she thought the thing they *needed to see* was so much as an inch of her body, then she had another thing coming. A fiery thing. Or maybe just an inexperienced fist to the face.

We wound our way through the beautiful streets of Erishwar until the buildings abruptly stopped and the Obsidian Desert took over once more. In the distance, behind a wavering heat shimmer that distorted my vision, I was almost positive I saw an oasis—a small chunk of lush green vegetation amid a barren land. Then again, it might've been a mirage...

She pointed to the spot. "We'll cross the desert and enter the oasis. Then you can see a chimera with your own eyes."

Speaking of eyes, mine widened to the size of saucers. "Are they dangerous?"

Camilla grinned and shook her head. "Only if you get in their way. They're very *Eristani* in that regard."

My saucered eyes narrowed immediately. Was that a low-key threat? Like, stay out of my way, bitch, or I'm going to get dangerous?

Well, back at ya, desert flower. I am this fucking close *to plucking you like the weed you are and tossing you out to wither in the sun.*

"Besides," she continued, glancing over at Speedy by my side, "you have a protector. You should have nothing to worry about."

As if I wanted Ash to get between me and a fucking chimera...

Camilla led the way, followed by Ben, Cal, and Dan. Rob and Speedy waited for me to go ahead of them.

I took a deep breath and wrapped my scarf around my face, protecting my pale cave-dweller skin from the sun, and started walking.

By the time we reached the other side, I was out of breath and panting. If I ever bitched about the Blackwood heat in the dead of summer again, it'd be a miracle. The oasis was even tinier than I imagined, just a greenish pool surrounded by a ring of palm trees. There didn't appear to be any houses or buildings of any sort, so clearly not a place for humans or harpies to dwell.

A massive shadow suddenly appeared across the surface of the pool, and I looked up just in time to be blinded by the sun. Fuck, that desert glare was bright. I blinked a few times as all sorts of colorful spots burned into my vision; then I shaded my eyes and tried again. This time, I saw a chimera circling the air above our heads, and oh my gods, was it a sight to see. When King Solomon had told us about the tri-part creature, I'd tried to imagine it but had pretty much failed. Seeing it in person was extraordinary.

With the face, mane, and massive front paws of a lion, the chimera looked lethal. In the middle, the wings and feathers gave it a touch of delicacy and grace. And at the end, the clawed dragon feet and jagged dragon tail went back to making it appear absolutely terrifying.

It landed with a thud on the other side of the pool, watching us with predatory eyes.

"Stay still," Camilla commanded us. "Let him see we are not a threat."

She didn't have to tell me twice. I stayed as still as humanly possible, not even bothering to *breathe*. We all did. But the chimera still seemed to be set on edge.

"Your jaguar," she said to me, as if it had just dawned on her. "The big cat in him must see your pet as a threat. Go. Back away slowly and wait for me to come get you after the princes and I have our visit."

Fuck no, she wasn't getting rid of me so easily.

"I don't think so." I glanced down at Ash, and he nodded.

I'd rather her see that my "pet" was actually a man than for her to think for one second that she could steal away my Storms. But did I have what it took to slit his spotted throat, knowing it was Ash residing behind those feral eyes? I guess we were about to find out.

I reached down to the sheath at my thigh and gripped my dagger tightly.

"You think my *pet* is the problem?" I asked in an arrogant tone. "Fine."

I grabbed the fur on top of his head and sliced his neck, quick and deep.

"No more pet."

Nausea threatened to consume me as the sloshing sound of his blood assaulted my ears, but I forced myself to remain stoic. This was me asserting my dominance. I couldn't afford to look like a weak bitch *now*.

Anger hardened Camilla's face into stone, and for some reason, I was pretty sure she was way more pissed off that I'd willingly hurt an animal than she was that her plan to get rid of me had failed.

But then the jaguar dematerialized into golden dust and swirled back into the shape of a man. *My* man. Just like the other Storms were. Not *hers*.

Her features softened, and her lips parted in question. "Asher Storm? How?"

"Asher's *dead*," Rob said coldly, warning her to drop the subject. "This is Adam, Alexis's personal royal guard."

Fucking hades, Rob, now I *really* looked like a pansy.

Ash glared at Camilla, looking every inch the hulking predator he just was. "Stay away from the Storm brothers. They're taken by Princess Alexis."

Her eyes narrowed. "*All* four of them? I don't think my father will be very happy to hear that."

Ash shrugged. "I don't care. They already told your father they didn't want you as a gift."

She pursed her lips and turned back toward the chimera, flinging her long black hair in the process. I exhaled a sigh of relief. At least she'd dropped the subject quickly.

A set of shorts whizzed past my face and landed on Ash's chest before falling into his hands. He slipped them on, and I followed the path of their trajectory over to Dan, who shook his head and rezipped his pack.

"I never used to care that your magic left you naked, *Adam*," Dan said with a cheeky half smile. "But now that you're guarding our princess so closely, I find myself getting a little jealous every time she looks at you."

Ash chuckled and played along. "No need to worry about me, *Your Highness*. Who would choose a simple guard over a quartet of handsome princes?"

Dan cocked a brow in my direction. "Good point. Except, she's different, this one. Very unpredictable."

Ash nodded. "So I've noticed."

Dan strolled over and patted his shoulder. "Yeah, well, hopefully you haven't been *noticing* her too closely. I'd hate to have to kill you. You really are a damn good guard."

Ash's eyes widened, and the corners of his mouth twitched. I could tell he was holding back a grin. "Hint taken, Your Highness. You won't have any trouble from me." He paused and glared at Camilla's back. "And hopefully not from *her*, either."

She sniffed in mild disgust, telling me right away that she'd been eavesdropping.

Now that Ash was a man, the lion part of the chimera seemed much more pacified. He settled down in the sand and just sat there looking around, tail swishing almost cat-like in the air behind him.

After a moment, another chimera approached, creeping out of who knows where. The vegetation was not that thick. There couldn't have been many places to hide. If the lack of mane was anything to go by, then I'd guess this pretty creature was a girl.

"There are two of them," I murmured. "A male and a female. So why are they nearly extinct?"

Camilla answered without turning to look at me. "Because they need the Lunaley. It's their breeding and nesting ground. If they can't get to the Ley, then they can't lay their eggs. Plain and simple."

Which was basically what Ben had already suggested.

So, the harpies needed the land to save their beloved animal idols, and the fae needed the land in order to keep their magic and their lives. Personally, I felt the life of a person should always outweigh the life of an animal, but as an animal lover, I totally understood the conundrum. Either way, who was *I* to decide if one life was more important than the other? I resolved to simply treat them as separate but equal issues.

As the chimeras moved closer together, the male stood, and they touched foreheads. Afterward, they did a little prancing dance, circling each around other and fluffing their feathers. It was quite fascinating.

I leaned into Ash's side. "The next animal you shift into should totally be a chimera."

He chuckled and nudged his shoulder into mine. "Now that I know what they look like, I totally can."

"Is that how it works?" I asked, looking up at him in surprise.

He nodded.

"So, how'd you manage to pick a sloth?" I asked, confused. "According to Ben, they're not indigenous to the Blackwood area."

"They're not," Ben cut in, shooting us a stern glance over his shoulder. "The Storm King made us come here a few times on royal business, and obviously we had the protection of *the royal guards*, which is why *Adam*, here, had seen a sloth."

Ash bit his bottom lip. "Yeah, what he said. To be honest, I wasn't all that impressed with the slow-ass thing. I thought it was lazy and weak—one of the main reasons I chose it."

I nodded, filling in the gaps. He'd wanted to die quickly and return to human form as soon as possible; then I'd found him and basically held him hostage for six years.... Damn, I kinda sucked.

The others had been having a conversation of their own at the same time, so we missed the first half of their discussion. But when I tuned into the last half, I heard Cal ask, "So how far away is the Lunaley?"

"A week's journey north," Camilla said offhandedly. "I can take you, if you'd like, but you have to keep up. I move fast."

My nose scrunched, and my lip curled. I wasn't sure if it was a direct jab at me and my abysmal fitness level, but I totally felt attacked. My upper body was cut, thanks to *years* of working the jewel mines in Blackleaf, but distance—walking, running, sprinting—had never been my forte.

"Are you sure your father would allow that?" Ben asked, eyeing her almost suspiciously. "Last time I was here, you weren't allowed outside of the Erishwar city limits."

She scoffed and rolled her eyes. "I'm still not. But I'm old enough to not give a fuck anymore."

"Are you sure it wouldn't be safer for us to get a different escort?" Cal asked, glancing at me with a sympathetic smile. "Someone older, stronger, and more of an explorer type?"

At least they were *trying* to prove to me that they didn't want to be around her. Whether it worked or not, didn't really matter. I was just happy to have their support.

"No," she said flatly, glaring at Cal and then the rest of us. "Either you have *me* as an escort or you blindly feel around the desert for your own way."

Dan sighed, running a hand through his sandy brown hair. "I don't know... Ben, do you think you know your way around well enough?"

He pressed his lips together and shook his head as he thought. "The western half of the desert? Yes. The northern? No."

Camilla sniffed, and a half smile appeared on her face. "Have things really changed so much, Benson?"

She approached him with a swagger in her step that made my blood boil in an instant.

"Do you remember when we talked about uniting our kingdoms one day?"

I tried my damnedest to keep my face neutral, but I must've looked ten shades of pissed. It was news to me, shocking, gut-wrenching news that had my jealosaurus raging.

"Of course I do," Ben said, confirming her words with sickening ease. "I also remember you talking about uniting your kingdom with Hydratica—either of the twin princes would do, if I recall correctly. And Timberlune. You thought you could convince Titus that you were better than Bravia, do you remember that?"

At least Ben wasn't the only object of her desire. That made me feel a bit better. But then she wrapped her arms around his neck, and I was immediately back in ax-mode.

She threw her head back and laughed melodiously. "Ah, the good old days. Back when unions were nothing more than political ploys."

"Aren't they still?" Ben pulled back, leaning as far away from her face as he could.

"No. They're so much more than that now," she said, staring at his lips. "Kiss me once, and I'll stop trying to chase you."

Her eyes darted over to me, and she smiled. She obviously *wanted* to piss me off.

"I can't," Ben said, pushing her hips to gain some distance between them.

"Come on, Benson. One kiss. I just want to see what happens."

"*Nothing* is going to happen, Camilla," he said firmly.

She grinned and bit her bottom lip. "We'll see about that."

She made her move quickly, pushing up onto her tippy toes to mash her lips against his—only it never happened. She got close, but just before their mouths connected, a bolt of lightning tore down from the sky and zapped them apart. As soon as the electricity filled the air, I felt it in my heart, a stabbing pain that brought me to my knees.

All five Storm Princes clutched at their chests too, and Camilla stared in wonder from the ground where she'd fallen on her ass.

"Amazing," she muttered in awe. "So, that's what a blood bond looks like?"

Rob's eyes were wide. "Not usually...."

I turned to him. "What do you mean?"

"I mean—" He gestured to the sky and to each of us—intentionally avoiding Ash—and tried to encapsulate everything that had just occurred. "—this isn't normal. The bond keeps things from happening, yes, but not with fucking lightning."

"Maybe it's because of our powers?" Ben suggested, rubbing his chin as he thought. "Our bond is stronger because the magic used to create it was stronger."

"It's possible," Rob agreed.

Camilla still looked starry-eyed as she turned to me. "I'm sorry, Alexis. I just had to see for myself if the rumors were true. I honestly have no intentions of overstepping my bounds. I hope you'll forgive me."

It was an odd sensation, feeling the flames of your anger extinguish so quickly. For some reason, I couldn't bring myself to be mad at her anymore. Probably because I could feel her emotions, and I knew she was genuinely apologetic.

"It's fine. Just—" I sighed and stood up straight. "—don't try to kiss my Storms."

She smirked and raised a brow. "*Your* Storms, huh?"

I smiled and looked around the oasis from face to handsome face, even stealing a quick glance at Ash. "Yeah. *My* Storms."

She cocked her head and stood up too. "Fair enough."

"How'd you find out about the blood bond?" Rob asked her, sounding both suspicious and apprehensive.

Shit. He was right. If *she'd* heard about it, then it was possible *anyone* could have, even the Storm King.

She shrugged one of her shoulders. "Heard it from a demon during an exorcism the other day."

Ben smirked and raised a brow. "*You* exorcise demons? I find that highly unlikely."

"Not personally, no, but the priest passed the information along." She crossed her arms. "He didn't specifically use your names, but as soon as I saw the five of you, I had my suspicions."

"And you're the only one with suspicions?" Dan asked, prodding a bit further.

She scoffed and put a hand on her hip. "If you're asking if my father suspects, the answer is no. He only sees what he wants to see. Anything else may as well be invisible."

"Good," Rob declared, glancing at us with relief in his gray eyes.

If *he* was relieved, then *I* was relieved, because that most likely meant the Storm King wasn't yet aware of our bond. The longer he stayed unaware, the longer we could keep him from using it against us.

"If you're still game," Camilla said, "we can head to the Lunaley in the morning. I'll need to grab a few supplies tonight: canteens, some salted meats, camels..."

Ben turned to me and shrugged. "It's your call, Sailor. She doesn't have to lead us if you don't want her to. But I don't know my way around this part of the desert. It could end up taking much, much longer without her."

He stared knowingly at me.

As in, if we didn't allow her to lead us, we would run out of time to return home with a chimera egg, and the Storm King would start killing the people I cared about—possibly not my mother, because she was such an important bartering tool for him, but little Lilah and her mother, Aunt Janna, and my other extended family members... and Gemma.

Gods, I missed Gemma. I wished I never would have sent her that first letter. I wished I'd never brought her to the palace at all. Now, the least I could do was return home as fast as possible and pray to the gods she didn't suffer too much in my absence.

I turned to Camilla and nodded.

"Perfect." She grinned. "Meet me here, at the oasis, tomorrow. We'll leave at dawn."

CHAPTER 8

*G*EMMA

I awoke tied to a chair in the tallest tower, groaning as the Storm King's face came into focus.

Not again.

Blood from whomever had been in here before me still puddled on the floor at his feet.

"Rise and shine," he sang in a raspy tenor. His voice was hoarse, and he seemed quite happy. The beating he'd just finished with must have gone well. "Time for us to have a little heart-to-heart."

"You don't have a heart, so that's going to be really difficult."

His hand immediately connected with my face, stinging like a swarm of hornets. Black dots littered my vision, sucking me close to unconsciousness. Had he already knocked me out once before? It was hard to say, considering I didn't remember getting tied to the chair in the first place.

"I'd cut out your tongue if I didn't enjoy beating you so much for your insolence."

I nodded my understanding, feeling the pain slowly fade from my face like a fog.

He withdrew his favorite jeweled knife from his belt and stroked the sharp edge of the blade, pleased when a thin cut appeared on his thumb. "My sources tell me you snuck out the other night."

I took a deep breath and nodded. No point in denying it. His sources were never wrong.

"Where were you going?"

"To get laid, if you really must know."

His smirk never faltered. "Are you allowed to leave the servants' quarters after dark?"

"No, I am not."

Before I could blink, his blade slammed into my forearm, cutting through muscles, nerves, and bone and pinning me to the arm of the chair. My eyes went wide, and I screamed, trying to remain as still as I could, since I knew if I moved it would hurt ten times worse and possibly even cut deeper.

"*Then why were you out after dark?*" he shouted at the top of his lungs, a vein in his forehead bulging as his skin turned a furious shade of red. "Were you meeting with Ashlynn?"

I sucked in a deep breath and gritted my teeth, trying to keep from whimpering. "No, I was meeting a *guy*. My door doesn't swing both ways."

"What about Alexis?"

Gods, this guy didn't take a hint.

"What about her? I already told you I was meeting a guy."

"What guy?"

He twisted the blade a bit, and I cringed in agony as another wave of pain tore up my arm.

I gave him my best flippant eye roll, which probably looked way overly dramatic considering I was trying not to pass out and the little buggers were already halfway into the back of my head. "I don't know. I didn't catch his name."

He then decided to change tactics.

"Did you *see* Ashlynn when you were out whoring around?"

I wracked my brain for the correct response. I knew she wouldn't have told him about our conversation, but would she have mentioned seeing me? If she had and I said no, we'd both be screwed.

I shook my head. "No. I never saw her."

He let go of his dagger's hilt, trusting it'd keep me pinned where he wanted. Honestly, it was fucking overkill—I was already *tied* to the damn chair.

That's when he pulled out another blade—plain, with a brushed metal handle and no jewels.

"What do you know about a man named Crissen?" he asked me far too calmly.

I eyed the blade with growing terror. "Crissen who?"

His icy blue eyes narrowed. "You know *who*."

"Honestly, I don't. If you think that's who I was meeting up with, then I already told you, I don't know the guy's name."

The Storm King held up the knife, its shiny blade reflecting off the setting sun like it had its own hellish fire contained within.

"I'm going to enjoy prying the answers I want from you," he said, his voice thick and slimy as pond scum.

For the first time in a while, I thought about praying to the gods for strength or help.

But I knew they wouldn't come.

～

HOURS LATER, I FOUND MYSELF CURLED UP NEAR THE fireplace in my bedroom.

I was freezing cold from losing so much blood, and my body hurt so bad I could barely even move without vomiting. My chin quivered—actually, my whole body quivered—as I rang out a soft rag in a bowl of hot water. I'd added the special herbs and tinctures the harem ladies had given me weeks ago, and the whole mixture now smelled like a soup far too spicy to eat. Taking the washcloth lightly in my hand, I dabbed at the slashes and cuts on my arms.

Each millisecond of contact was full of scorching pain, and I couldn't help but gag even though nothing came up. Tears streamed down my cheeks, so close together I couldn't tell the individual droplets apart. They skated down my neck, passing more raw cuts before soaking into my dress in a brownish stain. Thank the gods servant outfits were green. It was a dark enough color to hide most of the red, or at least make it appear more brown than crimson.

I removed the cloth once a tingling mint sensation coated that particular part of my skin; then I dunked it in the bowl of herbal water and touched it to a new area of damaged skin. I knew from experience, this shit would take all night, but it was certainly better than allowing the wounds to fester. With this many cuts, if they got infected, I'd probably die in days.

A crunching sound met my ear to the left, and I spun to my opened window, the startled movement shooting waves of angry pain all through me. The moon was high in the midnight sky, and stars twinkled peacefully in the black. There wasn't a cloud in sight, and if it hadn't been for the unbearable pain I was in, it would have been a beautiful night.

I forced myself to smile as more tears poured from my eyes. I couldn't change what was happening to me, nor could

I change the hurt I now felt, but I could decide how I reacted to it all. I could decide whether it stole my happiness, robbing me of innocent moments like peaceful nights under the stars.

I wouldn't. I wouldn't allow him to take that from me. And that, above all else, was why I smiled.

The crunching noise sounded again, a bit louder this time. It was almost as if someone was climbing the palace walls, their boots meeting with the dusty stone bricks and twisting as they adjusted their footing.

I'd heard that sound before, but I wasn't ready for it now.

I closed my eyes and prayed to the absentee gods that it wasn't Tristan climbing into my room. He couldn't see me like this. He'd freak the fuck out.

Before I had my wounds properly cleaned, I wrapped my arms in a layer of gauze, hoping it took him at least another minute to make it to my window. When I was finished, my skin was absolutely burning, but I ground my teeth and retrieved my robe, pulling it over my nightgown with painstaking carefulness.

Sure enough, a minute later, Tristan's big, burly frame took up all the available space in my window before hopping into the room with a thud.

I forced another smile and gently crossed my arms over my chest, trying to appear casual and maybe a bit playful. "Excuse me, Mr. Martell, but why are you stealing into a lady's room in the dead of night? You might give her the wrong impression."

He chuckled and moved closer, pulling me into a tender embrace. My whole body fucking shook under the weight of the pain his hug caused me, but I held back my whimper and squeezed my eyes shut, willing the tears to stay away.

The Storm King would not steal my happiness. He would

not ruin this wonderful man's embrace and make it torture. I wouldn't allow it.

"I missed you," he said with a warm smile, his dark eyes twinkling in the firelight.

I reached forward, wrapping my hands around the suspenders that looped over his shoulders, covering a tight white shirt that did nothing to hide his rippling muscles underneath. "I missed you too."

"I'm sorry about the other night," he said, and I had a feeling this was the entire reason he'd come. To apologize. He was too fucking perfect. "I shouldn't have tried to pressure you into... *that*. I know it's dangerous and stupid and that there's only about a 1 percent chance that it'll work, so... I get it. I get why you'd rather not try. And I just want you to know that I'll be here for you, no matter what, no matter where we are. No matter how many times he breaks you into pieces, I'll be there to pick them up and put them back together."

Gods fucking damn it. My chin quivered and a traitorous sob escaped my lips. My eyes welled with burning tears, and they spilled like lava down my face. Before I knew it, I was bawling, tucked into his warm, broad chest, fighting to endure the pain clawing me on the inside and out.

"I'm sorry, baby," he apologized once more. "I didn't mean to upset you. That was exactly the opposite of what I meant to do. I'm just... fuck, Gem. I'm so sorry."

I pushed away from him, just far enough to study his eyes through the blurry puddles of tears. "Please stop apologizing. You're the best thing that ever happened to me, and I'm not at all mad at you. I'm just... so tired."

I sucked in a ragged breath and more sobbing ensued.

"I told myself he wouldn't break me, and so far, he hasn't. But I'm tired, Tris. He's wearing me down."

His eyes—far too intelligent for those of a stable boy—

slowly scanned my body, pausing once they settled on my arms hidden beneath the robe.

"You're bleeding," he said matter-of-factly. "It's leaking through your robe. Gemma..." He paused, his jaw ticking as he tried to remain calm. "Let me see your arms."

I shook my head, retreating into myself. He couldn't see me like this. He'd go crazy, try to attack the king and get himself killed. Or he'd force me to leave, and we'd get caught, and then we'd *both* get tortured 100 times worse.

"It's not bad," I lied, hugging my arms to keep them as far out of sight as I could.

"Gemma..." His voice was softer as he approached me again. He took my hands and traced delicate circles on my skin with his calloused thumbs. "Let me see your arms."

"I can't." My voice broke, and the words came out as a whisper.

His face was hard, but his eyes remained soft. "It's bad, isn't it?"

I closed my eyes and nodded.

By the time I opened them back up, Tristan was over near the fire, lifting my bloodied rag from the bowl of healing herbs with a detached look in his eye. I moved closer, unsure of what to think or do, unsure of what *he* was thinking or about to do.

Eventually, he sat down and patted the ground beside him.

I lowered myself onto the cold stone ground and tucked my legs up into my chest. There was nowhere safe to rest my arms, so I had no choice but to deal with the throbbing pain, wrapping them around my knees.

He slipped the green robe down my shoulders, but I caught it at my elbow, refusing to let it go any further. "Please don't."

His hand found my chin and gently coaxed me to look at him. "Let me take care of you."

And that was the moment I fell completely in love with him.

Something inside me snapped, and the fear I'd been tethered to simply floated away on a breeze of hope and happiness. I removed the robe the rest of the way and allowed him to peel back the gauze. He never said a word, though if his slightly murderous expression was anything to go by, then I was probably right in assuming he wanted to attack the king. It didn't matter anymore though, because I trusted him.

He took his time, silently cleaning my cuts, and studying the haphazard slashes that laced across my skin.

By the time he was done, the fire had burned down to glowing embers, so he got up and restoked it until it radiated warmth once more. He went to my bed and retrieved my blankets, laying them carefully out on the floor where we sat. Then he laid down on his side and carefully tucked me into his arms.

I had no idea how long we laid there before I drifted off, but I distinctly remembered the words that fell out of my mouth as I did.

"I'll go with you, Tristan. I'll follow you anywhere."

Then sleep graciously claimed me.

CHAPTER 9

$\mathcal{A}$LEXIS

"Do you trust me?"

Ben's words were soft but dangerous, spoken against the backdrop of a crackling fire.

It was dark, and people were laughing and dancing outside in the streets, smoking and drinking, completely oblivious to the fact that we were here.

I glanced around the tiny room, but it was empty aside from us, hosting only a kitchenette and a small smattering of pillows strewn out across the floor. Bare rafters lined the ceiling, and the sandstone slab beneath our feet was way more "sand" than "stone."

Apparently, Ben had rented the little shack for a few hours in order for us to... *talk*. I didn't know why, but I had a bad feeling that meant I was in trouble.

The other Storm Princes had agreed to go out and relax with a few drinks and a couple smokes, which gave Ben and me the alone time he required. Normally, I would have been a little worried about a set up like that, but since a *literal fucking lightning bolt* would prevent any girls from moving in on my men, I was relatively at ease with the situation.

Then again, girls were sneaky and seductive. Like *Camilla* —beautiful, confident, exotic.... Maybe I shouldn't have let them go out without me? The whole town might be fried to a crisp by morning. And that would only feed my stupid jealousaurus. I mean, come on. Of all the freaking men on the planet, why did I have to fall for the most sought-after men around?

Ben moved closer, tickling my skin as he gently traced a finger along my jawline. "Do. You. Trust. Me?"

"Yes." My voice was soft and breathless all of a sudden. It was like my body knew what was coming before my brain had a chance to catch up.

"Then stand up and turn around."

Slowly, nervously, I did as he said. My muscles shook with anticipation and a little bit of fear. I had no idea what this was about or what he had in mind, but I knew I was about to be dominated.

His hands found my calves and glided up my legs, bunching up the gossamer material of my mocha-colored gown. They slid over the crest of my ass and up my back, pausing at my shoulders for only a moment.

"Raise your arms."

I did, and by the time his fingers passed my elbows and wrists, my dress was nothing more than a puddle of fancy material on the floor.

He hooked his thumbs into my panties and slid them down, leaving me totally bare, and yet mostly unexposed considering my back was to him.

"Are you okay?" he asked, understanding this might've reminded me of my "wedding night." It was similar, in a way

—there was still force involved and an obvious lack of control—but it was intimate and different enough that I felt safe and secure rather than vulnerable and sullied.

I nodded, and his lips found the small of my back, kissing me tenderly as he slid a silken rope around my waist. He pulled it tight, crisscrossing it around my back, then twisted it beneath my breasts, kissing my back again.

"What are you doing?" I asked nervously as he strung me up like a corset.

He grabbed my ass and squeezed, lifting me slightly off the ground and forcing me to push into the wall for support. "Don't talk. Not unless I ask you a question."

I nodded sharply, and he continued twining the silky rope around my body, circling my breasts and cleverly wrapping around my thighs so they remained spread apart.

"You were jealous today," he said, kissing the side of my neck.

"Of course I was. Have you *seen* her? She's gorgeous, and she tried to kiss you."

His hand cracked my ass hard enough to make me yelp.

"That wasn't a question, Sailor," he reminded me, caressing the stinging flesh of my rear. "It was a fact. You were jealous. And as hot as it was, I don't like the fact that you didn't trust me."

I wanted to protest, but he hadn't asked me a question, so I kept my mouth shut.

"Lace your fingers and lift your hands over your head."

As soon as I did, he threw the rope around a beam in the ceiling and began threading down my arms, trapping me in a standing position. My heart raced. Being helpless in a bad situation was the worst feeling in the world, but being helpless in the hands of a man I loved was exhilarating.

When he was satisfied with his work and my body was a web of knots from my wrists to my ankles, he spun me around and looked deep into my eyes. "I don't want anyone but you, Alexis."

The use of my full name and not a nickname told me just how serious his words were.

"You're gorgeous and sexy as fuck." His hands caressed the delicate skin of my neck, trailing lower to brush my collarbone.

His touch was inebriating, making me dizzy with anticipation.

"You're fierce and sassy." His hands moved further down, circling the edge of my breasts around the rope.

Gods, his touch was amazing. I could barely think straight.

"You're resilient and caring." His thumbs grazed my hardened nipples, making me moan. "And you have my heart completely."

It was the closest he'd ever come to saying *I love you*, and the happiness it brought me burned through my blood like a fever.

His lips brushed my stomach and trailed featherlight kisses down to my navel; then he continued lower, pausing just before my pubic bone.

I was already panting like a dog in heat, hanging limply from my arms because my legs were too weak to fully support me.

"I want to kiss *no one* but you." He kissed my inner thigh, sending tiny jolts of heat rushing to my spread-open pussy. "I want to touch *no one* but you." His hand roamed up the back of my leg, and he squeezed my ass like he owned it. "I want to... *lick* no one but you."

I quivered in anticipation, but to my dismay, his actions didn't mirror his words as they had before.

"Do you understand me, Sailor?"

"Yes," I breathed out in barely a whisper.

"I mean it. I don't care who I look at or who I talk to or what I say. This passion burning in my veins? It's only for you."

His words were music to my ears, everything I wanted to hear and more.

"And I'm going to prove it." His eyes met mine, and a devious grin overtook his darkened features. "Usually, *I* like to be in control. I like *you* to fuck *me* exactly how I tell you to. I like to sit back and enjoy the show. But tonight, I'm giving everything to you."

He ran his fingers through the folds of my lower lips, spreading my wetness everywhere, especially my clit.

Dear fucking gods, I was a hot mess. I didn't know if it had something to do with the ropes he'd tied around me, the sexiness of his words, or the delicacy and precision of his fingers, but I was already seconds away from coming. I could feel the telltale tingles flooding through me, numbing my brain in preparation for wrecking my body.

Then his mouth was on me, hot and demanding, his tongue swirling around my clit like a cyclone. Seconds later, I was gone, crying out as every cell in my body exploded with ecstasy.

"Oh, Sailor," he groaned, biting my inner thighs. "So willing and eager to give it up to me. So perfectly pliable."

He pushed his fingers inside and rubbed a spot I'd only read about in romance novels. Over and over he circled, keeping the perfect pace and pressure. Then he stood and sucked on my nipples, making sultry eye contact with me until my mind went blissfully numb again.

"*Fucking hades,*" I moaned, thrashing against my bindings as I came apart once more in his expert hands.

"Do you believe me yet?" he asked, tweaking my nipples lightly as I gasped for air.

"Believe... what?" I couldn't think straight; I could barely even see straight anymore.

"Do you believe that you're the only one I want?" he asked, reiterating his question from a moment ago. "If you're still unsure, I could always fuck you into believing me..."

I smiled and bit my bottom lip as my eyes fell closed. "Oh, I'm still *very* unsure, Sand Prince. You're going to have to fuck the hell out of me before I believe you."

I peeked at him, watching as his pupils dilated.

"Is that right?"

"It is."

He liked that defiant streak in me. I was pretty sure it turned him on to imagine draining the disobedience out of me, moment by torturous moment.

He backed away, leaving me half hanging half standing but completely aroused. He reached behind his back and yanked off his shirt, exposing the dark shadows of his tanned abs. Then he unbuttoned his pants and kicked them to the side, saving his boxers for last as his cock sprang free.

He stroked himself as he slowly approached me. "Is this what you want, sweetheart?"

He'd never called me by an endearment like that, but given the context, I very much enjoyed it. I adjusted my arms above my head and nodded.

"Are the ropes getting uncomfortable?"

"Only a bit."

Suddenly, there was a dagger in his hand, and as he cut the rope above my head, I dropped into his arms. The bindings around me loosened, and we both worked to untangle my body as quickly as possible. Then it was just us. No barriers. No clothes, no ropes, no jealousy, no fear. Just love and a heavy dose of lust.

He laid me down on the pillows and hovered above me,

the muscles in his arms and abs strung out tight. Our eyes locked, and as we stared, he pushed deep inside of me.

It was... *intense*. Sensations were everywhere. Around me. Inside me. Mental, physical, emotional... I could hardly tell what I was feeling from one second to the next; they were flying so fast.

"You believe me yet?" he asked, as he thrust in and out of me, slowly, maddeningly.

"I'm starting to."

He smirked and kept up the leisurely pace. "Good."

After those first two wicked orgasms, my body was already primed for pleasure. It didn't take long for the decadence to build inside of me, to soak me up and wring me out.

When my moaning and the pulsing of orgasm number three subsided, Ben gritted his teeth and stared at me intensely. "Do you believe me now?"

It was getting harder for him to hold his orgasm back. I could sense it.

"Yes, I do."

"I'm serious, Alexis. I don't want anyone but you. I..." He swallowed hard, and his gaze softened. "I love you."

An uncontrollable smile lit up my face as I pulled his lips down to mine. "I love you too, Ben."

I rolled my hips up into his, pushing him those last couple steps over the edge.

He groaned and thrust harder, railing me like a hammer, but the pain felt good after so much pleasure. Eventually, he reached his own orgasm, and as his movements slowed, I was able to breathe again.

I kissed him gently and added, "I really do believe you. I won't doubt you again."

He lowered his forehead to mine, panting through a pearly smile. "Glad we cleared that up."

"*Mmm*. Me too."

Now we just had to "clear up" the misunderstanding between the fae and the harpies, starting by following the "desert flower" into the sandy wilderness first thing in the morning.

Lovely.

CHAPTER 10

"*W*hat do you *mean* we have to take a pit stop at Dryroot Canyons?" Camilla asked Ash through gritted teeth.

"I *mean* exactly what I *said*," Ash bit back with an even more menacing expression.

They were standing on opposite sides of a map, tracing potential routes with their fingers, while Rob looked on with a devious grin.

We were right at the edge of Erishwar, where the city abruptly met the desert, not-so-anxiously awaiting the start of yet another long hike through the Obsidian. While they argued and Rob looked on with laughing eyes, the rest of us leaned against one of the sandstone buildings and tried to soak up a bit of shade. Six camels grazed on a bit of dry grass nearby, already loaded up with our stuff, just waiting for *us* to climb aboard.

"Gods, it's hot," I muttered, feeling like I'd lost some hydration just by opening my mouth.

Everyone grumbled their agreement except Ben.

"The rainy season is coming soon," he said, glancing at the crystal-clear sky.

"Deserts have a rainy season?" I asked, suddenly interested in the weather.

"Not usually," Dan muttered.

"Some do, briefly, but they have a long one here," Ben finished. "The Obsidian Desert is sort of an anomaly. No one can figure out where the rain comes from, though many scholars have tried."

"Not even you?" I teased.

"Not even me," he replied with a cheeky grin.

"He's right, though," Dan continued. His eyes were closed, with his head tipped back as he leaned against the building. "Rain is coming. I can feel it."

"Well, thank the gods for *that*," I grumbled.

I remembered a time when I would playfully scold Gemma for such blatantly blasphemous comments. I'd told her the gods would make her pay for it one day. But now that I was part god, I didn't feel the reverence I once had anymore. And with all the shit I'd been through, and never once had they appeared to help me out, well... fuck 'em. It wasn't like they were ever coming back anyway.

"Is anyone else worried about Ash jumping off a canyon?" I asked as we watched their heated argument from afar.

Cal and Ben nodded, while Dan said, "Yes and no. I don't really want him to do anything stupid now that he's back, but at the same time, I honestly don't think we could die if we tried. So, is it really that big of a deal?"

"You don't know that for sure," I argued. "Besides, I'm afraid Rob's hoping it really will kill him."

Cal shook his head. "Rob is a hard-ass sometimes, but he loves Ash. He doesn't want him to die for real. He just wants him to pay a little bit for all the shit he put us through."

"Can't say I blame him," Dan added with a smirk. "I love

Ash too, but I have to admit, it's probably going to be extremely satisfying to watch his atonement."

I shook my head and snorted with laughter. "You guys are crazy. I don't want to watch anyone leap to their death—whether the death is real or not—and especially not any of *you*. It's just so... sadistic."

"Oh, it'll be fun," Dan playfully argued. "We could probably all jump, if we wanted."

I seriously doubted that. They might be feeling confident about their immortal status, but I was feeling even less so than normal.

"All right," Camilla said, rolling up the map as their trio broke up and approached us. "We're pit stopping in the Dryroot Canyons, but due to that enormous out-of-the-way endeavor, we're now also going to have to stop at Maltor to resupply."

"Sounds good," I said with a nod.

Her brows rose and furrowed. "Uh, sounds *terrible*, in fact. Maltor is the absolute worst town in Eristan. We'll be lucky if we escape that place with the clothes on our backs, let alone a sack full of supplies."

"I assured her we'd be fine," Rob said, rolling his eyes.

I was not so sure. "Why are we stopping *there* if it's so awful? Why not the next town over or something?"

"Because there is no *next town over*." Camilla glared at Ash and Rob. "This is literally the only place we can stop between here and the Lunaley—unless we forgo this ridiculous trip to the Canyons."

"No," Ash and Rob both protested at once.

As awful as the situation was, it made me smile. They were both so stubborn.

Camilla sighed and shrugged dramatically. "Then we're stuck with Maltor."

"Fine," Cal decided, grabbing the reins of a nearby camel. "Then let's get moving."

~

THE JOURNEY TO THE LUNALEY SHOULD'VE TAKEN JUST ABOUT a week—which was bad enough, considering we now had less than half a month to return to Blackwood with a chimera egg—but with the diversion to the canyons, it was going to take an extra two days.

We'd travelled nonstop, only pausing for a few bathroom breaks during the day and to sleep at night. By the time the infamous Dryroot Canyons *finally* came into view, I was sweaty, tired, and my thighs were freaking chaffed to hell.

I fell off my camel and sprawled out on my back in the sand. "Thank you, gods, we made it."

Everyone else dismounted a bit more gracefully.

As I lay there, I was smacked in the forehead with something wet.

"Ew." I swiped at it quickly, thinking one of the camels had spit on me, when I was hit with *another* drop of wetness, this time on my arm. I held it up and examined my skin. Cool, clear liquid drizzled down my flesh, looking for the life of me like... water.

Thunder rumbled softly in the distance, and when I glanced up, the sky was suddenly a light gray color rather than blue.

What the fuck?

I glanced at Ben who merely shrugged. "Guess the rainy season is here."

The wind picked up, gently tugging on my gown as I stood and spun in a circle. As far as my eyes could see, the landscape looked dreary. When the hell had that happened?

Rob and Ash had wandered over to the canyon's edge,

arms crossed, staring intently toward the bottom. Curious, I trailed after them, wishing almost immediately that I hadn't. I'd never been so high up, not even if I climbed the highest tree in Blackwood or the tallest mountain. The canyon walls consisted of layer upon layer of different colored dirt and rocks—orange, brown, red, cream, tan. And at the bottom was a river, but it looked like nothing more than a squiggly black line drawn in the sand.

"Bonus points if you hit the river," Rob told Ash, who scoffed and shook his head.

"Bonus points if I *survive*."

"Oh, stop being a pussy. Just get it over with."

The wind blew a bit harder, knocking off my equilibrium and making me feel dizzy and unbalanced. Gasping, I backed away from the ledge. "Please don't do this, *Adam*."

He chuckled and glanced at me over his shoulder. "I'll be okay, *Princess*."

"But what if you're not? I'm serious. *Please*. Don't do it."

"He better fucking do it," Camilla complained. "So help me gods, if we went out of the way for nothing..."

Rob smirked malevolently. "Oh, he's doing it all right." Then he turned to me and lowered his voice. "It's the only way he can get back into the group. He has to."

"Surely there's another way?" I begged.

But Rob shook his head. "Sorry, Jewels. A deal's a deal." Then he patted Ash's back and grinned. "Have a nice trip, *Adam*. See ya next fall."

"Ha. Ha." Asher responded flatly. He took a deep breath and started stretching out his limbs.

This was insane.

I ran over to Ben and took his shirt in my hands, whispering fervently. "Don't let him do this, Ben. There has to be another way to add him to the group."

Ben smiled warmly and put an arm around my shoulder,

leading me even further away from Camilla and the guys. "He's already in the group, Sailor."

My brows pinched together. *"What?"*

He nodded. "Remember the lightning bolt that enforced the magical rules of the blood bond?"

"Yeah."

He shrugged. "That never happened with Ash. And you've already kissed *and* fucked him."

"But... how is that possible?"

"He was there for the blood bond ceremony—in sloth form—remember?"

I hesitated. "Yeah, but that bond was forged in *blood*. I think we would have noticed Speedy cutting his paw and—*oh my gods*."

Ben's expression turned curious. "Yes?"

"Right before the ceremony, I was discussing the pros and cons of the blood bond with Speedy."

"You talked to that sloth a lot, didn't you?" he asked with a warm smile.

"More than you ever want to know," I assured him. "But while we were talking, he fell off my bed and cracked his head on the floor. Which, in hindsight, I realize that was him trying to turn back into Ash and tell me *not* to make the bond... but, regardless, the point is, I had his blood on my hand."

Ben's eyes lit up. "And when you sliced your palm, his blood mixed in with yours, and when you added your hand to the circle, his blood got included in the bond. Holy shit, that's amazing."

"Right?" But then my excitement died down again. "No matter how you look at it, this is pointless. If Ash is already in the group and in on the bond, then there's no reason for him to go through with this whatsoever."

"That's not true. I think he needs to do it. To prove

himself. If he doesn't, the other guys will always feel like he doesn't quite belong. It'll tear us apart."

I ducked out of Ben's grasp and shook my head. "You're all insane."

"Finally, someone who agrees with *me*," Camilla huffed mockingly.

The rain came down harder, slowly soaking through my hair and the gauzy material of my gown. I had to blink away the droplets collecting on my lashes in order to even see.

Then Rob's voice cut through the air, making me physically sick. "I'm going to count you down. Ready? Three..."

"No!" I cried, throwing both hands up to my mouth in terror.

Ash simply sucked in deep, calming breaths and honed his focus on the edge.

"Two..."

I was too scared to move, too scared to cry. I couldn't tell if my heart was hammering nonstop or if it had stopped completely. "Please don't!"

Dan came over and pulled me into his arms, trying to comfort me, but the embrace felt more like a restraint.

"One."

"*Asher!*" I screamed at the top of my lungs, watching in blood-curdling horror as he sprinted to the ledge and jumped out of sight.

CHAPTER 11

I tore myself from Dan's arms and raced to the edge, dropping to my knees and sobbing as Asher fell... down... down... down...

Then he hit the ground in a puff of golden dust.

My heart splintered. Shattered. I couldn't breathe. The pain was so intense it was almost numbing. The sobbing that overcame me was nothing short of volatile.

He was... gone. There was no way he could've survived that. After all this time, I'd finally gotten him back just to lose him again.

Toppling over, my face smashed gracelessly into the sand, mixing with the rain, snot, spit, and tears streaming from me like a leak in my fucking soul.

Rob took a deep, shaky breath and stormed off. "I'm going to search the astral plain."

Whatever the hell that meant. As if it even fucking mattered.

No one spoke. No one moved. The only sounds to be heard were the pattering of the raindrops in the sand and the bone-crushing wails emitting from my mouth. I couldn't stop them, couldn't contain them. They poured out of me like a grievous, off-key requiem.

Eventually, Camilla spoke. "Well... now that you morons are done with your stupid fucking suicide quest, we need to keep moving. We have to make it to Maltor by dark. I can promise you, you don't want to arrive there in the morning when their high has worn off."

But I still couldn't move, and it didn't seem as if the Storm Princes could either. We were all lost in a spectrum of pain, from sorrow to shock, agony to numbness.

Suddenly Rob's eyes snapped open, and he clutched at his arms as he shivered. "He's not there."

A huge, collective sigh passed through the group as my brows furrowed, and finally some of their voices returned.

"Thank the gods," Cal muttered, running a nervous hand through his blond hair.

Sniffling, I wiped at the sandy fluids caked to my face. "What does that mean? *He's not there?*"

"It means his spirit isn't on the astral plane," Rob explained quickly. "He isn't dead."

"Oh my gods," I gasped as I scrambled back over to the ledge. But I saw nothing at the bottom. No gold dust, no animal, no human. "Where is he?"

Minutes stretched by—long strokes of an invisible clock I wanted to tear right off an invisible wall. Then a black and blue butterfly slowly rose from the canyon, struggling to fly through the cascading raindrops. He had a single white dot on his ebony torso.

"Ash!" I whisper-shouted, covering my mouth with shaking fingers. "Shit. I mean, *Adam.*"

Camilla chortled, but no one paid her any mind. "Save it, Princess. The jig is up."

Rob's hands clapped together quickly, smashing the beautiful bug in an instant. When the magic kicked in and Ash returned to human form, Rob had him in a burly hug so tight he probably couldn't breathe.

"Thank the fucking gods you're okay," he growled out, burying his face in Asher's shoulder.

Ash chuckled and hugged him back. "I take it this means my debt has been paid. We're cool again?"

Rob held him out at arm's length and smiled wide. "We're cool, bro."

Dan threw an extra pair of shorts at him, and he quickly covered his nakedness. After that, we all took turns hugging him and welcoming him back to the group.

When it was my turn, he picked me up and twirled me around as the rain fell all around us. It was a magical sort of moment, one that would never fade from my memory. All five of my Storms were alive and well, and I would never take that for granted—even if we lived forever.

Camilla put a hand on her hip. "As touching as that was, we need to keep moving. We only have twelve hours to get to Maltor while it's still dark, and I have no idea if that's going to be enough."

Ash put me down and took my hand. I stole a glance at his brothers, making sure they were okay with our PDA, but they were all still smiling. We were just so happy that Ash had survived that we were fine with just about anything he did.

Rob glared at Camilla and pointed a finger in her pretty face. "Not a fucking word about Asher being alive, understand me? You risk his life like that, and I'll take yours."

"You mean like you just did?" Upon seeing Rob's expression darken even further, she held up both hands and took a healthy step backward. "Relax, asshole, I wasn't going to say anything."

"Good." His voice was hard and dark, as was the look on his face. If I were her, *I'd* sure as hell keep *my* word. Rob was hot as fuck when he was angry, but I did *not* want to be on the receiving end of his brutal rage.

"All right," I said brightly, trying to lighten the mood a bit, "let's do as Camilla says and keep moving."

∾

I HAD NO IDEA HOW LATE IT WAS WHEN WE FINALLY SAW THE first glowing bonfire at the edge of Maltor, but the sky was not nearly as inky black as we'd hoped. Dawn was creeping in, lightening the clouds just enough to be noticeable on the eastern side of the horizon. In other words, we'd only just arrived, and we were already running out of time.

Camilla tightened the scarf around her face, leaving only enough room for her eyes to peek out. "I'll do my best to gather supplies as quickly as possible. Make sure the camels are fed and watered while I'm gone. I'll meet you at the northern edge of town, near the clock tower."

She started to leave, then paused, spinning back around.

"Oh, and Storms? Try to stay out of trouble. I heard what my father said. *No magic.* I expect you to obey his commands while you're here."

Ben bowed his head. "And so we shall."

She disappeared down a side street, and I glanced at the group through a drizzle of rain.

Rob nudged Dan as soon as Camilla was out of sight. "If we get into any fights, we'll just have to kick some ass the old-fashioned way."

Dan chuckled darkly. "I haven't gotten into a fight in ages. It almost sounds fun."

Cal sighed and held up both hands. "No. No fights if we

can help it. We're supposed to be laying low. Maltor is the most dangerous place around."

"Way to be a wet blanket, *Calvin*," Rob muttered.

He sighed once more. "Trust me, I hate to be the responsible one all the damn time, but somebody has to be."

Ben grabbed the reins of two camels and cocked his head to the side. "Come on. Let's get these beasts watered. If they're anything like me, they're parched. Plus, the well is going to be a hot spot as soon as the sun rises, and we do not want to be vying for water against the locals. We need to remain inconspicuous."

Right. Inconspicuous. Easier said than done when most of us had skin as white as moonlight and all of us had a fucking full-grown camel trailing behind us. Blending in and keeping out of trouble sounded like a physical impossibility.

"We'll just stick to the outskirts of town," Ben continued, leading the way. "Hopefully we'll avoid any... trouble."

But his words trailed off as a gang of Maltorians cut off our path. They were dressed in harem pants, as most Eristani men seemed to, and in the same shirtless style. They carried long, curved blades and wore overconfident smiles. I got the feeling they were a seriously competent group of thugs, not often losing a fight. The dusky air was rank with the scent of unwashed flesh, and despite the slow drizzle of rain, it was already getting hot.

"Well, well, well. What have we here?" the leader of the gang said, scratching his stubbled chin with the edge of his blade. "Tourists, so early in the morning? It's our lucky day, boys."

The *boys* chuckled from behind him, setting the hairs of my arms on end. Shit. There had to have been at least fifteen of them and only six of us. Without magic on our side, I didn't like our odds.

"You don't want to do this," Cal assured them calmly, as if

we *weren't* about to get our asses handed to us. "You're looking at the Princes and Princess of Blackwood Kingdom. Attacking us will only result in your death."

The leader chuckled, revealing a hole where one of his front teeth should have been. "*Royal* tourists. And without any guards. Looks like the best catch we've had all week."

Rob turned around, daring to give the thugs his back, and he pointed to me. "Take the camels and get out of here."

I stood firm. I might not have had much training, but Taron and Tamara had taught me *some* shit. And I had a weapon strapped to my waist and my thigh thanks to Ben, so I wasn't entirely helpless. I didn't necessarily *want* to fight, but if the guys were going to risk their lives to protect us, then I needed to pull my weight too.

I reached down and unsheathed my sword, holding it nervously in front of me.

Rob glared at my defiance, and Ash seized my wrist. "I don't think so, Sweets."

But I yanked it right out of his hold. "*You* didn't listen to *me* when I begged you not to jump off that cliff, so I'm sure as fuck not going to listen to you now."

"*Oh*! Burned by our sexy fire girl!" Dan announced through a shit-eating grin.

"Peach, I think Rob and Ash are right. You need to—"

"Zip it, Cal," I snapped, gripping my sword even tighter. "You made me sit out the last fight, and I hated it. You're not going to make me miss this one."

"Double burn!" Dan declared, bending over in laughter.

I turned to Ben, raising a brow. "You said earlier that you'd let me fight whoever I wanted as long as it wasn't you guys. Were you serious?"

He blinked, and his brown eyes went wide. "I mean... yeah, as long as you're sure."

I turned to Dan. "And you?"

"I got your back, Sexy Lexi. *Always*. And usually your front too." He winked, and I couldn't help but chuckle.

The lead thug's brows were furrowed as he watched our encounter like an unwilling hostage. "Are you through? Can we get to the actual fighting now?"

"You bet we can," Rob growled as he launched at them.

Soon, chaos broke out. We quickly became a writhing mess of swinging arms and slicing blades, ducking here, jabbing there. Surprisingly, I wasn't even scared. There was no time for fear to infiltrate my system, not with pure adrenaline pumping through my veins.

I reared back and sliced down in front of me, cutting into the skin of the nearest thug's shoulder. He didn't scream, as *I* would have; he simply gritted his teeth and came at me like a hungry bear. He didn't hold his knife like I held mine. He gripped the handle and jabbed it forward, nearly impaling me through the stomach. Luckily, I hopped backwards at the last second.

I studied my fingers on the hilt and realized I must've been holding my weapon incorrectly. I tried to adjust my grip, but the blade just felt all sorts of wrong in my hand.

My moment of distraction gave the thug another chance to attack. He jabbed at me again, this time slicing through the shimmery fabric of my gown and drawing a thin line of blood from the skin of my stomach. It stung, but it wasn't unbearable, thank the gods.

A moment later, that man's head rolled right off his shoulders and the rest of his body crumpled to the ground, revealing Rob right behind him.

"You okay, Jewels?" he asked, staring darkly at the dick who'd cut me.

I nodded, eyeing the decapitated guy a little nauseously.

Rob quickly grabbed the back of my head and pulled my forehead to his lips. "Be careful."

Then he found another thug and got back to kicking ass.

He'd let me keep my dignity by allowing me to fight, then he'd protected me when I didn't even realize he was looking, and now he was once again allowing me to have my freedom. I knew we were in the middle of a fight, but I couldn't help falling a little further in love with him.

"Your boyfriend was right," another oily thug taunted, drawing my attention. "You should have run away when you had the chance."

"Which boyfriend was that again?" I asked, trying to keep him from concentrating too hard. "I have five."

He glanced around to where the guys were battling it out with the rest of the thugs. The odds didn't look bad anymore, but I still wouldn't call them good. We seemed to have about a fifty-fifty chance at winning or losing.

"A foreign whore. Maybe I should get in on that action, eh?"

"Sorry. My schedule is full."

He grinned, revealing a row of snaggle teeth. "I have a feeling your schedule is going to be *wide open* here in a few minutes."

Numbing fear overcame me, and I struggled to even think straight. Losing this fight was no longer an option in the slightest—not with *that* on the line.

So, using the method that felt right, I retaliated by hacking my blade at him once more, missing most of the time because I wasn't nearly close enough.

Suddenly, Camilla leapt from a nearby rooftop and rolled across the sand, joining the fight. "Somebody get that girl an ax!" she shouted.

"A pickax?" I asked, brightening up. I didn't particularly miss swinging the heavy thing around all day, but there was a degree of familiarity to it that would have been comforting right about now.

"No," she said, swinging her sword around and slicing at least three guys in a row. "An *ax*. One you could swing *like* a pickax, but that has a broad blade with the ability to fell trees and men alike."

As Camilla and the guys worked to take out the last of the thugs, I began to see her in a slightly different light. She was wickedly skilled in combat, light on her feet, and quiet as a mouse. Maybe she wasn't my competition; maybe she could be my instructor? A trainer in the place of Taron and Tamara while I was away?

I stared in awe as she yanked her sword from the chest of the last thug on the ground. Everyone was panting and sweating and had some form of a cut, red mark, or bruise. Everyone except her.

Camilla raised a brow at me. "What?"

I raised both brows. "*What* what?"

"You're looking at me weird."

"Am not," I argued.

"Are too."

"We're not adding her to the group, Lexi," Dan said flatly. "No matter how sexy you think she is."

I laughed and shook my head. "It's not that. I was just..." I turned to her. "I was wondering if you might be willing to teach me some fighting skills along the way?"

She wiped both sides of her sword on her baggy black pants, the blood blending in seamlessly with the dark fabric.

"I don't see why not. Every woman should be able to fight, to defend herself if need be." She sheathed the long blade once it was mostly clean, then pointed her finger at me. "But if I'm training you, then I'm picking your weapon, and I'm choosing an ax."

"Done," I agreed. "Where do we get one?"

She sighed, then climbed back onto the roof, retrieving a pack she'd left up there before she joined the fight. After shouldering it, she leapt from the edge and opened it. "I was able to get us some meats and some canteens—"

"Oh, thank the gods," Dan muttered, snatching one of them out of the bag and chugging it.

"—but I still need to gather up some weapons. I'll make sure I find you an ax before I'm done."

I smiled. "Thank you."

"Seriously, this time," she said, turning toward the guys, "take the camels to the well and *stay out of trouble*. I can't keep coming back to bail you out of fights."

"We'll be fine," Rob assured her with a glare. "We would have been fine without you during that last fight too."

She rolled her dark eyes. "Maybe. Maybe not."

Then she disappeared down an alley once more.

Ben sighed and walked over to the camels, which had scurried off to the far left, away from the fight. They'd found some grass peeking through the sands, but it was plastered flat to the ground thanks to the rain, so they had to root extra hard for it.

We'd just placed their reins in our hands when another thug approached. He looked just as vile as the others, but if his purple bandana was anything to go by, I'd guess he was from a different gang.

He held both hands up in goodwill, a yellowed piece of paper tucked between his middle and index fingers, but he sported a wicked grin that warned me he had no good intentions.

"A message came for my leader today," he said smoothly, "and he asked me to pass it on."

The thug dropped the paper to the ground, grinned a little wider, then disappeared back to the hell from which he'd come.

Cal shot us a grim glance then strode over and picked it up, unfolding the edges a little too slowly and carefully for my liking. I was antsy, itching to know what sort of bullshit awaited us this time. Though, I had a bad feeling I already knew who it was from.

The color drained from Cal's face, confirming my theory.

"It's from the Storm King."

CHAPTER 12

"*W*hat's it say?" Rob demanded in a growly voice. Cal took a calming breath and read the note aloud.

"MY DEAREST CHILDREN,

I hope you're enjoying your vacation abroad. Your mothers are worried sick about you. They're barely eating. I told them you were fine, much safer than anyone they knew, but they don't seem to care. I hear it's the rainy season over there. Hopefully it's also nesting season. I look forward to seeing you in two weeks' time.

Until then...

King Zacharias."

DAN SCOFFED. "SO BASICALLY, 'I'M STARVING YOUR MOTHERS, and you have two weeks left to bring back the egg.'"

Cal nodded grimly. "Basically."

"Gods fucking damn it!" Rob shouted, yanking on his dark hair. "I'm so tired of this shit."

So was I. I couldn't imagine having to deal with that kind of mental torture for twenty years or more. It was a miracle they were all as sane and normal as they were.

I thought of the unsent letters I'd written to Mom and Gemma, and I was suddenly grateful they were still in my pack. I had a bad feeling any correspondence between me and them would only piss the Storm King off worse, inadvertently exacerbating their situation.

Ash and Ben looked a mixture of sad and angry, and I imagined I looked about the same.

"Come on," Ben eventually said. "Let's feed and water these damned camels before we get attacked *again*. We really need to keep moving if we hope to be out of this kingdom in less than two weeks." He said the words flatly, as if even he didn't believe the quest was possible anymore.

We were heckled and harassed on our way to the well, but thankfully not attacked.

"Foreign scum isn't welcome here," a man shouted, brandishing a fist in the air.

"Go back where you came from," a woman sneered, lifting her nose at us.

"How many coins did you pay for your whore?" another man taunted, thrusting his hips in a crude gesture.

That last comment was apparently the straw that broke the camel's back. Rob and Ash both spun around in unison, prepared to knock the guys teeth out, but Ben and Dan grabbed a hold of them and held them back.

"Ignore them," Cal insisted. "Their words mean nothing. You know that."

"Yeah, well they still piss me off," Rob seethed, ripping his arm from Dan's grasp but thankfully not going after the guy.

"What kind of men are we if we don't protect our girl's

honor?" Ash bit back. "I won't tolerate anyone calling her a whore, Maltorians or not."

"Agreed," Rob said, glaring at everyone.

Apparently, the only thing that'd make them put their differences aside was *me*. Odd, considering the main reason they were fighting was *also* because of me.

"Is she a whore?" Cal asked rhetorically. "No. Are we scum? No. So just let it all slide."

No one argued against his words, but the electric tension in the air spoke louder than words ever could; they were pissed at each other.

When we reached the well, the camels lapped at the water as we refilled our canteens. There was a striped canopy shielding us from the rain that reminded me of the rind of a tropical fruit. Glares met us from every direction, men and women filling up jugs and vases, their hate and distrust for us almost a physical presence.

I found myself nervously wandering to the edge of the desert, hoping Camilla would return soon.

Speak of the devil, she suddenly sprinted into our midst like a wild beast was on her tail. She yanked the scarf from her face and shouted, "Let's move!"

She didn't have to tell me twice. I clambered up onto my camel's back and snapped the reins, giving his rear a nudge with my foot. I didn't want to hurt him or anything, but I sure as hell didn't want the Maltorians to catch up to us. Thankfully, my camel seemed to understand. He bellowed quickly and kicked into a long-legged run.

I had a feeling that Camilla's means of procuring supplies was actually *stealing* them. I couldn't even condemn her for it; it seemed to be the way everyone did business around here. Shit didn't cost coins or jewels; it cost nerve. If you had the balls to steal something and the skill to get away with it, then you may as well have been rich.

We rode hard and fast for at least an hour before Camilla felt safe enough to slow down. She took a deep breath, glanced behind us one more time, just to be sure, then tossed me a golden ax. It was heavy, but the weight felt familiar in my hand. The hilt was wooden and etched in strange, intricate carvings. The head was sharp and glittered in the sunlight. I'd never been one to drool over weapons, but this one was actually quite beautiful. In Blackwood, it would have cost a *very* pretty jewel. Here in Eristan, it probably cost more nerve than I possessed. Camilla had risked a lot—probably even her life—to secure me this ax. I totally owed her.

"It fits your hand," she commented with a smile. "And your grip is flawless. How'd you learn to hold an ax without also learning combat skills?"

I chuckled. "Before I became a princess, I was a jewel miner. I've been handling pickaxes for years."

"Nice. How exactly does one go from being a lowly miner to becoming a luxurious princess?"

The guys were up ahead paying us no mind, so I figured it couldn't hurt to chat with her a bit. Besides, it wasn't like the whole thing was a great big secret.

"I suppose all it takes is... a magical almost-dead guy transferring his powers before keeling over. I never would have become a princess if it weren't for magic."

"You used your magic to secure the crown?" she asked, genuinely curious rather than condescending.

"No, the Storm King found me and tried to kill me. I didn't die. When he found out I had magic, he ordered me to marry one of his sons. He wanted our children to strengthen the Storm family line for generations to come."

"And you married Prince Calvin, right?"

I reached into the top of my gown, pulling out the necklace with my ring threaded through, allowing it to dangle between us.

"Yes. I married Cal."

Her smile faltered slightly, and a look of confusion crossed her face. "So, when the Storm brothers say they're taken, what they mean is..."

"They mean by me. I may have been forced to marry Cal, but as you've no doubt noticed earlier, we all have a blood bond that means much more to us than ink on a parchment or a stone set in metal. We're committed to one another, heart and soul, no ifs, ands, or buts."

I tucked the ring back into my bosom and glanced at her from the corner of my eye.

"Fair enough," she said, cocking her head. "I don't know if my father will be quite as satisfied with that answer, though."

I raised a brow and narrowed my gaze. "He wants you to marry Ben, doesn't he?"

She tittered airily, the tinkling tune of it practically echoing across the sand dunes. "Benson is the most eligible bachelor on the planet. No one is as perfectly attractive as he is."

I grinned and shook my head. As far as I was concerned, *all* the Storm brothers were striking. As far as everyone else seemed to care though, Ben was the cherry on top of the world's ice cream sundae.

"So, he *does* want you to marry Ben?"

She nodded. "He does. And I certainly wouldn't mind it. But I can see why it would be impossible. You'll have to think of another way to appease my father when the time comes."

Yes, we would, because there was no way I was losing one of my Storms. I didn't give up on Cal, and I wouldn't give up on Ben. Even though I knew he wasn't interested in her— he'd made that abundantly clear the other night—I refused to sit back and do nothing as the Eristani king tried to tear us apart.

My cheeks flushed as I remembered the last night I'd

shared with Ben, and I faced forward, trying to hide my grin from Camilla. Of course, I only ended up focusing on the back of Ben's head. His dark brown hair was wet and sexily mussed thanks to the incessant drizzle from the clouds. His white shirt clung to the thick muscles of his broad back, and droplets raced across the tan skin of his neck and arms before soaking into his form-fitting pants.

He really *was* incredible.

My gaze moved over to Cal, the biggest, most muscular mountain of a Storm. His blonde hair somehow managed to look like sunlight kissed it despite the rain, and his features were handsome yet carefully contained. Ever the perfect gentleman.

Then I glanced at Dan, who was only slightly shorter than the rest, but just as broad. Any inch he lacked in height was made up for by his charm, allure, and extreme good looks. When he flirted with me, I felt like the only girl in the room —the only girl in the world.

I shifted my stare over to Rob, who was dark and brooding as always. I was pretty sure the guy had a resting bitch face, but it was sexy as sin. The dark stubble along his jaw, coupled with the tattoos that covered most of his body, made him almost impossible to resist. When I added in his delicious protective nature, then it really *was* impossible.

Then I turned to Ash, the newest inclusion to the group, yet the longest holder of my heart. Ash was like a dream— handsome, strong, hilarious—though, I hadn't seen much of his humor since he returned to his human form. He was probably too pissed off from being stuck as a sloth for six years and from trying to prove himself to his own brothers.

Ash rode next to Ben, the two of them laughing and joking around as they caught up on each other's lives. Dan rode next to Rob, both guys chatting about one thing or another with dark and cocky grins on their faces. And then there was Cal, all alone at the head of the group, the leader fulfilling his duty, shouldering the burden alone.

It was a strange thought to be having, but I suddenly wished there was *just one more* Storm, to balance things out, so that Cal could have a brother as a best friend too.

Then I realized that would turn the number of Storm guys into an even one, and I quickly let the thought die an ugly death.

"Whoa," I heard Cal mutter to his camel, bringing our group to a stop.

My camel spit as I tugged on his reigns, and I was suddenly glad I was behind him rather than in front.

Ahead, stood a cloaked figure walking toward us with his hands out in front of him.

"Turn around, travelers," the man said. "Nothing but death awaits you at the Ley."

Were we that close? I thought for sure we were still days away.

"No worries, old man," Cal called out amicably. "We're plenty capable of protecting ourselves no matter where we're headed."

The old man's eyes were sharp, far sharper than an old pair of eyes ought to look. "But that *is* where you are headed, no? The Lunaley?"

Cal nodded, apparently unfazed by the old man's nosiness.

"Turn around," the man repeated. "There are demons living in that forest. Hellish creatures that will pluck out your eyes and suck your very soul from your bodies. Evil beasts that will slice you to ribbons and eat your flesh for breakfast."

Rob chuckled and turned to face those of us in the back row. "Are you hearing this dude?"

I nodded, but I wasn't sure if I should grin or grimace. I

wanted to believe he was exaggerating, but I couldn't sense his feelings, so I couldn't be positive that he wasn't telling a terrifying truth.

As if on cue, Cal turned to us and nodded. "He believes what he's saying. I think the heat's gotten to him." He reached down and handed over his canteen to the poor guy. "Here. I think you're dehydrated. This should get you to the next closest town—Maltor. It's a dangerous place, but I still think you'll have a better chance of survival there than wandering the desert alone."

The man took the canteen and tipped it to his lips like a drunk might swig at a bottle of whisky. As he shuffled along and we passed him by high up on our camels, I felt a strange sensation of magic. It was difficult to describe, but it set the hairs of my arms on end and filled my chest with something lighter than air. I spun around, about to ask the man who he was or what he'd just done, but he was gone.

"Uh... guys," I said, scanning the desert but finding nothing but soggy sand dunes. "He's gone."

"What do you mean he's gone?" Cal asked, turning around.

"Like he's dead?" Dan supplied, peering around me.

I shook my head. "No, like he's fucking *gone*. Nowhere to be found. Just a figment of our imaginations."

"Couldn't be," Ben decided. "We all saw him, and there's no such thing as mass hallucination. There's *mass hysteria*, and there's *folie a deux*—a very interesting disorder shared by *two* people—but not a group."

"Okay," I agreed, knowing better than to doubt my human encyclopedia, "then what the hell happened to the guy?"

But nobody seemed to know. We searched the sands in every direction, calling for him, but it was just as I'd said—the man had simply disappeared.

Nothing but death awaits you at the Ley...

His words echoed in my mind, and whether he was real or imaginary, I hoped beyond hope that he was wrong.

~

"WHO GOES THERE?" A GUARD ASKED, STAMPING HIS SPEAR into the ground.

Dirt not *sand*, I noted as I glanced around at our surroundings in bewilderment. There were trees ahead of us, tall trees with pink-and-purple-striped bark and mist floating between their trunks. It was impossible to tell what lay beyond that, because all I could see was misty trees fading into a gray abyss.

I turned back to the guard, who was shirtless with dark skin and big black wings that spread out behind him. So, clearly he was Eristani. But where the hell were we? At the Lunaley already? And if so, when the hell had we gotten there? The last thing I remembered was the desert stretching on and on for miles.

"Prince Calvin of Blackwood," Cal announced, answering the guard's initial question. Then he gestured to the rest of us. "Along with Princes Benson, Robert, and Daniel."

He hadn't mentioned Ash.

I glanced around and was stunned to find a sleepy sloth curled up in my lap. What the fuck? I most certainly didn't remember him turning into an animal along the way. What the hell was going on?

"And Princesses: Alexis of Blackwood and Camilla of Eristan."

The guard immediately dropped to a low bow on the ground. "Forgive me, Your Highness, I did not know it was you."

Camilla smiled and told him to rise. "It's all right. You

weren't supposed to. I don't want word of this getting back to my father."

The guard smiled and stood. "I won't tell a soul, Your Highness."

"Good." She patted his chest, and his dark cheeks flushed a rosy red. "How's the fight going?"

"It's difficult to say, Your Highness. There seems to be a bit of a... time delay issue."

Camilla quirked a brow and shared a glance with me before she turned back to the guard. "Time delay? How so?"

"Yes, Your Highness. I know it sounds strange, but—" He shook his head. "—soldiers will go in, then *minutes* later, stumble out disoriented as if they'd been gone for weeks. Entire battles happen in the blink of an eye. It makes planning a strategy quite difficult."

"I'm sorry," Dan said, smiling gracefully and shaking his head. "Did you say *weeks*?"

The soldier nodded sharply. "Yes. And sometimes months. One group even swore it had been years that they were lost inside."

Holy shit.

Genuine fear curled up in my belly, much like the sloth in my lap, though not nearly as warm. If we went in there—correction, *when* we went in there, we could be lost for... years? But not actual years, just minutes... minutes that felt like years.

This was so fucked up. My mind could barely comprehend the idea of it.

A slow-rolling wave of mist escaped from the Ley and breezed across the ground, gathering at our camels' cloven feet and sending the fear of the gods into them. They bellowed and squawked and trotted away, carrying us with them.

The soldier jogged over and offered to take their reigns.

"You will need to leave your camels here." He glanced at me. "And probably your sloth. Animals are skittish of the Luna-ley. They won't go anywhere near the mist."

I clutched Speedy close to my chest and dismounted rather gracelessly, falling on my ass and jarring my tailbone. *Fuck*, that hurt. I stood and rubbed the spot, glaring at the guard as if *he'd* done it. "My sloth is coming with me. I would never leave him behind."

The guard lifted both hands and shook his head. "Fine. Just wait. You'll see how he claws at you to escape if you dare to bring him too close."

Camilla's brows furrowed, and she glanced around the group as if just now noticing Ash was missing. "The sloth is... special," she told the guard. "I don't think he'll give us any trouble."

The guard shrugged. "Very well. We have a base set up inside the Ley—though I have no real means of estimating the time or giving you any direction. All I can say is, just keep walking straight until you find someone."

Well, that was... comforting.

I sidled up next to Cal. "Are you *sure* we have to go in there?"

"We told the king we'd help save the chimeras." He glanced around nervously. "I don't see any way to do that from out here."

Ben came up beside us and nodded. "The chimeras are probably deep within the Ley where the magic is strongest. We need to observe them, study their behaviors and their environment, and then determine the best course of action."

"Even if it takes years?" I asked, almost desperately. "We only have two weeks."

At least, I *thought* we did. It was hard to say how much time we did or didn't lose between here and Maltor, considering I didn't remember a damn bit of it.

Ben smiled softly. "You heard the guard. Years in the Ley equates to minutes out here. Even if it takes *years*, we'll still have enough time."

Oh, gods, I didn't like this one little bit. I snuggled Speedy even closer to my chest, knowing he was probably getting freaked out at the rapid beating of my heart.

Cal stepped forward, and the rest of us followed. Even me, though I wasn't sure how my legs were able to move; I'd have sworn they were frozen in fear. Camilla stepped forward too, only to be halted by the guard.

"My apologies, Your Highness, but I cannot let you in there. It is far too dangerous. Your father would have my head. He'd have *all* of our heads."

The guards stationed nearby, who'd clearly all been eavesdropping on our conversation, nodded their heads solemnly.

Camilla paused, seemingly contemplating whether to fight him on the issue or not. Then she reluctantly nodded. "I'll wait here for you. It shouldn't take long, anyway."

Cal nodded in return. "We'll see you in a few minutes."

And then we stepped into the forest...

CHAPTER 13

CRISSEN

I STROLLED THROUGH THE STREETS OF BLACKHAVEN, A BOUNCE in my step as I whistled an old drinking tune.

Men and women smiled and waved as I passed, and I grinned and nodded in return. It was going to be a good day. The king had commissioned a thousand swords, giving me and my crew work for months, and today was pickup and payday.

I told myself I was most excited about the mountain of jewels I was bound to receive, but in reality, I was eager to come face-to-face with my father for the first time. Yeah, I'd been to a couple of the smaller-scale royal balls, ones held by the princes, but I'd never technically been *invited*, and I'd never once met the man and the legend, Zacharias.

I'd heard so many stories of what a great man he was, and I secretly hoped that once he met me, he'd be so impressed with my workmanship and my character that he'd recognize me as a true prince of Blackwood. My mother might have given me the surname Storm, but it meant nothing if not acknowledged by the king.

I'm not exactly sure why he decided to pick the swords up personally, but I wasn't about to look a gift horse in the mouth. This was karma and good luck pulling through for me. Today was the day I'd finally be accepted.

"Morning, Criss," a homeless man named Ted said from his perch on the corner.

I reached into my pocket and handed him a coin. "Morning, Ted. Sleep well?"

He rubbed his lower back with a bony old hand and grumbled. "I think I slept on a rock."

I grinned. "I think most people sleep on pillows."

"Well, I ain't got no pillow, do I?" He was sassy for an old man, even if he did appear rather cheerful while he complained.

I crossed my arms and smirked. "I don't know, do you? I distinctly remember buying you a pillow once."

He waved my comment away. "I sold that pillow months ago for a barrel of ale."

"Of course you did." I rolled my eyes and pointed to the coin in his hand. "Why don't you buy a new pillow with that?"

"Because I just finished my last drop of ale last night. I need to buy a new barrel."

I sighed, contemplating him with a little smirk. "What if I gave you an extra coin? Would you buy a pillow, then?"

His white eyebrows rose, and he smiled, revealing all three of his teeth. "I could... or I could buy *two* barrels of ale. That would last me *twice* as long."

I chuckled and shook my head. "I'll see you later, Ted."

"Bye, Crissen," he said, his hand waving in a wide arc above his head. "And thanks again for the coin."

"Don't worry about it," I called over my shoulder as I continued toward my shop.

My guys were already hard at work: pouring metal into molds, hammering the steel into perfectly smooth blades, carving designs into the hilts, and cutting sheaths that fit each sword just right.

I said my good mornings to them as I passed, heading toward the warehouse where the king's order of swords had been stowed. All thousand blades were there, glimmering in the early morning sunlight that slipped in from the second-story window, plus a hundred or so extra in case there were any imperfections in the first go. I'd checked and rechecked them at least five times, but you never knew when you'd miss something.

After that, I strolled into my office and shut the door behind me, staring at myself in the mirror propped behind my door. My hazel eyes looked worried, so I forced myself to take a deep, calming breath, watching as my chest rose and fell shakily. I smoothed a hand over my wavy brown hair and wrapped it in a band at the nape of my neck. There was a wrinkle in my decorative blue jacket, so I flattened the material with my hands, using them as an iron of sorts, and then did the same to my white dress pants. Normally, I'd never dream of wearing white to the forge, but today was a day for first impressions, and I wanted to make a great one.

Speaking of impressions... had I made a good impression on Alexis at the ball? I couldn't tell. I knew she'd married Prince Calvin weeks ago in a whirlwind ceremony, but I couldn't help but think about her still. She was stunningly beautiful, her tiny body fit perfectly into mine as we danced, and she was so easy to talk to. I couldn't believe I'd spilled my guts to her about my royal heritage, but since she took it all so gracefully, I didn't regret my confession.

Did she ever think about me?

I scoffed and turned away from my own reflection. Of course she didn't. She had four strapping Storm princes biting at the bit to satisfy her every whim. She didn't need a bastard Storm drooling after her too.

A knock sounded at my door before Jenson, my hilt worker, came bursting in. His wild, curly hair was halfway in his face. "The king is almost here. There's a procession of carriages rounding the bend."

I swallowed hard and nodded. "Thank you. I'll be out in just a moment."

Holy fucking gods, this was it.

My heart hammered as loud as my workers pounding at their blades and at least five times as fast. I took another deep breath, but it did nothing to calm the nervousness icing in my veins.

Do not freeze, Crissen. Do not mess this up. It might be your only chance.

A moment later, I strolled from my office with a confidence and ease I did not feel whatsoever. I was grateful that I could fake it on the outside, though—a skill that would no doubt serve me well if I ever became a prince.

Standing at the front of the shop, I crossed my arms behind my back, straightened my spine, and patiently waited as the carriages rolled to a stop in front of me. Guards surrounded the procession, riding on the backs of strong black steeds, glaring at me like I was a criminal.

I adjusted my footing. *Did they look at everyone like that?* Friendly bastards.

A servant opened the door of the carriage in the middle and proclaimed, "All hail the King of Blackwood."

My five-man crew and I dropped to one knee and placed our fists over our hearts as the king—my father—emerged from the coach.

My heart beat wildly, and my lungs pumped like mad.

Sweat broke out across my brow, and nerves triggered my hands to shake.

This is him, Zacharias, the man and the legend.

He stepped out, pulling a pair of black gloves off his jeweled hands as he assessed his surroundings with an appreciative eye—thank the gods we'd spent the weekend cleaning the place. His hair was silver, but his expression was sharp, his features handsome and bold. There was a confidence, an aura of poise about him that made me proud to be his son—even if he didn't know that I was.

"Crissen, is it?" he asked as he approached. Even his voice sounded rich and regal.

I stood at the mention of my name and bowed my head. "Yes, Your Majesty."

"Are my swords ready?" he asked, holding steady eye contact with me.

I swallowed hard. "They are, Your Majesty."

"Show me."

I led him over to the warehouse and swung open the door, allowing more light to glint off the numerous blades lying in wait. He strolled inside, every so often picking up a sword and testing its balance, weight, and plumbness. After a few minutes of this, he spun around and nodded to his guards. Immediately, they filed in and collected the swords, stowing them away in the extra carriages.

The king put his arm around my shoulders and squeezed. "Let's talk money, shall we?"

I ducked down, since he was shorter than me, and smiled brightly. "Absolutely, Your Majesty."

He led us over to his carriage and gestured for me to climb inside. Since most financial transactions were conducted in private, I thought nothing of it. He stepped in behind me, and a servant shut the door. Then, he got straight to business.

"I am prepared to offer you fifty thousand jewels." His voice was calm and collected. "That's fifty per sword. Do you accept?"

I nearly sputtered out loud. That was ten times what I expected to make. "Yes, Your Majesty, thank you very much."

He nodded, apparently pleased with my reception, and he glanced out the window. "There's a rumor going around that you are my illegitimate son. Have you heard anything of this?"

I couldn't tell from the tone of his voice if he was curious or pissed off; the pitch was so carefully neutral. It set my nerves on edge.

I glanced at the velvety purple rug on the carriage floor. "Yes, Your Majesty, I've heard of them."

"Did *you* start these rumors?"

My leg started to bounce. "No, Your Highness, my mother did. She says you spent a single night together some twenty-eight years ago that resulted in... me."

I glanced up, suddenly caught in his intense blue gaze, and immediately wished I hadn't.

"What was her name?" he asked lightly, as if carefully containing his emotions.

"Charity, Your Majesty. Charity Haventon."

"*Haventon*," he muttered, stroking his silver beard. "The founding family of Blackhaven. Yes, I believe I do recall spending a night with the governor's daughter." He stared at me a moment longer. "You have her eyes. Clear blue and innocent."

I smiled, relieved beyond belief that he'd not only remembered her name but also her eyes. If he'd admittedly been with her, then he was, in a sense, acknowledging the possibility that I was truly his son.

"I'll be back tomorrow, if you don't mind," he said, nodding to himself. "I'd like to get to know you better."

My smile stretched even wider. I couldn't believe my unimaginable luck.

"Yes, Your Majesty, I'd like that very much."

He smirked and his eyes crinkled at the corners. "Please. Call me *Father*."

CHAPTER 14

$\mathcal{A}$LEXIS

ONCE WE CROSSED THAT MAGICAL THRESHOLD INTO THE Lunaley, it was as if the place we'd just left behind was nothing more than a memory of a dream.

Magic thrummed through the air; I could feel its pressure weighing on my skin, its energy vibrating the very cells of my body. It hummed through the earth and the nearby stream, which was an electric, glowing blue. I clutched Speedy and stared at our surroundings, absolutely fascinated as we made our way deeper into the woods.

The soil beneath our shoes was strange, squishy and soft, yet dry and sturdy. It sank beneath each step we took, but the surface layer never broke or suctioned to our feet.

"Are we still going straight?" Rob asked skeptically.

Cal glanced over his shoulder with one golden eyebrow arched. "Of course we are."

"How can you be so sure?" Dan asked, pausing to look around. "There's not exactly a path."

Ben knelt down and touched the base of a nearby tree. "If the moss on this tree is anything to go by... then, yes, we're still going straight. And as long as we continue to follow this river, we should *stay* going straight."

Cal smirked. "See? Told you."

Rob rolled his gray eyes, which appeared lighter in the Ley than they ever had outside it. "You were totally fucking guessing."

"Think what you will," Cal said, and continued in the direction we'd been traveling.

"What are we even doing here, anyway?" Dan asked, scratching his head as he spun around in a circle.

I squinted, trying to remember the specifics. "I'm not sure."

"We're walking straight," Rob supplied.

"Right," Dan agreed, "but *why?*"

Rob shrugged, and Cal shook his head. "I don't know. I just really think we need to keep going straight. I'm pretty sure there's something waiting for us up ahead."

"A good something? Or a bad one?" Dan asked, but none of us were able to answer. We couldn't seem to remember much of anything.

I looked down at the mist floating around my ankles and knees, trying to remember as much as I could. We'd been right outside the Lunaley, talking to a guard. The same mist that surrounded us now had been hovering through the trees at the edge of the sand. Camilla had been there... but I couldn't remember exactly who Camilla was. She was waiting on us, though. I remember her saying that she would be there when we returned. But returned from *what?*

"We're in the Lunaley," I said aloud. "I remember talking to a guard at the border of the Obsidian. He's the one who told us to go straight. And there's a girl named Camilla waiting for us."

"Who's Camilla?" Rob asked, crossing his tattooed arms suspiciously.

Ben's gaze narrowed. "The Eristani princess. But why the hell would *she* be waiting for us?"

I shrugged. It was like I knew the answer, but it was buried under a mountain of sand. "No idea."

Cal's lips thinned as he thought. "If the Eristani princess is waiting on us to return, then this must be an important quest. So, regardless of the reason, we better keep walking."

~

HOURS LATER—OR MAYBE DAYS—WE'D FOUND NOTHING BUT more and more trees. The sun never rose higher, nor set. I couldn't even see it through the overcast sky, but I could tell its general position based on the brightness of the clouds. It was as if time stood still. Our feet moved, the trees rolled by, the river meandered onward... but we got nowhere.

Eventually, I stopped walking and put a hand on my hip. "Are we even getting anywhere?"

No one seemed to know.

Speedy wriggled in my other arm. Asher was apparently ready to come back.

I held him out at arm's length. "Can someone kill Speedy? I don't have the heart to do it."

I might've killed him in jaguar form, but in sloth form? He'd been my pet for so many years. It pained me to think of hurting him, even though I knew it was actually *Asher*, not Speedy.

"I damn near killed him at Dryroot Canyons," Rob muttered halfheartedly. "I can't do it this time."

"I snapped his neck once already," Cal added.

Which left Dan and Ben.

Ben cocked his head at Dan. "He's my best friend, bro. Don't make me do it."

Dan heaved an annoyed sigh and pulled out his sword. He lined his blade up with Speedy's neck, and in one swift slice, the golden magic was swirling through the air once more.

When Ash had returned to human form, his eyes were wide and alight with clarity and excitement.

"Everybody use your magic," he commanded quickly. "It clears your head, lifts the fog. I can remember everything perfectly now. Try it."

Rob, Ben, and Dan used theirs right away, manipulating the astral plane, the nearby trees, and the flowing stream. But Cal hesitated and glanced at me. "Just a *little* bit of magic, Peach."

I glared at him, suddenly feeling fiery. "You need to stop telling me what to do, especially where my magic is concerned, Calvin Storm."

His blue-eyed gaze narrowed into a dark stare. "I'm only trying to be responsible. An orgy in the middle of the Lunaley is probably not the wisest idea."

"I can handle it," I insisted for arguments sake. "Rob deals with pain and extreme cold, and Ben loses all five of his senses. I'm pretty sure I can deal with a bit of horniness by myself."

His lips thinned into a tight line. "Fine."

"Fine," I shot back in irritation. "*Fire*."

As I spoke the word, peach-colored flames curled out across my arms. They swayed happily, dancing to their own silent tune as they burned. I saw my blaze reflected in Cal's eyes, giving a hint of madness to his angry stare. And like the mature adult I was, I stuck out my tongue in response.

He shook his head and called on the sky, sending a gust of wind blowing through the trees, battering our hair and clothing. When his wind eventually stopped, I followed suit, squeezing my fists and cutting off my flames.

Ash had been right. Upon using my magic, clarity immediately overcame me, my memory becoming crystal clear. We were on a mission to save the chimeras on behalf of Eristan and to reinstate the Treaty O' Ley in order to save the fae. We needed to find and steal a chimera egg on behalf of the Storm King, and we needed to do all of this in less than two weeks.

Perfect. I almost wished I hadn't remembered.

Just beneath the clarity, lust stirred hot as a branding iron. I glared at Cal, half hating the fact that he'd been right, half wanting to rip the clothes off his body.

Ash glanced upward, drawing all our gazes, as a chimera lit in the tall branch of a nearby tree. It didn't appear to be watching us; it simply paused to lick its paws, wiping them along its lion-like face, before yawning and pushing back up into the air.

When I glanced back at Ash, he already had a puff of gold swirling around him. "I'm going to change into a chimera. I want to know what it's like."

Then he was gone, replaced by a chimera that was taller than I was, with a dark mane and a golden circle of fur at its chest. Its wings stretched out wide, as if testing the reach and flexibility, and its feathers ruffled. At the rear, its dragon claws dug into the ground and its jagged tail swished anxiously.

He sniffed the air, and his pupils narrowed into thin slits, his head turning in the direction of a gnarled tree with purple and pink striped bark. He rubbed his head against the trunk, then his wings, and his tail, spinning in a circle around the tree's base, trying to get as much bodily contact as he could.

The whole thing was strangely fascinating, but I still couldn't stop stealing furtive glances at Cal. He was side-eyeing me in return, proving my magic had most likely affected us *both*.

Ignoring the lust yanking at my heartstrings and lady bits, I looked up, noticing the leaves of the tree in question were dark blue and crescent shaped. They tinkled in the breeze, a soft metallic sound like wind chimes. Instead of stretching tall, the branches spread out wide, curving and clawing into a bowl of sorts, so that the entire plant stood only about twenty feet high but equally as broad. It was the only one of its kind in these parts, and I had to wonder if there were more somewhere, perhaps further in?

I swallowed hard, choking down the burn of desire, and stole another glance at Cal. He'd moved a little closer. I could practically reach out and touch him. My body ached for me to do just that.

"You can't handle it, can you?" Cal asked, his voice raspy.

I took a heavy breath and glared at him. "Of course I can."

Cal smirked, stepping even closer, running his broad hands up the outsides of my arms and cupping my neck in his warm palms. His thumbs brushed my jaw, causing my lips to part. "That's only a half truth."

"Ah, fuck," Rob muttered. "Jewels used her magic."

Dan and Ben grunted sounds of agreement and understanding, and the three of them wandered a little further ahead, giving Cal and me some space.

At least there'd be no awkward proposals, considering we were already married.

He stared deep into my eyes, trying to figure out the part that was a lie. "You can handle it, *but...?*"

I let out a heavy breath and stared at his lips. "*But...* I don't know if I *want* to handle it. To hold it back, control it, or contain it."

He took another step, bringing his hard body right up to

the curve of my chest and hips. "I don't know if I want you to, either."

Then his lips were on mine, hot and demanding, soothing that lustful ache that had drilled its way through my very skull. He stepped forward, pushing me back until my shoulders and ass crashed into the bark of a nearby tree. With nowhere to go, he pressed his body into mine like molten steel, molding perfectly against me.

"Why are we always having fast and furious sex?" he muttered, tearing my dress over my head. He bit my bottom lip as he unhooked my bra; then he worked my undies down my legs. Next thing I knew, I was in his arms and my legs were wrapped around his waist. He still had his pants on, which was a serious problem for me and my raging hormones.

"Probably because your bossiness makes me *furious*," I replied, fumbling with the buttons of his pants before removing his cock and stroking him.

He lifted a brow in challenge. "And the *fast* part?"

I smirked as I pulled off his shirt and threw it. "Fast to make me come undone?"

"Good answer."

I ran his dick through my soaking wet folds and positioned him right where I wanted him. A few firm thrusts were all it took for him to claim me completely.

"We're always fucking against shit too," I moaned as he pumped into me, trapped between him and the rough bark of the tree. "The first time was a pillar."

He chuckled and whipped me around, lowering us onto the forest floor, so that I was the one on top. The mist enveloped us so completely, it was difficult to see beyond each other's faces.

"There. Now, we're not always fucking against things. Sometimes we fuck on the ground."

I rolled my hips, loving the control he'd given me. I moved the way *I* wanted to, hitting all the spots *I* liked. And when I started getting close, I put my fingers down to my clit and took *my own* pleasure from his body. It was so fucking empowering.

He lay beneath me, mesmerized with my every move— my free hand as it tangled in my hair, the rhythmic rolling of my hips against his, the curve of my spine as my back arched and my moans became desperate pants.

"Yes," Cal groaned, reaching up to roll my nipples between his thumbs and forefingers. "Come for me, Peach."

I don't know if it was his sexy command, the nipple tweaking that sent sensations straight to my clit, or the touch of my own fingers, but a second later I was crying out my release. I rode him until my first orgasm blended into a second, even stronger one, and I moaned even louder.

I could hear the guys groaning up ahead, and I could just imagine their cocks swelling at the thought of me being so horny and vulnerable. It was probably torturous. I wanted to call them back and have them join us, but we didn't really have time for that. Technically, we didn't even have time for *this*, but my magic made it impossible to deny.

"How do you want me?" I asked, circling my hips. Now that I'd gotten off, I wanted to help him do the same.

His blue eyes were dark, and his facial features strained. "Right where you are, don't stop."

I leaned down and pushed my hands against his massive chest, riding him hard until he lost all control. As he ground out a string of cuss words, he grabbed my hips and pumped me up and down, slowly milking every last drop from his body.

When we were both blissfully spent, I climbed off him and quickly realized gravity was not on our side. My inner thighs had cum dripping all over.

Cal chuckled and reached for his shirt on the ground, handing it over to me for cleanup. "I should start calling you *Peaches and Cream.*"

I stuck my tongue out at him. "It's *your* cream."

"My favorite kind to dip you in." His lips curved seductively, turning me on once more with no encouragement from any magic.

I grinned and crawled over to him. "Want to go for round two?"

He bit his bottom lip, and despite the fact that he'd just come, his cock jumped at the thought.

Just then, Speedy screeched, a cry that didn't sound scared or threatened but that still seemed significant. He was alerting us to something. He jerked his lion-like head up, and his gaze darted forward, seemingly searching the forest for noise or an image that none of us had heard or seen. He leapt from the branch and took to the air, soaring high above the trees and moving deeper into the forest. His body tipped side to side as his wings caught the sky's current, and he disappeared from view.

"Come on," Cal said, lifting me up and handing me my dress. "We don't want to lose him."

He balled his dirty shirt up and stuffed it into a pack, retrieving a clean one from the top. After my gown was back in place and I had a clean pair of panties on, we were once again on the move.

The five of us rushed after Ash, sprinting through the undergrowth as fast as humanly possible without tripping over roots or hanging ourselves on vines. After a few minutes, I saw a puff of smoke rising above the trees, a slightly darker shade than that of the dreary clouds. Between the trunks, I saw a camp of sorts. The trees in the area had been chopped down, their ends whittled into spikes that guarded the perimeter. Soldiers—Eristani from the looks of their baggy pants and shirtless upper bodies—were huddled around fires eating soup, strolling between tents, and napping on pillows on the ground.

Speedy lit in the top branch of a tall tree, scattering leaves onto a few of the soldiers' heads. They glanced up, then looked right back down, immediately paying him no mind, getting back to spooning in mouthfuls of soup. Apparently, the appearance of a chimera in these parts was not all that rare or surprising.

"This must be the camp that guard was telling us about," Dan muttered, as we all crouched behind a bush and spied on them.

"I wonder if there are any chimera nests nearby?" I said, scanning the forest for more of those strange trees. I'd hoped to find one holding some oversized eggs, but I saw none.

"Why are we hiding, anyway?" Cal asked. He straightened his posture, tugged the wrinkles out of his shirt, then smoothed back his golden hair. He strolled right up to the camp's gate, smiling amicably at the guard who pointed a spear at him in return.

"Who goes there?" the guard asked in a deep, rich voice.

"Prince Calvin Storm of Blackwood, my wife: Princess Alexis, and my brothers, the Princes of Blackwood: Daniel, Benson, and Robert."

The guard's dark eyes narrowed. "There is no reason for Blackwood royalty to be traipsing through the Ley. Turn around. Leave while you still can."

"*While you still can?*" Rob mocked with a smirk. "Is that some sort of threat?"

The guard planted his spear in the ground and stepped closer, lowering his voice. "There are demons in this forest, boy. Demons that will rip your spine from your body and use it as a toothpick after they've devoured you whole."

Rob shook his head. "Demons always get such a bad rap."

I glanced at him. "Do you have demons living in your quadrant?"

He nodded, still grinning at the guard's serious expression. "Take us to the demons, *soldier*, and I'll reason with them."

The guard scoffed. "You can't *reason* with demons. It doesn't work that way."

"I assure you, it does. Let us through the gates, take us to the demons, and we'll be out of here by nightfall."

But the guard simply shook his head. "One, we're not going anywhere near the demons. And two, it's never nightfall here, nor is it morning. It's always... the same."

Ben and I shared a glance, his mind *whirring* a mile a minute behind the brown depths of his eyes. I could tell he was trying to figure this place out. Me? I had no clue where to even start.

"Whatever," Rob said, shaking his head. "Just tell us the direction the demons are located, and we'll be on our way."

The guard rolled his eyes and pointed to the opposite end of the camp. "It's your funeral."

Rob smirked. "You say that like it's a bad thing. Like it's *the end*."

"Death *is* the end."

Rob chuckled. "Death is only a bridge, a pathway between this world and the next."

The guard picked up his spear and went back to his post. "Have fun crossing that bridge, then."

Since we hadn't been invited into the camp, we skirted around the spiked perimeter until we reached the other side. Ahead, the forest seemed to grow even darker and mistier than before, so I had a bad feeling we were headed in the right direction.

"Are you sure we have to do this?" I asked, hating the fear

in my voice. I couldn't help it, though. This place totally freaked me out.

"Of course we have to." Rob glanced around the group, as if realizing for the first time that not everyone might've agreed with him. "They're probably lost in here with no way out. You'd want someone to save you, wouldn't you?"

Dan nodded right away, as if the answer was obvious. Then Ben, who'd no doubt taken time to thoroughly think it through first. Then me, a little reluctantly. And finally, Cal nodded too—*very* reluctantly.

"We still need to find a chimera nest," Ben stated, mostly to me and Cal. "May as well kill two birds with one stone. Save the demons *and* steal an egg."

Rob grinned and started walking.

"That's the spirit. Now, let's go find us some demons."

CHAPTER 15

*S*peedy followed us from tree to tree, waiting until we were well out of sight from the camp before tucking his wings and diving to the ground, landing with a *thud*. He opened his lion-like jowls to roar, but an earsplitting screech screamed out instead, much like an eagle—an eagle with oversized vocal cords.

I backed away slightly, intimidated by the thing whether it was Ash or not.

"Do you think he wants us to kill him again?" Dan asked. "Because I refuse to do it this time. Someone else can murder the bird from hades."

Rob stepped forward, his bravery shining through as he unsheathed his sword. "I'll take care of it. Everyone else just stand back."

He didn't have to tell me twice. I scurried backward and clutched onto Dan's arm, inadvertently using his body as a shield.

Speedy lowered his head so that he and Rob were face-to-face, and even though he appeared to be yielding, it still looked terrifying as fuck.

Rob put his free hand out, barely touching the creature's neck, then jabbed his sword forward, puncturing its chest and twisting the blade for maximum damage.

The chimera screeched maddeningly, flopping to the ground and flailing about as if it no longer had control over its body. Blood gushed from its chest in waves, slowly but surely draining the life from its eyes. As its head went limp, it let out one feeble squawk, then died at Rob's feet.

The golden magic swirled to life then, transforming the creature back into an angry, glaring Asher.

"You are never allowed to kill me again," he decided, jabbing a finger at Rob.

Rob flung his arms out in defense. "It was a clean kill!"

"It was neither clean, nor quick," Ash argued. "It was slow and painful."

Rob rolled his gray eyes, trying to hide a grin. "Don't be a pansy, Ash."

But Asher had already moved on, turning to Ben. "I'm going to fly ahead. See if I can spot any demons lurking in the woods. I'll also be on the lookout for nests and eggs." He paused as another thought seemed to come to him. "Did you see how I acted back there at that one tree?"

Ben nodded, perking up at the chance to puzzle something out. "Yeah, the one with the moon-shaped leaves? Does it have a special sort of magic flowing through it? Something that drew you in?"

Ash grimaced and shook his head. "I don't know. I don't think chimeras even like magic."

"What do you mean?" Ben's brows furrowed in intrigue.

"I mean, my chimera form wanted to avoid you guys at all costs. It took every ounce of control I had to get that close to Rob without accidentally clawing him through the chest."

Ben's lips pursed. "How do you know it was because of

magic and not just the fact that we're *humans* and you were an *animal?*"

Ash shot him a flat look. "I'm in animal form *a lot*. I think I ought to know what it feels like. Besides, I didn't feel any aggression toward the Eristani soldiers back at the camp. And while you guys were following the glowing river, my chimera form wanted to fly as far away from the magical water as possible."

"So, they don't like *magic*, but they live in the *Lunaley?*" Rob asked doubtfully.

Ash shrugged. "It is what it is, bro."

Ben shook his head. "Let's get back on track, shall we? What attracted you to that strange tree?"

Ash's cheeks flushed a gentle pink. "Its ability to hold a big nest."

Rob burst out laughing. "You were house shopping? How cute."

"Hey, I can't help it I take on the natural instincts of the creatures I become, dickhead. The chimera only seemed to care about two things: finding a tree fit for holding a nest and finding a female chimera fit for laying eggs."

Rob laughed even harder, and against all rational sense, my jealousaurus reared her ugly head. I placed both hands on my hips and narrowed my brows. "You were looking for a piece of ass this whole time?"

"Sweets," he groaned, holding his arms out to me. "It's not like that. It was an instinct, not a deliberate choice."

My eyes narrowed further. "How many sloths did you fuck over these last six years?"

He rolled his amber eyes. "How many sloths did you see hanging out in Blackwood? I'll give you a hint: *I was the only one.*"

I pursed my lips. He had a point. He probably couldn't even jack off as a sloth. Not only would his motions be far too slow to be productive, but he wouldn't even want to *think* about touching his junk with those long claws. I know I sure as hell wouldn't have. Sloths probably didn't masturbate anyway.

Did they?

"Besides," Ash continued, taking a few steps closer to me, "I have a feeling that if my chimera even tried to... I don't fucking know... *mate* with another chimera, a lightning bolt would tear from the sky and burn us both to a crisp."

I smiled despite myself and crossed my arms. "Good."

He grinned and shook his head. "You're feisty right now, aren't you?"

"She's feisty *all* the time," Cal assured him with an exaggerated eye roll.

I turned to the Sky Prince. "Just because you're bossy and I don't like to do as you say does not mean that I'm feisty all the time. It means I'm a person with my own thoughts and ideas."

Again, Cal rolled his eyes, a small smile tucked into his lips.

"And you"—I pointed to Ash—"are getting my fiery attitude because you literally just admitted to wanting to fuck another woman."

"An *animal*!" he corrected me in a shout, and all the guys sniggered.

They knew how ridiculous I was being. Even *I* knew. I couldn't hide the smile that crawled up onto my face at his outrage.

Ash glanced from face to face as we all chuckled. "You're fucking with me, aren't you?"

"I don't know," I admitted. "I wasn't at first, but then I realized how stupid I was being."

He shook his head, unwound my crossed arms, and

155

pulled me into a tight embrace. "I love you, Sweets. You're the only girl for me—human or animal alike."

My heart warmed at his use of the word *love*, but I still wasn't ready to say it back. Of course, I still loved him; I'd never really stopped, even after all these years. I just didn't want to make any waves for the other Storms. They'd welcomed him back to the group, but the situation was still so new. I couldn't risk doing anything that might make them change their minds or regret their decision. That ultimately meant that things with Ash had to progress *slowly*—magical lust orgies aside.

"Good," I said again, kissing his cheek. I pulled away from his embrace and forced my eyes onto the imaginary path ahead of us, moving into a determined stroll. "Let's find these demons and get that egg so we can get the hell out of here."

❧

Turned out, finding the demons was far easier than I ever expected. We just kept walking forward, deeper and deeper into the misty gloom where the trees grew taller, blocking out most of the sky. And after a few hours, give or take—who could actually tell?—Speedy squawked and dove to the ground.

"Are the demons up ahead?" Cal asked him.

The chimera nodded and screeched again, prancing his feet impatiently as he waited on someone to deal him a fatal blow.

Cal sighed, knowing what needed to be done next but clearly not wanting to do it.

Rob held up both hands. "Sorry, bro, but you heard the man. I'm not *allowed* to."

Cal turned to Dan. "You're best at it."

Dan blew an obnoxious raspberry that morphed into a

sarcastic chuckle. "I'm best at it? What the fuck kind of a compliment is that?"

"I don't know," Cal growled. "Just kill the damn thing so we can keep moving."

Some of us already *had* kept moving, though.

Rob left the cover of the trees and entered the little meadow where the demons had set up camp. There appeared to be five of them, each with shadowy humanoid forms that glowed red from their eyes, mouths, and joints as if there was actual fire inside of them. Three sat around a round table playing a game of cards, one was sprawled out on a log tossing a ball in the air, and the last one was roasting something that looked strangely like a human arm over a fire.

"How's it going, guys?" Rob asked.

They recognized their prince immediately, and as the demons scrambled to their knees and bowed down before Rob, Dan sliced his blade across Speedy's throat. Blood gushed out like a crimson waterfall, turning my stomach in an instant.

Gods, I didn't think I'd ever get used to the gurgling sound of death.

"Prince Robert! Thank hades!" the demons shouted in the background. "We're saved!"

"I don't know about *saved*." Rob chuckled. "But you *are* lucky we found you. Is... is that a human arm on a stick?"

The demon that was spinning the limb rotisserie-style above the fire paused and looked up. "Um..."

Rob crossed his burly, tatted arms. "How many times have we been over this? You can't eat humans. It's socially unacceptable."

"But there was nothing else to eat!" the first card player complained, gathering their finished game into a big pile to be collected.

"Yeah, we would have starved!" the second card player chimed in, not helping the first guy clean up whatsoever.

Rob cocked a brow and pointed skyward. "Birds."

"Oh, gross," the third demon spat. "You try eating a bug instead of a chicken."

Rob sighed. "Humans are not equivalent to chickens."

"They taste like them," the demon by the fire added nonchalantly.

Ash had apparently finished turning back into a human, because he chose that moment to place his hand on my shoulder, startling the hell out of me. I gasped and clutched at my throat, accidentally drawing the curious gazes of all five demons.

"Who's over there?" one of them asked, craning his neck to see above the bushes.

"Have you brought us dinner?" another questioned excitedly.

"Absolutely not," Rob growled. "That's Jewels."

"Jewels?" the demons groaned. "Like shiny rocks? That's all you brought us to eat?"

"No, Jewels is a person—one you *can't* eat."

While they moaned and groaned, Dan shot us a cocky grin and emerged from the bushes with a swagger in his step. "Untrue," he said to Rob and the demons. "I have, in fact, eaten Jewels already. Three times, actually."

Oh. My. Gods. I was going to kill him.

As Rob's features morphed into a deadly glare, I popped from the bushes and interrupted the shitshow before it could happen. Cal, Ben, and Ash followed me.

"Hi!" I said with an overly enthusiastic wave. "I'm Alexis, the one your dickhead prince likes to call Jewels. I'd appreciate it if *no one* talked about eating me in any way, shape, or form." I leaned in and whispered, "It makes me a bit uncomfortable."

158

"No, right, of course," the first demon said, pocketing his cards once he'd stuffed them back into their box. "I wouldn't appreciate being discussed as a dessert right in front of my face either."

"I wouldn't want to be a dessert at all," another demon added, scratching his charcoal-colored hair. "Could you imagine how burnt and disgusting I'd taste?"

They all muttered their agreement.

Dan stole the ball from the demon lying on the log and initiated a lazy game of catch. "How'd you guys get stuck out here anyway?"

They all glanced at one another. "Well, we heard scrambled chimera eggs were even better than scrambled human brai—"

"Okay!" Rob shouted, cutting them off before I gagged. "You mean to tell me, you travelled all the way from southern Blackwood up to the fucking Lunaley on a wild goose chase to find an egg?"

It sounded absurd, yet there *we* were, doing the exact same thing.

The third demon slapped a hand to his face and dragged it down his shadowy skin. "No, Your Highness, not a *goose* egg, a *chimera* egg. Weren't you listening?"

"Hades give me strength," Rob muttered to the sky above his head. "Were you at least successful?"

"Yeah, we found an egg," the fifth demon said as he continued roasting the arm. "But it was not nearly as delicious as—"

"Right, we know," Rob said. "Where exactly did you find this egg?"

They pointed ominously into the ever-darkening trees. *Great.*

Rob sighed. "Well, pack up, boys. You're going to take us to that chimera nest."

A loud round of complaining and arguing broke out, but Rob silenced them quickly. "Do you want to get the hell out of here or not?"

They nodded eagerly and laced their sharpened fingers into a stereotypical begging pose, complete with a lip pout. It was almost cute.

"Then you have to take us to the chimera nest first. We need an egg too, and we're not leaving until we get one. So, you better get your asses moving."

"But those chimeras are dangerous!" the laziest demon shouted. "There were ten of us at the beginning of this journey."

Rob glanced at us then back to the demon, his arms still crossed. "Half of you died trying to get the egg?"

"Well, not exactly," said the demon who'd pocketed the cards. I was pretty sure he was the leader of their little crew. "Two of them died before we ever even reached the Ley. Got sidetracked, tried to possess a couple bodies.... Let's just say there were crosses and holy water involved, and it was *not* pretty."

Rob rolled his eyes but couldn't hide his grin.

"And then one of them died in the crossfire of the fighting," the demon by the fire added. He removed the arm from the blaze and blew wildly at a finger that had accidentally gone up in flames.

My stomach twisted, threatening to spill what little contents it had in there, and I covered my mouth. "Please tell me you're not going to eat that."

The demon in question glanced between me and Rob, back and forth, until finally sighing and tossing the whole limb into the blaze as if it were a damn shame to waste it.

"What happened to the other two?" Rob asked.

This time the demon playing ball with Dan spoke up. "They killed each other. Got into a fight over who could burn who the hottest. Both of 'em went up in flames. They were nothing more than piles of ash by the end of it."

"Gross," I accidentally grumbled out loud.

Rob ignored me. "So, no one actually died in the procuring of the egg?"

"No," the leader admitted. "But chimeras *are* dangerous."

"See!" the lazy one shouted, glad to finally have some support. If anyone would bother calling *that* support.

"We're just lucky we caught the chimeras when they were fighting *each other*," the lead demon informed us. "Too busy to notice us when they were ripping each other's throats out, eh, boys?"

The other four demons muttered words of agreement.

Rob turned to Ash and grinned, his brows waggling wickedly. "You know what that means, don't you?"

Ash shook his head, his lips curling up at the corners. "Looks like I'm going to be our diversion."

"That's right," Rob agreed. "While you're fighting the chimera, one of us will sneak in and grab an egg."

Cal frowned. "And what happens to Ash once we steal the egg and run? I won't leave him behind. What if he dies and turns back into a man?"

Rob shrugged. "Then he'll just have to turn back into a chimera and try again."

Cal's blue-eyed gaze narrowed. "I thought we agreed to never again put Ash's life in danger like we did at the canyons?"

Asher chuckled darkly. "I wasn't in danger at Dryroot, and I won't be in danger here. Honestly, I don't even know if the word *danger* means a damn thing anymore."

Cal looked like he wanted to argue, but Rob didn't wait to hear what he had to say.

"Demons!" the Spirit Prince shouted. "I told you to get your asses moving."

They snapped into action as if Rob had cracked a whip, disassembling their tents and tables, grabbing pots, pans, clothes, and blankets, and shoving it all into a few oversized rucksacks. All in all, I was quite impressed with their speed. Though, to be fair, I had no idea how fast a demon usually moved.

"Ready, Your Highness," the leader announced with a salute.

Rob gestured to the darkened woods before us. "After you."

And we all disappeared into the trees once more.

CHAPTER 16

"So, what are your names, anyway?" Dan asked the demons after we'd already been following them through the woods for hours, or so I guessed; it was hard to see the sky beyond the dense canopy above. Even through the leaves and the clouds, the sun didn't appear to move much, so it was difficult to tell how much time might've passed.

The lead demon spoke up first. "I'm Hugh. That over there's Kel." He pointed to the demon who'd been tossing the ball to himself.

"I'm Bob," the lazy demon chimed in.

"Larry," one of the ex-card players said, lifting his hand into the air.

And then finally the demon who'd been roasting the arm spoke up. "Sue."

"What the fuck?" Dan asked, clearly amused. "You're all guys, right? Why do two of you have girl names?"

Hugh, the leader, turned around and glared at him. "Did *you* choose *your* name upon birth?"

"Well, no," Dan conceded, "but if I'd been named Sue, you can bet your ass I'd be changing it as soon as I could."

Sue merely shrugged. "I like my name. It's unassuming. I can get really close to people before they realize I'm a demon."

"And by really close," Cal asked, "you mean...?"

Sue waggled his brows and licked his shadowy lips.

My nose curled as my stomach flipped. Dear gods, these things were disgusting when they talked about eating people.

"Besides," Bob argued, pointing at Asher, "you have a guy with a girl's name in your group, too. *Ash*. That's short for Ash*ley*."

Ash glared at him. "Yeah, or Ash*er*."

Suddenly, a loud screech tore through the air, rendering us all silent.

Hugh tucked his shoulders in and glanced wearily overhead. "The nest is close."

Bob, the lazy demon, latched onto Hugh's arm and shrank down even lower. "That's the sound she made last time we got too close."

Ben nodded, taking in the few bits of important information they'd divulged. "A warning call," he decided.

Then all at once, everyone turned to Asher.

He took a deep breath and shrugged. "Guess that's my cue."

I strode over to him and pulled him into a tight hug. "Be careful."

He chuckled, the sound rumbling into my ear that was pressed to his chest. "No worries, Sweets. I'll be fine. Just like last time."

I kissed his lips and let him go, hating the feeling that every time I kissed him might be my last.

Ash turned to the others. "I'll circle the nest when I see it, so it'll be easier for you to find."

Cal put a hand on Ash's shoulder. "We'll get the egg as fast as possible. And as soon as we do, you get the hell out of there, okay?"

Ash nodded.

Hugh crossed his shadowy arms and raised a brow. "That's the big plan?"

Rob cut in. "You have something better? What was *your* plan when you got your egg?"

"Our plan was simple," Larry said with a half shrug. "*Get the egg.*"

"So why is our plan any less acceptable?" Rob asked, glancing between Larry and Hugh.

Bob rolled his glowing red eyes and sighed. "Let's just get on with it."

"Right," Ash agreed, quickly morphing into Speedy in a cloud of swirling gold dust. He pushed off the ground and took to the air in one swift motion, scanning the horizon for the nest.

Ben looked around, biting his lip as his brows furrowed. I could tell he was studying something, so I glanced around too. The forest was teeming with those pink-and-purple-striped trees, the ones with the blue crescent leaves that tinkled musically in the breeze. Only, here, deeper into the forest, they grew taller, as if the magic of the Ley grew stronger in the center. Or, you know, as if the tree simply needed to grow taller in order to reach the sunlight and survive. Whichever.

"Those trees are significant, aren't they?" I asked him.

Ben nodded. "We just need to figure out *why*."

Suddenly, a second earsplitting screech echoed through the trees from high above, followed by another, slightly deeper one that I assumed belonged to Ash. Mama chimera must've noticed him.

It was time to move.

I tore off into a run, and everyone else did the same—well, everyone but the demons. They dragged their feet and pretended to jog, in no apparent hurry to meet the frightening beasts a second time. It was ironic to me that the humans thought *they* were the fierce beasts, while the demons were scared of a beast that the humans didn't fear at all.

I couldn't see Ash above me, so I had no clue if he was circling a nest or not, but I could certainly hear them screaming at each other, so I just did my best to follow the noise through the woods.

The screams and screeches grew louder, along with the sound of flapping wings and clashing claws. They were clearly getting into a fight above the clouds. I didn't know how difficult it'd be for Ash to hold off a mother chimera hell-bent on protecting her eggs, but it couldn't be an easy endeavor. We needed to get there as fast as humanly possible.

Ahead, the nest came into view—a dark blue thing, largely made up of the crescent-shaped leaves of that strange tree. There were also twigs, feathers, and random pieces of grass and vines intertwined, but the nest itself was positioned in the wide bowl of that striped tree. I wondered if all chimera nests were built in those trees or if all nests used those leaves. That would certainly explain their significance.

The eggs were the size of ripe watermelons, with white shells and pale brown spots. There were three tucked safely into the nest, waiting on their mother to return and keep them warm. I had a sudden pang of sadness, and guilt gripped me. If Ash killed their mother, they would die. But I sure as hell didn't want the alternative. Hopefully they could just battle it out and one could retreat without their dignity but with their life intact.

Rob turned to us, and I knew already he was planning on being brave. He couldn't help it.

"No," I said, before he ever even spoke. "You're not going in there alone. You need backup."

"I'll go," Dan volunteered, stepping forward to stand beside Rob.

Ben and Cal glanced between us and the aerial fight overhead with grim expressions on their faces.

"Make it quick," Cal decided. "That chimera looks aggressive as fuck."

I glanced up again too, sickened to see blood dripping from Ash's head, throat, and chest. The female was bleeding too but not nearly as bad. She only had a few shallow scratches on the side of her shoulder.

I stepped forward and kissed each of them—just in case—and watched with a pounding heart as they raced toward the unguarded nest.

By that point, the demons had finally caught up to us.

"You guys are doing great," Hugh panted as he put his hands on his hips, puffing out his chest.

"What took you so long?" I asked, knowing full well they'd been dawdling on purpose.

"Bob," Larry said, shaking his head. "He's always so slow."

"It's true," Bob added, as if it were more of an excuse than an insult.

As soon as Rob and Dan made it to the nest, they grabbed an egg and took off running like lightning was about to strike behind them. They sprinted through the undergrowth, dodging tree trunks and vines with more skill than I'd ever be able to mimic, but I was damn well going to try.

Cal and Ben each took one of my arms, tugging me forward as Rob and Dan reentered our midst. They blew through our circle and blasted into the lead, leaving us struggling in the dust.

"Come on!" Hugh shouted, and all five demons ran like the wind after their prince.

"Always slow, my ass!" I shouted at their backs, pushing my legs as fast as they'd go.

I stole a glance behind me... just in time to see Ash falling to the ground in a heap of bloodied feathers.

"Ash!" I cried, stopping abruptly.

But Cal and Ben pulled on my arms.

"He'll be fine!" Ben assured me.

"Keep moving!" Cal demanded.

But something wasn't right. The magical dust was sluggish to billow up around him, and once it passed, he didn't get up. He just lay on the ground, a permanent grimace etched into his handsome features as he clutched his side and chest.

"Asher!" I screamed even louder. This time there was an evident hint of hysteria in my tone. I whipped around and sprinted back toward the nest far faster than I'd been running away from it.

He groaned and rolled side to side, as if trying to get up but failing. When I reached him, I crashed to the ground on my knees, staring in horror at his blood-soaked chest.

"Oh my gods, what the fuck is happening?" I shrieked. "He's not healing!"

Cal and Ben appeared beside me in an instant. I had no idea if Rob, Dan, or the demons were coming back or not. They could have been a mile away for all I knew.

The mama chimera swooped down again, narrowly missing the tops of our heads. Apparently, this fight wasn't over until the threat to her eggs was totally eliminated; and *we* were that threat.

"I'll take the chimera. You guys save Ash," Cal growled, leaping into the air as his sky powers took over. Then he was gone, circling the female with vengeance burning brightly in his eyes.

Oh my fuck, what were we going to do?

I might have screamed that out loud, because Ben immediately answered me.

"Use your fire to singe part of his flesh; it'll stop the bleeding. Afterward, I'll stitch the wound shut."

I cupped my hand and did as he asked without question or hesitation. "*Fire*."

When the peachy pink flames emerged in my palm, I quickly traced a line of them down Ash's chest and side, cringing as he hissed in pain and gagging as his flesh seared, my head swimming with fear and disgust. It left an ugly, charcoaled gash, but at least it wasn't hemorrhaging anymore.

"Okay, that's enough," Ben decided, reaching for an overgrown blade of grass. Using his magic, he split the green fibers into thin strings, then turned the final strand into something that looked like a pine needle. He hooked them together, knotted the end, then pushed it through Ash's skin.

It dawned on me then; he'd made a makeshift needle and thread.

He got to work stitching Ash's wounds shut just as Cal fell out of the sky. He crashed through multiple tree limbs, their branches splintering under his weight, before he hit the ground with a menacing *thud*.

"Oh, gods!" I screamed again, scrambling over to him. He, too, had bloody claw marks streaked down his chest, along with the cuts and scrapes from the branches he'd fallen through. "Ben!" I cried.

"Coming!" he shouted, but he stumbled a bit on his way, and I could tell his powers were already stealing away his five senses—the price of using his magic. He blinked a few times as he knelt by Cal's side, as if trying to clear his vision. "Same drill, Sailor. Light it up."

"*Fire*," I called, and my curly flames once more shot up into my palm.

The first time I'd used my power must not have been enough to stir the lust within me. Either that, or I was just too petrified to react in a sexual way. But, after this second time, I could feel it slowly building.

Just as I was about to use the flames on Cal, the mother chimera swooped down and raked a claw across my shoulder. It burned like a branding iron and stung as if a blade of pure salt had been wedged in the wound. My eyes squeezed so tightly shut, I thought the little orbs might burst. The pain was excruciating.

"*Fire!*" I called, and while the curling flames did race up my arm, they did *not* heal me as usual.

Oh my gods, we're going to die.

Ben rushed over, sweat beading across the tanned skin of his forehead as he tried to patch me up too. I shook my head, apparently in some sort of shock, because all I cared about was him helping his brothers.

That's when Rob and Dan came running back, charging the chimera with an aggression I hadn't seen in them before —not even the brooding badass.

"Go back!" I cried. "Don't leave the egg!"

"Fuck the egg," Rob growled, landing a bare-handed punch into the side of the chimera's lion-like head.

"The egg is safe. The demons have it," Dan elaborated as he swung his blade at the chimera's throat. It nicked some skin, drawing blood and a nasty scream from the wild creature.

Gods, he really *was* good at slicing throats. It was fucking weird and also slightly terrifying, but at the moment, it was more like a godsend.

"The demons will *eat* it," I protested, my voice slurring slightly.

A chill suddenly crept across my skin, sinking into my

muscles and bones. I shook and shivered, my teeth chattering as my eyes grew heavy.

"Stay with me, Sailor," Ben demanded loudly as if he could barely hear, squinting at my wound as if he could barely see.

It must've been far deeper than I'd realized.

I watched in a daze as Rob, Dan, and finally Ben took hits from the beast's wicked claws, their blood spraying through the air like a fan of crimson and spattering on the nearby leaves.

My heart physically ached, a ferocious pain in the center of my chest. The blood bond fought to keep us alive and intact, but with all of us wounded, it had nowhere left to draw strength from.

I homed in on a few blades of tall grass blowing gently in the wind in front of my face. Then I lost focus completely and everything went black.

CHAPTER 17

C RISSEN

I AWOKE THE NEXT DAY LIKE AN EARLY BIRD GLEEFULLY greeting the dawn.

This was the day.

My *father*, the *king*, was coming back to Blackhaven to spend time with me.

I knew I must've sounded like a needy little boy, but in a way, there *was* still a child inside of me longing for the presence of his dad in his life—to play ball with, to go hunting together, to teach me how to be a man, or how to treat a lady. I knew all those chances had already come and gone, but the longing remained.

I put on the same white pants and the same blue dress shirt because they were the finest items of clothing I owned. I ran a hand through my wavy brown hair and once more tied it off at the base of my neck. I wasn't sure what time he would arrive, so I decided to be prepared at *all* times.

I stared in the mirror, trying to find some sort of resemblance between the face of the man I met yesterday and the face of the man staring back at me now. Perhaps we had the same straight nose? Or maybe the same bluish-hazel eyes? There had to have been something.

Suddenly, and without warning, extreme pain assaulted my entire body, and I dropped to the floor, writhing in agony. It filled my chest with a pressure so intense I couldn't even cry out. I just lay there, every muscle in my body clamped down tight, with my mouth open wide and no sound coming out. It was like someone had cut through my chest, ripped open my rib cage, and squeezed my fucking heart with their bare hands until it was about to burst.

The pain eventually subsided enough for me to breathe, but it took every last ounce of my energy and strength with it. I was so lethargic and disoriented I could barely comprehend what was happening. My heart beat slow and faint, faltering every now and then, and I was certain it was about to give out entirely.

Was this death? Was this what death felt like?

The thought crossed my mind as my eyes drifted closed and peace overcame me.

If this is death, it's not so bad.

I lay there for a few minutes before my eyes snapped open and realization dawned on me. I was no longer in pain. I was no longer weak or weary. I sat up and held out my hands, but they weren't shaking as I'd guessed they'd be; they were strong and sure.

What the fuck just happened? Was it...? I wracked my brain, trying to come up with something that didn't sound insane. *Was it a heart attack? An anxiety attack? Had it even truly happened, or had I imagined the whole thing?*

I had no fucking clue.

I climbed back up to my feet and studied myself once

more in the mirror. My skin was much paler now, clammy with sweat, and had purple bags hanging like nooses around my eyes.

Something had clearly happened.

I rubbed my face, trying to bring back a bit of color. It was an anxiety attack. I was sure of it. I'd been nervous about meeting up with my father, anxious to impress him, eager to get back all that lost time, and it must've just been... too much.

Taking a deep breath, I regathered my courage. *You're fine now, Criss. Just get to the shop and wait for the king. Simple and easy. No worries.*

I strolled outside, passing Ted along the way, but was surprised to find him sitting on a pink, square pillow.

"Ted, you old dog, I can't believe you actually bought one."

He smiled and gave me a nod.

In the background, behind his white, mostly hairless head, I saw a barrel, and my brows furrowed. "I only gave you one coin. How'd you manage to buy both?"

His wrinkly old hands skimmed down across the front of his body in a totally failed effort to look... gods, I didn't know, *sexy*? It was slightly terrifying.

"I sold my body for an extra coin."

He didn't even look ashamed. In fact, he seemed quite impressed with his own ingenuity.

I choked on the image that had suddenly filled my mind, then coughed to cover it up. Who the fuck would seriously *pay* to tap an old wrinkly ass?

As soon as the thought came to me, I dismissed it. Honestly, I was probably better off not knowing.

I tossed him another coin and backed away slowly, a grin sneaking onto my lips. "In case you don't get any customers tonight."

He caught it and kissed its shiny face. "Thanks, Criss. You're the best."

"No worries, Ted." I waved without looking and continued down the road.

It didn't take long for that same nervous feeling to wash over me once more. Thankfully, though, this time it didn't hurt or bring me to my knees. It just swirled around in my chest and gut, making me seasick.

Already, a carriage sat at the front of my shop, surrounded by armored guards on horseback. The Storm King stood at the open carriage door with his arms folded neatly behind his back. There was a knowing look in his eye, one I couldn't quite place.

"Take a ride with me," he ordered through a cocky grin.

Nerves bounced around inside of me like sparks from a forge, but the nausea was now replaced with excitement. As long as I didn't have any more anxiety attacks, I'd be fine. I could totally get through this without looking like a total dumbass.

I jumped into the carriage, and the Storm King climbed in behind me. A servant shut the door, and soon we were bounding down the cobblestone streets.

As I smiled at my father, sitting regally in the seat across from me, I couldn't help but feel like this was the beginning of something amazing.

CHAPTER 18

✤

$\mathcal{A}$LEXIS

I SLOWLY OPENED MY EYES, BUT THE WORLD WAS A BLUR.

Darkness huddled in the space where I lay, and some sharp, spicy scent lingered on the air like a bucket of cold water for my brain.

I snapped awake, sitting up far too quickly and regretting it instantly. Agony flared to life in my shoulder, white hot. I hissed as I collapsed back onto the bed, forcing myself to hold as still as possible, hoping that my lack of movement would stop the pain. It didn't—it only dulled it.

Suddenly, my memories came flooding back. *The chimera.* It had attacked us. Ash had fallen. Cal had fallen. So had Dan, Rob, Ben... and me. How could I have forgotten? Actually... how could I have *survived*?

I cracked my eyes open once more, glancing around the tiny room I'd found myself in. The roof seemed to be thatched, with bits of grass patched together by vines and sealed shut with mud or clay. The walls were made up of thin shoots of wood, and they were lined from grassy floor to domed ceiling with rows upon rows of shelves. Each shelf was filled from end to end with vials and bowls and strange objects. An ivory horn from some wild animal. A massive, triangular tooth. A wooden doll. A dead newt floating in a jar of fluid.

Where the fuck am I?

I decided to risk sitting up once again, moving much slower this time. The world swam before my eyes, and I struggled to stay afloat in a sea of unconsciousness and pain. Sweat broke out across my brow, but I somehow managed to *not* pass out *or* fall down.

A bloody fucking miracle.

"She's awake," a voice stated. It was a woman's voice, deep and wizened.

I turned, blinking as my eyes filled with light from the doorway. A short, plump woman with suntanned skin stood off to the side, allowing a hoard of demons to filter in. Her face was long and stoic with a strong nose and calm eyes. There was something peaceful about her but also hard.

"Oh, thank hades," the leader—Hugh—declared, dropping his head onto my leg and hugging it. His skin was flaky and charcoaled and hotter than a fever.

I pulled away and scanned their faces, cheerful as ignorant little children. "Where are the guys?" I croaked.

"In the other huts," Hugh replied before turning to the older woman. "If *she* woke up, *they* should be waking up soon too, right?"

My eyes snapped open wider. "They haven't woken up yet? How long have we been here?"

The old woman shrugged. "A couple weeks, give or take."

"*Weeks!*" I shrieked. Oh my gods, it was already too late. We failed to bring the egg back to Blackwood in time. Our loved ones were probably already dead, Eristan and Timber-lune were no doubt still fighting over the Lunaley, as they would continue to do until the fae eventually died out.

And it was all our fault.

"Relax," the woman cooed, the sound coming out of her throat in a gentle vibration. "Time works differently in the Ley."

I took a deep breath, fighting to calm the erratic thumping of my heart, and let it out slowly. She was right. I knew that. I'd just forgotten. My hands raked through my hair with quivering fingers. Gods... this trip had been *awful*.

"None of them are awake?" I asked, feeling small all of a sudden.

She shook her head, as did all five demons.

"But they *will*?" I clarified nervously. "Wake up, that is?"

She shrugged nonchalantly, as if the death of my precious Storms would mean almost nothing to her. "It's possible. I've never known anyone to survive chimera wounds of that magnitude, but the five of you are far stronger than anyone I've ever come across."

"That's because they're part god," Larry explained to the woman, who I was beginning to think might've been a voodoo doctor or something.

She quirked a brow at the demon. "So you've said."

"They're not all high and mighty, though," Bob added. "Not like angels, the pompous pricks."

The old woman chortled, a sound that seemed to vibrate through her stout little frame. I got the impression that she was on much better terms with demons than she was with angels. An interesting woman indeed. Though, to be fair, I'd never met an angel, so I had no idea how they acted. They really might have been the arrogant dickwads the demons seemed to think they were. Nothing would surprise me at this point.

"Where are we?" I asked, glancing behind the woman to peer into the trees—normal trees, not the striped ones with the crescent leaves. We were still in the Lunaley, she'd basically just said so, but it was clearly not the place we'd been knocked out.

"The western side of the Ley, near the fae border. Magic is stronger over here. It helps me with my spells and rituals."

Spells. Rituals. A powerful sorcerer... or *sorceress*?

My gaze darted back to her face, studying her suspiciously. "You don't happen to know the Storm King, do you?"

Her wrinkled lips puckered into a frown. "Everyone has heard of the Storm King."

"But have you met him?"

"Not personally. Why?"

I ignored her question and asked another of my own. "So, you've never made a spell or a potion for him?"

"No. *Why?*"

I shook my head. "Just curious."

"*Just curious?* You think she's telling the truth?" Bob asked his fellow demons.

Kel said nothing, which seemed fairly standard for him, while Larry stared me down as he contemplated Bob's question.

"I don't know," Larry hedged. "She looks pretty serious."

"Yeah, but no one's ever *just curious*," Bob pointed out.

I rolled my eyes and forced my focus back to the sorceress or voodoo doctor or... whatever. "What's your name?" I asked, hoping I could quit referring to her by vague occupational monikers.

"Shellaka."

"Ooh, can we call you Shelly?" Larry asked.

"Got any human meat, Shelly?" Sue eyed her shelves of strange jarred objects as if they were fucking grocery items or something. "Like this eyeball, perhaps?"

She grunted. "That's an eye of a fae."

Ugh, gross.

Sue's lip curled in disgust. "Fae are too sweet for my taste."

"Mine too," Shelly agreed with a small smile.

I had to hope the old biddy was talking about their *personalities* being too sweet rather than their *persons*. Otherwise, what kind of fucking world did I actually live in?

"Anyway," I stressed, trying to get the conversation onto a different track. "Can you take me to see the guys? I need to know they're all right."

She grunted and nodded. "This way."

I rolled off my pillows and tried to stand, but dizziness swarmed my head along with nausea. I waited for just a few moments as the vertigo settled, then staggered onto my feet and followed Shelly and the demons out the little hut door.

There were multiple shacks outside, including a bigger one on the left, which I assumed was Shelly's, and four littler ones, about the size of mine, curving around to the right. The slapdash way the five little huts had been constructed made me think they were very recent additions—as in "built just for us" recent.

I approached the first hut and found Ash lying inside. A meaty red slash trailed across his chest, looking blistered and possibly even infected. Sweat clung to his hairline, and his brows were furrowed tight, as if he was having a nightmare.

This whole thing felt like a nightmare.

I left the first hut and checked the second, which held Cal but only barely. His mountainous frame took up the entire diameter of the cylindrical hovel. His head and toes were skimming the walls, and his broad shoulders looked even wider packed between the walls. He had animal furs draped over top of him and pillows piled underneath. He, too, was sleeping, and he shook like he was freezing, despite his rosy cheeks.

Why the fuck were we not healing properly?

After checking on Dan, Rob, and Ben, I exited the final hut and found Shelly and the demons sitting on logs gathered around a fire. It was not cold in the Lunaley, so I assumed the fire was mostly for cooking rather than warmth. Sure enough, she flung a big black pot that looked strangely like a witch's cauldron over the flames and plopped back down.

A screech tore through the air, alerting me to the presence of a chimera.

"Run!" I shouted, darting toward my hut as the lion-eagle-dragon lit on the ground with the grace of a butterfly. "Hide!"

My hut didn't have more than an animal skin sheet for a door, but I hid behind it anyway, peeking through the crack to where Shelly laughed near the fire. *Laughed?* What the hell was wrong with her?

The demons had crowded in with me, lining up behind me as if I would somehow protect them. As if *anyone* could.

"Run, Shelly!" Hugh cried, waving his black-clawed hand wildly behind the curtain. She couldn't see him, but he didn't seem to care.

The chimera strolled closer to Shelly, and she held out her hand. There was nothing in it, no food or water for the beast, but still it came nearer. A strange cooing sound fluttered out of his mouth, almost like the call of a dove or an owl, and it pushed its face into her palm, allowing her to stroke its head.

What. The. Fuck?

The same breed of beast that had damn near killed me and my immortal lovers was also calm and caring enough to be *petted?* It didn't add up.

"I found your egg," Shelly muttered, shooting me a stern glance. "I thought about giving it back to the mother you stole it from."

The mother had lived? Unbelievable....

"Please don't," I begged, pulling back the curtain a bit more so I could speak to her easier. "We almost killed ourselves trying to get that egg. The Storm King will surely finish the job if we fail to bring it to him."

Her dark gaze narrowed. "You are on an errand for the king?"

I glanced at the ground, no longer wanting to meet her gaze. "Not of my own free will."

"Everyone has a choice."

"Not where the king is concerned."

She paused, her palm resting gently on the chimera's broad snout. "There is *always* a choice."

"You wouldn't understand," I scoffed. Not only that, but I wasn't really at liberty to discuss the issue with her. I decided to change the subject. "How are you able to get so close to the creature without it trying to kill you?"

She tittered, the lightest sounding thing she'd uttered since I woke. "They're quite gentle when they're not defending their nests and their young."

I shared a skeptical look with the demons and slowly exited the hut.

The chimera turned to me, growling low. I put a hand onto my golden ax—just in case I needed it for a hurried defense. It kind of surprised me that it was still on my waist at all; I thought for sure I'd have lost it in the woods when I blacked out.

Shelly put her hand up, and I froze. "Stay. You have magic in your veins."

"So do you," I argued. At least, I was pretty sure she did.

But she shook her head. "I can create small amounts of

magic through potions and spells, but I am not inherently magical. The energy does not flow through my veins as it does yours."

Ash had said earlier that he was pretty sure chimeras didn't like magic, that his chimera form didn't want anything to do with us. In fact, he had struggled to keep himself from slashing us with his talons. But why?

I released my ax, allowing it to hang loosely at my side once more. "Why do chimeras hate magic and magical beings? And if they hate it so much, why the hell do they live in one of the most magical forests to ever exist?"

"Chimeras do not *hate*," she specified, standing up and tossing a few orange-and-white-striped roots into the cauldron. "They simply act on instinct. Magic and magic users are their natural enemies. Their claws, fangs, and tail spines emit an anti-magic poison when their foe's skin is breached. For a normal person, the poison is totally harmless; the wound is just like any other cut or scrape. But for a magical being, it can be lethal until the poison runs its course."

"How do you know this?" I asked, daring to hedge a bit closer.

The chimera watched me with darkened eyes, but the growl was absent for the moment.

"I love the chimeras," she said plainly, going back to petting the beast's head. "I love watching and studying them. I've seen the extent of their uses and their harms. I understand their behaviors and instincts. It took years, though."

"So, why do they choose to live in the Lunaley?" I asked, reiterating my question from before.

"Because they refuse to nest in any tree other than the Luna Tree."

"The ones with the dark blue crescents?"

She nodded. "That's the one."

"So, the Eristani people need the *trees*, not the *magic*," Ben muttered, emerging from his hut in a stumble.

"Ben!" I said his name in a desperate whisper as I rushed to him, wrapping him carefully but completely in my arms.

He hugged me back, tighter than I was expecting, and it gave me hope. The stronger he was, the stronger the likelihood was that we would *all* survive this nightmare.

At the sight of *two* magical beings around the fire, the chimera growled and took flight, disappearing beyond the canopy.

Good riddance.

"Correct," Shelly said, answering Ben's musings. "The leaves and vines are used to make the nests. The Luna Fruit are used to feed the hatchlings when they emerge. The stone-like bark is used to sharpen their fangs, talons, and spines. They need these things, and so they risk living here, despite the fact that the forest is magical."

Ben rubbed his face and pinched the bridge of his nose, as if trying to stay alert. "If the trees can survive without magic, then that's all we need—some saplings to bring back to Eristan. If we plant them in the oasis near Erishwar, then the chimeras should naturally repopulate."

"They can," Shelly said, sounding sure of herself and her knowledge. "This world survived many years without magic before the gods came and went, and it will continue to survive regardless. The trees will be fine."

"Then we know what we need to do," Ben said to me.

"Yeah," Dan replied, staggering from his hut and plopping down on a log, "dig up some stupid trees."

"Dan!" I sped over and sat down on the log beside him, snuggling into his chest. "Thank the gods you're alive."

"Thank *yourself* we're alive," he chuckled gruffly. "The gods don't give a fuck."

"How *are* we alive?" Ben muttered to no one in particular.

He might've just been talking to himself. "It doesn't make sense, not even with the blood bond taken into consideration."

"Blood bond?" Shelly asked. "No wonder the chimeras dislike you so much. That's strong magic."

Dan turned and glared at her. "Who are you again?"

"Shellaka. The woman who saved your lives."

"But you can call her Shelly," Larry said, smiling, completely oblivious to the suddenly sour atmosphere.

"What did you mean about the blood bond?" I asked Ben. "You *do* remember how I included sharing in each other's strength and power as a last-minute addition?"

He nodded. "I do, and that's exactly what I mean. We were all weak and dying. Even if we relied on one another in a magical way, it *shouldn't* have been enough. So how did we live?"

"Maybe we're more powerful than we thought?" Dan suggested.

Ben shook his head and paced around the fire. "Maybe..."

The Sea Prince put his arm around my shoulders and kissed the top of my head. "Speaking of the blood bond, have you been keeping things fair? That was the number one rule we all agreed on, if you recall."

I laughed. "Seriously? You just woke up from a near-death experience, and the first thing you think about is sex?"

He grinned cheekily. "I'm *always* thinking about sex."

"Me too," Larry agreed. "You ever possessed someone then fucked their significant other? It's some intense shit."

My mouth fell open, and I was momentarily stunned into silence.

"No, Larry," Dan said slowly. "We've never once possessed someone, let alone used their incapacitated body to fuck with."

Bob shrugged, ignoring the hint of repulsion in Dan's tone. "It's too much work if you ask me."

"*Breathing* is too much work for you," Hugh retorted.

Bob put up both hands in agreement. "Exactly! That's why I don't do it."

"*No,*" Larry argued, "that's why you always get caught. Human bodies need to breathe in order to appear normal. Exorcisms are painful, you jackass. Why risk it?"

I took a deep, calming breath, inhaling the intoxicating scent of Dan's spicy skin. Then I exhaled slowly, tuning out the demons chattering, and got back on topic.

"Cal's ahead," I admitted to Dan. "I owe everyone else some private time. Especially you and Ben."

His smile stretched wider. "Good. You, me, and Ben can hang out here while Rob, Cal, and Ash go and collect the trees."

"No, no," Ben protested. "Sorry, Sailor, but I think I need to be with the tree-extracting group. I need to make sure it's done properly so that the saplings don't die during the journey home. We can't take any chances."

Dan grinned, looking rather smug. "All right, then. I'm down for some one-on-one Sexy Lexi time. Maybe we can reenact the last time we were alone together..."

I blushed, my lady bits tingling at the remembrance of that night on the lake, but no one else seemed to pay any mind to his naughty suggestion.

"Fine," I agreed. "We can stay here and catch up on some time together. We already know that time kind of ceases to exist here. I suppose there's not really a reason to hurry."

Ben was still pacing around the fire as if he were deep in thought. "It still feels urgent, though, doesn't it? The time thing is difficult to wrap your head around, even for me, and I've studied relativity and a bit of quantum physics."

"Yeah, it does," I said, agreeing with his first statement,

even though I had no fucking clue what he meant by the second. "But at the same time, so much has happened to me that was supposed to be impossible, that this kind of just feels like any other thing in my life."

"Totally understandable," Dan said, kissing my head once more.

Shelly put a hand on her rounded hip. "Are you even going to ask if you're welcome to stay? Or if I'd be willing to share my food and water with all of you?"

Kel chuckled at her ridiculous question, which started Larry and Sue laughing, and finally Bob. Hugh didn't laugh, but his smile was huge.

"Good one, Shelly," Hugh said. "I mean, of course they're welcome here. We wouldn't have gone through the trouble of building the huts if they weren't."

She raised a brow at the demon. "It still couldn't hurt them to use manners. I thought they weren't as pompous as angels?"

Bob crinkled his nose and scratched his head. "She has a point."

Hugh huffed and glared at Ben. "Prove to her you're not an arrogant asshat."

Ben paused his pacing and blinked, glancing between Hugh and Shelly. "Um, may we stay for a few more days?"

"See?" Hugh said, crossing his arms haughtily. "Told you they were fine."

Shelly rolled her eyes and shuffled over to stir the soup. "I suppose you can stay then."

Something shifted in one of the huts, and soon the curtain to Ash's space slid open. "Do I smell something cooking?" he asked, his voice groggy from sleep and exhaustion.

Dan removed his arm from my shoulder, allowing me to stand up and hurry over to his brother.

"Are you okay?" I asked, carefully tracing the scarred lines across his neck and chest. "How are you feeling?"

I wondered if our wounds would ever heal *completely*.

"I'm okay," he rasped, tucking me into his side. "Just tired as fuck and sore all over."

"The soup will help," Shelly added somberly. "There are special ingredients in it."

Hopefully not fae eyes and newt balls.

"Soup?" Cal asked, emerging from his hut. "Thank the gods. I'm starving." He glanced around the fire. "Where's Rob?"

"Right here," the final brother answered, pulling back the animal skin sheet and bracing himself on the doorway of the tiny hut for balance. I was surprised the whole thing didn't topple right over. "How long have we been out?"

"Weeks," Shelly reiterated for those who'd shown up late. "But do not panic. Time acts differently in the Ley."

"Who are you?" Rob asked, rubbing his sleepy gray eyes.

Bob sighed loudly. "Her name is Shelly. *Shelly.* One more time for the people in the back—Shelly. Now let's stop asking all the damn time."

Rob glared daggers at the demon, and I immediately knew which one *I'd* rather not piss off.

"You might've been enjoying your little lawless vacation in the Ley," Rob threatened in a dangerously low voice, "but I won't remind you again that you are currently speaking to *your prince*. You're one smart-ass comment away from getting that attitude knocked right out of your charcoaled head. Understood?"

"Yes, Your Highness," Bob apologized quickly. "I definitely wasn't talking to you, though. I was, uh, talking to the others because... *Kel*, here, forgot the witch's name *again* even though she told us a thousand times. Right, Kel? Your memory is about as bad as my sluggishness."

"You mean *laziness*," Larry muttered, and I totally agreed.

Kel's eyes went wide before he glared at Bob. "Nuh-uh."

"Uh-huh," Bob argued, shooting him a glare that screamed "Shut the fuck up."

He didn't have to tell Kel twice. The poor demon was already quiet as it was. Now he appeared to be almost caving in on himself.

"It's *Shellaka*," Shelly clarified for the group as she grabbed a pile of wooden bowls and dipped them each into the pot.

"Well, thank you for your help and hospitality, Shellaka," Cal said, resuming his usual political pleasantness as he sat down on a log. "We are in your debt."

Finally, she smiled, apparently satisfied with our gratitude, or at least satisfied with *Cal*. I walked over as casually as I could and sat down beside him near the fire—*just in case* the voodoo doctor got any funny ideas about my Sky Prince.

As we ate, talked, and slowly regathered our strength, I finally started to feel optimistic again. We might've been battered by this impossible mission to the desert, but we hadn't yet been beaten.

We had the egg, the solution to the harpies' endangered species problem, and soon we'd have the Treaty O' Ley back in place.

All we had to do was collect a few saplings, and we could be on our way. Easy-peasy.

Right. As if it'd ever be that easy.

CHAPTER 19

A few days later, we were totally healed. *Thank the gods.* The magic might not have worked instantaneously as usual, but at least it worked at all.

That evening, I found myself standing in front of a small pond not far from Shelly's shack. Its magical blue waters sparkled, its surface miraculously free of the near-constant mist floating along the Lunaley's forest floor.

Ben, Ash, and Cal had already left to collect the Luna Tree saplings, and as promised, I was on a date with Dan. Rob had insisted on tagging along too, and since neither Dan nor I were known for turning down a good time, we graciously obliged. The prior had chosen the location—*obviously*, considering it was near a body of water. But the latter had chosen the activity—drinking games.

In order to gain a little privacy from Shelly, who'd graciously sold us some of her homemade Luna fruit wine in exchange for some jewels, and from the demons, who were more than a little irritated that they wouldn't be able to drink with us, we'd wandered off just far enough to not get lost.

"Perfect," Dan declared with a contented sigh, looking about the place.

There was flat ground nearby that would make for an excellent picnic lunch, fallen logs to sit on, and the water was just deep enough to reach my chin with my feet on the ground, so I could go out by myself without fear of drowning. I found that out from Dan, who apparently knew the pool's depth just by looking at it.

"Agreed," Rob replied to his brother, as he carefully deposited our barrel of wine. "It's pretty damn perfect."

Yes. *Barrel.* As in, a giant-ass barrel. I didn't know whose alcoholism I was more impressed with: Rob's or Shelly's.

Dan spread out a soft fur blanket he'd borrowed from the shack, and we all three sat down, making ourselves comfortable.

"So, what's the first game we're going to play?" Dan asked as he leaned back and threaded his hands behind his head.

Rob grinned, his luscious lips tugging into a delicious pout. "I'm thinking... truth or shots."

"How do you play?" I asked. Considering I'd never been invited to parties back when I was a peasant, and only rarely had I attended any as a princess, I was pretty much a drinking-game novice.

"It's where I ask you a true or false question, and if you choose not to answer, you have to take a shot instead."

Dan's lips tugged into a devious smile. "So basically, it's tell the truth sober, or get shitfaced and spill the truth later anyway."

Rob chuckled. "Basically."

"What happens if you do answer?" I asked.

"Then the person who asked the question has to drink."

I wiggled my brows at them. "This sounds like fun."

"Oh, it will be," Rob decided. "You ready?"

Dan and I nodded, and he filled up three small glasses with an inch or so of wine.

"I'll go first," the Spirit Prince said. "Alexis, true or false: you were a virgin before Cal."

"False," I said, grinning as Rob grumbled and downed his shot of wine.

"It was Asher, wasn't it?" he asked.

I rolled my eyes and nodded. "He wasn't the *only* one before Cal, though."

Dan groaned, and his head fell back. "Why do I have the sudden urge to find these guys and beat the fucking shit out of them?"

"It's okay, I do too," Rob agreed. He refilled his glass, then nodded to his brother. "All right, Dan, true or false: your first time was in the water?"

The Sea Prince raised his glass. "False, actually, though I do prefer it in the water. Drink up, bro."

I giggled as Rob drank again.

"My turn," Dan said, before I could beat him to it. "Alexis, you were masturbating that day in the tub when we were waiting to take you to magic training. True or false?"

A heated blush burned my cheeks, but I nodded anyway. "True."

"I knew it!" Dan shouted right before he downed his shot. He refilled it and turned to Rob. "Your first time was with a vampire. True or false?"

"True," Rob admitted, drinking another shot. "It was almost with a ghost on the astral plane, but we got caught before it could get any further."

"How do you have sex with a *ghost?*" Dan asked.

"How do you have sex on the *astral plane?*" I added, suddenly enormously curious.

Rob shrugged. "I guess you'll have to ask me somehow. It's your turn."

I grinned. "True or false, Rob, sex on the astral plane is all in your head."

"False," he said with a grin. "The astral plane is a real place that almost no one can get to. But anything that happens there generates actual bodily reactions."

"Fascinating," I muttered, wishing I could somehow see the plane with my own eyes. I quickly took my shot, refilled it, then turned to Dan. "True or false, you enjoy watching me get with the other guys."

He raised his brows suggestively. "True. It's hot as hell."

Rob raised his glass and drank right along with me. "I agree."

I sputtered a bit as I laughed while trying to swallow my wine. "It wasn't your turn!"

"Oh, I don't give a fuck." Rob laughed. "Let's play a different game. Let's play... never have I ever. I'll start. Never have I ever had a dick in me."

Dan's head dropped to the blanket, and he covered his face as he laughed.

I glanced between them and smiled curiously. "So, what happens now?"

"Anyone who *has* ever done the deed in question, has to take a shot."

I pursed my lips. "And I'm the only one who's had a dick in me."

"Yep," Dan said, sitting back up and folding his hands in his lap. He looked way too pleased at the direction this game was headed.

"Fine," I said, and swallowed my wine. "Never have I ever eaten pussy."

They both chuckled and clinked glasses before downing them at the same time.

"All right, my turn," Dan said, pursing his lips as he thought. "Never have I ever... drawn blood during sex."

193

"Ooh," I groaned. "Low blow."

This time Rob and I clinked our glasses and drank together.

"All right," Rob said, pinching his plump bottom lip as he thought. "Never have I ever lost a fight."

"Oh, bullshit," Dan shouted, "you just got your ass handed to you by a chimera."

Rob rolled his eyes and specified, "With a *person*."

Dan glared at his brother but drank a shot. "You know it was only that one time that I lost, right?"

Rob chuckled. "Sure do, but I love rubbing it in."

"Who did you lose to?" I asked, crossing my ankles out in front of me as the alcohol slowly swam through my bloodstream.

Dan licked his lips. "A guy named Jonas. Rob and I met him when we were kids sneaking out into the local villages and pubs at night. I'd never been in a fight before, and he was like a solid foot taller *and* wider than me."

Rob held up both hands and shrugged. "I mean, *I* didn't lose my first fight..."

Dan shook his head and chuckled. "Whatever, man."

"I want to play another game," I decided, curling my legs underneath me.

"And what's that?" Dan asked.

I tapped my chin in thought. "I don't know. Surprise me."

"All right," Rob said, propping himself on an elbow as he lay on his side. "How about we play mirror mirror?"

My smile pulled extra wide, and I subconsciously leaned a little further into the middle of our triangle. "And how do we play that?"

Rob leaned closer too. "It's where I do something to you, then you mirror that action on Dan. Then he does something to you, and you have to mirror it on me."

My mood instantly turned smoldering as heat rushed to

my lady bits. Just the thought of the naughty game turned me on.

"Okay," I agreed breathlessly.

Rob ran his fingers up my arm and then back down to my fingertips. So, I turned to Dan and slowly caressed his arm up and down. Dan bit his lip in reaction to my touch, and even more heat flooded through me. He ran his fingers through my hair and tugged slightly. So, I turned to Rob and raked my fingers through his hair, pulling until he let out a little moan.

Fuck, this is my new favorite game.

Rob ran his hands up my thighs and squeezed, stopping just shy of any erogenous zones. I turned to Dan and ran my hands up his thighs, careful not to touch his growing erection.

He took a long, hard drink of his wine and shook his head. Then he leaned in and dragged his tongue up my neck, nice and slow, tantalizing the fuck out of me with every hot, wet inch he left behind. I shivered as heat raced through my body. Then I turned to Rob, tasting his salty skin from his collarbone up to his ear.

Rob chugged a whole glass of wine before standing, kicking off his shoes, then bending down to take mine off.

I figured the wine chugging was optional, so I skipped that part. I turned to Dan, crouched down, and removed his shoes. When I stood back up, he took a deep, calming breath and slid off his pants. Then he knelt in front of me, staring deep into my eyes, and dragged my panties down my legs.

Poseidon almighty. They were probably damp as fuck.

I swallowed hard and turned to Rob, my insides pooling into molten heat when I caught the darkened look in his eyes. I was pretty sure he wanted to ravage me right then and there, and the restraint he was clinging to was thin as a thread. I dropped to my knees and unbuttoned his pants, sliding them over his raging hard-on, down his strong legs, and over his feet as he stepped out of them.

We were running out of layers.

The realization made my anticipation soar to new heights.

Rob licked his plush lips, drawing my gaze as he reached behind his head and yanked his shirt off in one swift motion. My mouth watered. That move was sexy as fuck, and the muscles and tattoos it revealed were hotter yet. He strode closer, bunching his hands in the material of my emerald dress and pulling it slowly up over my head. By the time he was done, I was left wearing nothing but my bra.

I turned to Dan, panting a bit as the heat of Rob's touch still coursed through my veins. I ran my hands up under the material of his shirt, feeling his abs tighten as I lifted it higher and higher until it was off his head and on the ground.

One layer left. Dear gods, I was fucking ready.

He bent down and removed his boxers, stroking his swollen cock like he just couldn't help himself. Then his hands were on me, unhooking my bra with the ease of an experienced playboy and sliding the flimsy material of my straps down my arms, leaving me completely bare. His eyes grazed my body as hot as any touch, making my nipples harden.

I slowly turned around, watching heatedly as Rob eye-fucked me, too. My breathing grew heavier as I hooked my thumbs in his boxers and pushed, gliding them down his legs until my face was even with his rock-hard dick. I contemplated licking him, taking his head in my mouth and sucking away the salty fluid that dripped from the tip... but before I could open my mouth, he kicked his boxers away and lifted me up.

The next thing I knew, Dan was behind me, pressing me between their heated bodies. "Wanna go for a swim?"

I nodded, too breathless to speak.

Rob took my hand, and I took Dan's, not quite sure if we were still playing the game or not. He led us into the pond, which, like the river nearby, glowed a magical blue. It was warm to the touch, caressing my skin like silk as I waded in up to my chin. The pool's surface touched just below the guys' pecs, and as they both strode closer to me in the water, the image was hot as hades.

Immediately, Dan's lips met my collarbone, trailing gentle kisses up and down my neck while his tantalizing hands grazed lightly along my sides. Rob moved in behind me, pulling my hair until my head fell back onto his chest, and with his other hand, he moved across the front of my hip and settled his fingers between my legs.

Fucking gods, this was perfect.

"Spread your legs wider," Rob whispered into my ear.

I did, and as he slipped into my pussy from behind, Dan dipped underwater. Between Rob's cock stroking in and out of me and Dan's tongue swirling all around my clit, I knew I wouldn't last another minute. Then Rob's hands were cupping my breasts and squeezing my nipples almost painfully hard, and the pressure was more delicious than I could have predicted.

"Oh fuck," I moaned before coming hard, my body spasming despite the fact I was still wedged tightly between them.

Dan resurfaced after the waves of my orgasm ebbed, and he took my mouth in his. As he kissed the life out of me, Rob continued to move in and out from behind, slowly building the pressure all over again.

"Turn around," Rob growled, slipping out of me and waiting until I was facing him before thrusting back in.

Dan's hands found my thighs and ass, caressing me sensually as Rob pounded mercilessly, sending choppy waves scattering all around us. As usual, the pain he gave was quickly overridden by pleasure, and soon I was approaching another orgasm.

"Jewels," he said, calling me back to the moment, and I knew what he was silently asking.

He wanted pain.

I leaned forward and bit the meaty flesh between his shoulder and neck, dragging my nails down his back as I did.

He moaned loudly, driving me wild, and I bit him again, scratching my nails back up his spine—probably hard enough to draw blood. *Again.* "Fucking hades, I'm gonna come."

That made two of us. He rooted deep inside of me, groaning as his orgasm consumed him completely.

Before the pulsing of my second orgasm was even finished, I was back in Dan's arms. "What do you want, my queen? I'll give you whatever your heart desires."

I smirked and lowered my forehead to his. *"My queen? Where did this come from?"*

He bit his bottom lip as he stared at my mouth. "It came from my desire to worship your body like a slave to a queen. It sort of just felt right on my tongue when I said it. Are you cool with it?"

"Abso-fucking-lutely." I pulled him to me and kissed him as hard as I could.

When we came up for air, he smirked and looked down at me. "Tell me what you want."

"I want you to fuck the hell out of me until you come *hard.*"

"You got it, sexy girl."

And he did exactly that, thrusting deep and seductively, over and over, until the pressure of another amazing orgasm built. Rob came up behind me, squeezing my breasts and biting the side of my neck, pushing me right over the edge. Dan and I moaned as we both came apart together.

After, the three of us floated leisurely for a few minutes as we caught our breath.

By the time we left the pool, lying naked out to dry on the fur blanket, we were completely spent and blissfully content. We laughed and teased each other, getting back to our silly drinking games, when all of a sudden...

Pain assaulted me. My eyes flew open wide, and I curled in on myself, crying instantly as I tried to breathe through the agony. Dan and Rob doubled over too, growling and gritting their teeth, trying their damnedest to endure the discomfort without shouting.

"What the fuck is going on?" I ground out, trying to clutch my heart through my ribs.

But the pain kept on coming.

CHAPTER 20

"*T*he blood bond," Rob growled, jumping into action. He dragged his boxers and pants up his legs in one swift motion. "It has to be."

"Are they in trouble?" Dan asked, roughly yanking his shirt over his head.

I shook my head in disbelief as another wave of pain sailed through my chest. "Voodoo Shelly said the chimeras would leave us alone as long as we weren't stealing their eggs."

"Well then, *Voodoo Shelly* either lied, or she was wrong," Rob growled, wrenching his shirt on as he pushed through the trees, on a mission to somehow get to the guys.

"What if they went after another egg?" Dan asked, tossing me my dress before hopping into his pants. I tugged the stretchy material over my head, and we both caught up with Rob as quickly as possible.

The Spirit Prince shook his head, ducking under a wayward branch. "Why would they? We already have an egg."

"Unless the demons ate ours," I muttered.

Rob shot me a furious look over his shoulder. "I'll fucking kill them if they did."

"What if the guys didn't go after another egg," Dan reasoned aloud as we strode over fallen logs and clumps of brush, "but the chimeras remembered them from all those weeks ago? Do you think they'd attack us out of spite?"

My eyes went wide. I didn't trust those feathery fuckers as far as I could throw one, and that sounded like exactly the sort of thing they'd do too.

Extreme pain and difficult terrain be damned, I started running. I wasn't even sure if I was headed in the right direction; I just hoped the ache of the blood bond would somehow pull us the way we needed to go.

We ran through the woods for a while before I was out of breath and panting. The scenery all looked the same, and yet different enough that I couldn't quite tell where the hell I was.

Rain pattered onto the leaves above us, slowly filtering down to soak the underlying plants, but it wasn't heavy enough to do more than dampen our clothes. The pain in my chest had lessened, and I wasn't sure whether to be relieved or terrified as fuck. That might've meant they were now okay; it also might've meant they were dead. It was impossible to tell.

Ahead, the faint glow of an illuminated archway caught my gaze, and I faltered to a stop. Rob stopped just short of my back, but Dan crashed into Rob, and like dominos, we all went down. They quickly rolled off me and helped me up, apologizing profusely and asking me what the hell had made me stop so abruptly.

All I did was point.

Their eyes went wide, and they too remained silent.

We moved closer, slowly examining the archway with suspicious gazes. So far, the Lunaley seemed to hold nothing more than vicious creatures, an Eristani soldier camp, and a lying voodoo lady who kept demons for company. Whatever this archway belonged to, I had a feeling it wasn't good.

There was music thumping from somewhere, even though no one and nothing else was around. The beat and the instruments were like nothing I'd ever heard before, and it rumbled the ground at my feet.

I shared a curious glance with Dan and Rob and crept forward quietly. The arch was nothing more than giant rectangular stone slabs stacked on top of one another and plastered together with some sort of hardened dust—much like the smooth, ground up cobblestone streets that the richer towns had.

The closer we got to it, the more I realized this was much more than a simple arch. From the side, it appeared to be a lonely archway leading to nothing, the Lunaley stretched out forever in every direction all around it. But once you moved to the front, getting a head-on view, there was suddenly a very different picture.

At the proper angle, I could see lights flashing in the mostly dark space beyond, and this seemed to be where the music was coming from. Occasionally, I could hear the voices of people talking or laughing, but the words were indiscernible. A slight hint of alcohol rode the breeze, and I had the sudden image of a strange party going on in there.

"What the fuck?" Rob muttered. He stepped closer, touching the stone, making sure the archway was real and not just a figment of our imaginations.

We circled it. There was nothing on the back side. No flashing lights, just an empty archway leading to more forest. Then we came back around to the front again, and the room beyond the Ley reappeared.

"How is this possible?" I asked them breathlessly.

I mean, I was pretty fucking sure this was, like, another

dimension or something. Either way there was definitely magic involved. How else could a random door appear in the forest and lead to nowhere and yet somewhere all at once?

Suddenly, a man walked past the archway, pointing up ahead as if he were talking to someone. "Hold that thought, I'll be right back."

We dove into the bushes as he backed up, stopping in front of the archway and gazing out into... What? Was he looking out into the Ley? It sure as fuck looked like it. His eyes narrowed and he sniffed, as if he'd somehow caught a whiff of us on the breeze.

What. The. Fuck?

"Dion? Did you leave the door open again?"

A voice replied, but it was muffled beneath the sound of the music and the chatter of the party.

The man in the archway shook his head and stepped closer to us. I gasped and ducked even further beneath the bushes for cover. He poked his head *through the archway*, over into our side of the magical fucking barrier, and suddenly I couldn't breathe. He looked left, then right, pausing for just a moment before grabbing onto an invisible doorknob.

"Next time, remember to shut the fucking door."

And he did just that.

In the blink of an eye, the archway turned into nothing more than empty stone with no noise, lights, or people beyond the frame. The Ley became visible once more between the stones, and the mist that crawled so heavily at the forest floor began to dissipate.

"What the fuck was that?" Dan whisper-shouted, jabbing a finger at the arch.

"Was that shit even real?" I asked, unable to believe what I'd seen. "You guys saw it too, right? A room, a person, music, lights..."

Rob nodded, his expression hard like he was ready for a fight should the door reopen.

The mist retreated even further, vanishing from the ground and evaporating into thin air. Suddenly the atmosphere seemed... normal, like any other forest. It was a strange shift of the ambiance, almost as if something had changed on an energetic level, something too small for me to see, but strong enough to feel.

"You don't think the guys are in there, do you?" Dan asked, glaring at the arch.

"They fucking better not be," Rob decided in a growl, "because we just lost our shot at getting them out."

"Or did we?" I asked, approaching the arch hesitantly, as if it were a living creature capable of striking. I felt around, trying to grasp a handle or a knob, or possibly even contact the physical wood of the door even though I couldn't see it, but my hand went right through. In fact, I took a few steps forward... and I went right through as if there was never anything on the other side.

"Surely they wouldn't have gone in. Ben's too smart for that, right?" Dan asked.

"Right," Rob and I agreed. I just had to hope Cal and Ash were smart enough to listen to him.

"Maybe they didn't even come this way," I said, dragging my nails through my hair nervously. "We should keep looking."

Rob shot a final glance at the darkened archway and shook his head. "Yeah, let's just... keep looking."

We wandered around for another hour or so, no freaking clue where we were or where we were going. It was impossible to know where the guys might've been and equally as impossible to find our way back to Shelly's camp. A lump formed in my throat and slowly sank to the pit of my stomach. We were lost. Lost in the Ley. People could get misplaced forever in these woods, and no one would even realize they were gone. Who would ever find us? And how would we ever find them?

A soft snapping sound caught my ear in the distance, like an animal stepping on a twig. More snaps followed, suggesting the creature was running rather than walking. Then more crackles and pops as if there was *more than one* creature. Finally, Cal, Ben, and Ash came into view as they dashed toward us through the woods.

"What's going on?" Cal shouted. "Are you hurt?"

The three of us darted over to meet them in the middle, taking turns wrapping each other in tight hugs. "No, we're not hurt. Are you?"

They shook their heads, confused.

Cal glanced at Ben and Ash before turning back to us. "The blood bond... it pulled on us. It was as if you were in physical pain. We were terrified."

I nodded. "It happened to us too. We thought maybe you'd been attacked by the chimeras again."

Cal shook his head and held up a sapling in his hand. It was only about three feet tall and maybe an inch wide. The crescent-shaped leaves dotting the top of the branches were tiny and more of a pale blue than a midnight. Then Ben and Ash did the same, holding up their own saplings.

"We had no trouble at all," Cal said, tucking his lips in as he shook his head. "I don't understand. What the hell does this mean?"

Dan shook his head and crossed his arms. "I vote we just get these trees to Eristan and get the hell back to Blackwood as fast as possible. We'll deal with figuring this blood bond shit out later."

"Agreed," Rob chimed in.

Cal glanced around and pointed in the direction they'd

come. "Shelly's hut is this way. Let's grab the demons and get out of here."

My brows furrowed. "How do you know the hut is that way?"

It used to be damn near impossible to tell.

Cal looked around, nodding; then his eyes met mine once more. "I don't know. I can just tell. It's like my sense of direction has come back and things suddenly seem clearer. Speaking of *clear*, where is the strange mist?"

We filled them in on the weird archway we'd found and the even weirder events that happened beyond the frame, explaining that once the invisible door had been shut, the mist had disappeared.

"The mist was magic," Ben decided at once. "Whatever that doorway had led to, it left our world open to receiving magic in return. Now that the door is shut, the magic is gone."

My blood went cold. "What do you mean *the magic is gone?*"

Ben quickly reached for a twig and turned it into a striped fruit that fit in the palm of his hand, exhaling in relief. "Not *all* magic is gone, but... the magic that influenced this *place*? The entire Lunaley? It's gone."

Oh fuck. We needed the magic in order to save the fae. If the magic was gone, then...

"Son of a bitch," Cal ground out, yanking at his golden hair in frustration. "We need to get that door back open."

I shook my head, as if in a daze. "We can't. I tried. It's like it was never even there."

Suddenly, a chimera perched on a branch above our heads, shrieking at the top of its lungs and filling me with dread. Its call alerted another chimera, a bigger one with a shaggy brown mane, which landed on a branch across the way.

Oh shit. Mommy and Daddy are about to get revenge.

I pulled out my ax and prepared to fight, but Cal shook his head quickly.

"Just run!" he shouted, and our whole group scampered through the brush as fast as our legs could go.

My feet caught and tangled in tiny vines and bushes, but I somehow managed to stumble and remain upright. Cal was in the lead, and I was last. Ash and Dan each grabbed one of my arms and pulled me forward, tugging me through the trees far faster than I could have gone on my own. But it still wasn't enough.

The male chimera swooped down up ahead and slashed Cal from behind, knocking him to the ground in a tumbling mess of brambles and blood.

The female had apparently chosen *me*, the weakest one, as her target. I raised my ax and swung at her as she moved in on me, but even though I made contact, it didn't stop her attack. I turned and ran once more, but she caught me in an instant. Pain laced up my spine, white hot and maddening, as her claws tore through me. I crashed to the ground, cringing as thorny bushes cut my face and my mouth filled with dirt, cutting off my screams.

Poison flooded my bloodstream—an extra potent dose. They were seeking revenge, after all, so it made perfect sense. As it coursed through me, my vision wavered and my hearing muffled. My skin went cold, and my nerve endings went numb. All I could taste was the muddy dirt coating my tongue, and all I could smell was the iron tinge of my own blood on the air.

I didn't know how far the others might have gotten. Had they turned back to help Cal and me? Had they stopped to fight? I didn't know how long I lay there before darkness claimed me.

But claim me, it did.

CHAPTER 21

*C*RISSEN

During our carriage ride, *Father* and I chatted about everything under the sun.

What my life had been like growing up, what my mother was up to nowadays, funny childhood stories I recalled, and my future hopes and dreams. I didn't mention it was my greatest aspiration to become a prince of Blackwood—I didn't want him to think I was fishing for a crown; though, truth be told, I really did want the prestige. Being a prince was the most admirable occupation I could hope for, and I knew I would do the title justice if it ever bore my name.

After an hour or so of driving around, he knocked on the window and the carriage rolled to a stop.

I looked through the glass, noticing we were still in the middle of the woods. Perhaps he'd had enough of talking to me and we were turning around? But then the carriage door was pulled open by a servant, and my father gestured for me to step out. Maybe he simply needed to stretch his legs after sitting for so long?

I exited the carriage, trying my best not to frown as I scanned the empty forest around me. There was something decidedly unsettling about this situation. Had I read the signs all wrong? Was he not pleased with having another son after all?

"Are you magical?" he asked me with a cunning smile.

I glanced from left to right, watching as his guards crept closer, surrounding us. "*Magical*, Your Majesty?"

"I told you already, call me Father. That's who I am, right? Your father?"

I hesitated, afraid to somehow say the wrong thing. "Yes, you are my father."

He nodded, then folded his hands behind his back and paced around in front of me. "Here's the thing, Crissen. All my sons have been blessed by the gods, a sure sign of their divine right to rule. If you have magical godlike powers too, then I would have no hesitation in making you a legitimate prince of Blackwood. My other sons are on a mission in the east anyway, and who knows *when* or *if* they'll come back alive? It would be nice to have another successor—just in case."

My mouth was dry as cotton. I was scared to death to ask, but I needed to know the alternative. "And if I *don't* have magical, godlike powers?"

Because there was no doubt in my mind—I fucking *didn't*.

He sighed and stopped pacing. "Then you're just another bastard dog, clawing at my robes and begging for scraps. I don't tolerate strays, Crissen. I put them down."

The king nodded, and pain suddenly exploded in my left side, hot as a molten metal. I dropped to my knees and clutched at my side, trying to stem the ache, surprised to find blood pouring over top of my fingers. It dripped down my nice white pants, the stain growing larger by the second.

I turned left, staring in numb shock at the bloody dagger clutched in one of the guard's gloved hands.

My world shifted, and I lost balance and focus, crashing to the dirt before the king's feet. My lungs burned, and my heart thudded wildly, growing weaker by the second. My skin turned freezing cold all the way down to my bones, and I shivered convulsively. I was losing strength and losing consciousness...

The king sneered and spun on his heel. "Dump him in the woods."

So, this was it. The moment I'd been waiting for my whole life... come and gone in one disgusting moment of disappointment and regret.

I supposed it was my own fault. I should have been more content with what I had: a roof over my head, plenty of food to eat, a metalsmith shop of my own with men who respected me, and a mother who loved me and raised me well.

Now, I had nothing.

My eyes fell shut. But just before I blacked out, something *strange* overwhelmed me. A rush of air gusted into my lungs, and my heart rate picked up, growing in force. The pain in my side diminished to a dull ache, and the icy cold in my veins melted. I pushed onto my feet and fought off the guards with more strength than I had even *before* I'd been stabbed.

It was... a fucking miracle.

The king stopped walking and turned back around, eyeing me with a gaze sharp as steel. "Lift his shirt."

Before I could blink, the same guard who'd stabbed me was ripping my shirt from my back, the expensive blue garment nothing more than a tattered piece of cloth at my feet. I glanced down to where the stab wound had been.

Yes. *Had been*. Past tense. Because to my sheer and utter disbelief, the wound was now completely healed. A shiny white scar and the drying rusty blood on my skin and pants were the only indication that I'd been stabbed at all.

The Storm King smiled wickedly.

"Send for his mother," he said to a guard. "It's time for a new addition to the harem."

Then he turned to me, his evil smile widening further, lending a madness to his eyes. "Welcome to the family, *Prince Crissen*."

CHAPTER 22

$\mathcal{A}$LEXIS

I AWOKE WITH A START ON THE COLD, SANDSTONE FLOOR OF the Eristani palace.

The *palace*?

I glanced around, surprised to find at least twelve sets of eyes looking down on me from every angle.

"She's awake," King Solomon muttered with a bright white smile. "Thank the gods."

The features of four Storms came into focus then, along with a beady-eyed sloth who must've been Ash. I also saw Princess Camilla and five men I didn't recognize who had strangely vacant expressions on their faces.

I sat up, rubbing my temples as they throbbed with the force of a sudden and massive headache. "What... what happened?"

"After the chimeras attacked us," Cal explained, "a few of the king's soldiers found us lying in the woods. They brought us back to their camp, where—" He paused, as if trying to find the proper way to say what he needed to. "—*these five Eristani gentlemen* escorted us back to the palace."

My gaze slid to the five strangers staring into the distance, and suddenly it clicked. Hugh, Larry, Bob, Kel, and Sue had possessed a handful of bodies in order to remain unnoticed.

Fucking hell, it was creepy.

He must not have wanted to mention what they truly were in front of King Solomon. Maybe demons and harpies didn't get along well? Honestly, the harpies only seemed to get along with chimeras, and I knew from personal experience how fucking friendly and pleasant *they* were. I supposed the two were made for each other.

"Well, thank the gods we're all alive," I muttered, accepting Ben and Dan's hands as I struggled to my feet. Then I bent down and scooped up Speedy, snuggling him under my chin for emotional support.

"There's more," Cal said, swallowing hard.

Fear instantly gripped me, cutting off the wind to my lungs, and I swayed a bit where I stood.

"Let's discuss this in a more appropriate location," King Solomon suggested. "Can you walk?"

I wasn't sure, but I nodded anyway.

He led us to the throne room, where he immediately made himself comfortable in his massive sandstone chair. Pillows were brought out for the rest of us to sit on, and I was grateful for the reprieve from standing. I'd only just become conscious; I wasn't ready to trek all over the palace on wobbly legs. Sweat was already beading on my brow from that cute little journey, and my stomach was rolling.

The king then nodded to Cal, permitting him to continue whatever the hell he'd started to say back in the medical wing.

"It took a week for these five to get us back to Eristan," Cal said nervously, "and another two weeks after that for us to wake up."

My eyes went wide as dread and realization hit me like a hammer to the chest. If three weeks had passed—three *real weeks*, outside of the Lunaley—then we were already out of time to finish the Storm King's task.

"Your fevers raged for days," King Solomon added. "I thought you were as good as dead, but you held on. Strong as monsoons, you Storms are." He smiled wide and pointed at Ben. "Which is why I insist upon you marrying my daughter."

Every eye in the room went wide—even Camilla's and the mostly vacant demons'.

Ben pressed a hand into his chest. "*Me?*"

King Solomon laughed as if the Sand Prince had just told a hilarious fucking joke. "Yes, you! Who else would be deserving of my desert flower? No one, that's who. Except maybe your brother." He gestured to Rob, who's gray eyes also went wide.

"Father, I must object—" Camilla started in a nervous voice, but King Solomon cut her off.

"Nonsense. Refusal is out of the question. I shall begin preparations for the wedding tonight!"

"*Tonight?*" I choked out, finally finding my voice. "Your Highness, that's impossible."

"Nothing is impossible for a king," he said, staring down at me from the bridge of his nose, a look of contempt surfacing in his dark eyes.

"Actually, this really is," Camilla argued, trying once more to talk some sense into her father. "They're blood bonded. Physically, mentally, and *magically* unable to commit to anyone other than each other. I..." She glanced down at the floor. "I experienced it firsthand."

"What do you mean?" King Solomon's voice was harsh,

his lips set in a thin line as he turned to stare at his daughter. "Experienced it *how?*"

I could tell she really didn't want to say. "A lightning bolt."

His eyes went wide, filling to the brim with fury. He spun on us. "You attacked *my daughter?* With *magic?* After I specifically commanded you not to? Guards!"

"No, Father, wait!" Camilla shouted, rushing to latch onto his arm. "It wasn't an attack! It was an accident!"

A moment later, at least thirty guards filed into the room, surrounding us at spearpoint. We jumped from our pillows and put our backs together, protecting ourselves on instinct. My heart hammered fearfully in my chest, and I knew I was only a few moments away from catching on fire involuntarily; I could already feel the magic swimming in my bloodstream.

"Stop this *now!*" Camilla shouted, drawing everyone's eye.

She marched to an open-arched window and jabbed a finger toward the oasis resting peacefully across the sands. It was now a strange bluish-purple color rather than jungle green.

"Your deal with the Blackwood royals was to save the chimeras from extinction in exchange for the Treaty O' Ley going back into effect—*not* in exchange for a marriage to *me*. The chimeras are saved; the trees they brought back have already attracted new chimeras to the oasis, and there are at least five nests with eggs, plus more under construction. They kept up their end of the deal, now you keep up yours."

The king stared at her, that hardened, angry look still carved into his face, but he held up an arm to keep his soldiers at bay. "The *deal* was that they save the chimeras, and we let them have an egg."

"Okay, whatever," Camilla argued. "It still had nothing to do with marriage."

"But it also had nothing to do with the Treaty O' Ley. So, why bring it up?"

"Father," she groaned. "We don't need the Lunaley anymore; can't you see that? That's my point. The chimeras are thriving. If you continue to fight over the Ley, then you're senselessly condemning your people to an unending war. To death. To being lost forever in that cursed forest with no hope of ever returning."

The king paced around the room with his fingers on his lips, contemplating her words.

I held my breath. I had no idea what would happen, but I was afraid if I so much as breathed wrong, everything would go straight to hades.

"My daughter is right," the king eventually conceded. "I was... getting ahead of myself."

He moved back to his throne and picked up a still-smoking roll of weed and inhaled deeply. As the smoke puffed from his lips in a cloud, he waved a flippant hand at the guards, and they reluctantly dissipated.

Sighing heavily, he pursed his lips. "I will reinvoke the Treaty O' Ley, as an act of good faith and appreciation. But I have not yet given up on you as a suitor for my daughter. Either of you. What was forged in blood, can be unforged in blood."

He stared knowingly at us all for a couple endless seconds before snapping his fingers. Then a servant entered, carrying a scroll, a quill, and some ink. How the hell they were able to have the document ready and waiting so quickly was absolutely beyond me.

King Solomon quickly scrawled his name at the bottom of the scroll then deposited the quill in the ink jar. After the signature dried, the servant rolled up the document and handed it to Ben.

"Many thanks, Your Majesty," Ben said with a warm smile.

Solomon nodded, then shot Camilla a slightly disapproving glare. "You will make a fine queen one day. It would be my greatest wish that you have a Storm by your side."

She smirked and nodded her agreement, despite everything she'd just said. "We will find a king worthy of the Eristani throne."

King Solomon smiled at her. "We already have. It is simply a matter of time."

I absolutely hated the way he was talking about Ben and Rob, right in front of my face, as if I wouldn't be keeping them forever. As if, one day soon, I'd be forced to relinquish one of them into the hands of the *desert flower*.

I sneered. *Yeah right, buddy, over my dead body.*

He turned back to us, homing in on Rob. "Have you forgotten the other half of our deal?"

Rob shook his head. "No, I have not, Your Majesty. Are you ready?"

The desert king nodded almost nervously.

To be honest, I was a little nervous myself. I'd seen Rob converse with ghosts before—well, I hadn't actually seen *the ghosts*, but I had seen them pass a knife into his hand, which was convincing enough for me—but I never thought I'd come face-to-transparent-face with a spirit.

"Let's sit."

We all did as Rob suggested, lowering ourselves once more onto the satiny pillows and sitting cross-legged on the floor in a circle. I plopped Speedy into my lap and threaded my fingers around his fuzzy stomach.

"Have you ever seen him do this?" I whispered to my old pet.

Speedy bleated and, for once, didn't try to flop from my arms and crack open his skull.

"Yeah, me either," I replied.

Then Rob got straight to business.

"Here's what I'm going to do," he said matter-of-factly. "I'm going to pull the astral plane as close to our plane as possible. I have a few contacts on the other side who can help me locate Queen Nefiti, and once she's found, I'll pull the three of you even closer together and establish a faint connection. That will allow you to hear and see each other."

Rob glanced at the rest of us who were all staring in excitement.

"You guys will probably be able to see her too, but you won't be able to speak to her, and honestly, you talking would just fuck with my concentration. So please don't."

We all nodded our understanding and agreement, already practicing the *no talking* thing.

Rob took a deep breath and cracked his neck. "All right. Let's do this."

He closed his eyes, and as we all sat there in pure and utter silence, cool shadows and dim white lights began moving across the floor. The longer we sat, the darker it got, like the sun had somehow set already, but it was bright too, like stars twinkling vividly in a midnight sky.

It was the most beautiful, most magical thing I'd ever seen in my life.

Semitransparent figures quickly flitted in and out of perspective. One of which came much closer than the rest, pausing to wait for... something. Then the stars blurred, and lights flashed all around us. When it stopped, we were back to watching more translucent figures.

It was like Rob was controlling the whole scene. Like he was a spirit on the astral plane, and we were simply seeing that world through his eyes somehow. It was incredible.

Not long after, a solitary figure came into view in the distance. The scene jumped, skipping closer in the blink of an eye, and a woman stood right in front of us. She was beautiful with dark skin, green eyes, and tight copper curls.

King Solomon stumbled to his feet and reached out toward the vision with wide eyes. "Nefiti? Is that you?"

Camilla stood too, crying almost instantly. "Mama?"

The woman smiled and nodded to them both. She said something, but I couldn't hear so much as a whisper.

Not wanting to intrude on their moment—not that I actually could, since I couldn't hear half of it, but still—I decided to turn my focus onto Rob. He was sitting cross-legged on his pillow, eyes closed with a tight-set jaw, and he was shivering like he was in the middle of a blizzard rather than a desert. Every muscle he possessed was strung tight, and every once in a while, I could hear him groan in pain.

The longer he held the planes together, the more pain he seemed to endure. His tight-set jaw eventually turned into a bared-teeth grimace, and his groans of discomfort ultimately morphed into cries of agony.

I didn't know what to do. Part of me wanted to rush over there and wrap him in my arms to comfort him, but the other part of me wanted to obey him—to let him concentrate and stay the hell out of his way.

Solomon and Camilla were both crying by the time Rob lost his hold on the astral plane. Our world snapped swiftly and brightly back into focus, and as the rest of us blinked and adjusted to the light, Rob shook violently from the internal cold that only he could feel.

I passed Speedy to Dan and scrambled over to Rob as quickly as I could. Carefully, I sat in his lap, curled my legs around his waist, and wrapped my arms around his neck. He was freezing cold, but I would give him every spare ounce of heat my body possessed because he was fucking incredible.

I wanted to tell him how amazing he was. How selfless he was to offer them the closure they so desperately needed at the expense of his own health and comfort. How his gift made him beautiful rather than freakish, which he'd always been called growing up.

But, as a tear of happiness and pride escaped my eye, the only words I could utter were, "I fucking love you, Rob."

His eyes remained closed, and his body kept on shaking, but he smiled and pulled me even closer. "I love you too, Jewels."

Cal, Ben, and Dan stood and shook hands with the king and princess, exchanging words of appreciation and good-will. Then they helped Rob up with me tucked stubbornly into his side.

"A million thanks, Spirit Prince," the king gushed, but Rob merely offered him a painful half smile and nodded.

"Sorry, Your Majesty," Ben explained. "He's in too much pain to really speak."

The king nodded his concern and understanding. "Yes, of course."

"If you don't mind, Majesty," Cal began, "we really need to take our leave now. Our father expected us home weeks ago. I'm sure he's simply sick with worry."

"No doubt he is, Storm Prince," the king said assuredly. "Please take your leave as well as my blessing for safe travels home to Blackwood. I might even consider reopening a few trade routes to the west."

Cal grinned and bowed his head. "That would be wonder-ful, Your Majesty. Thank you."

We turned to leave, but Camilla's stopped us.

"Storms!" she called out, and since she could have been talking to any of us, we *all* turned around. "Take care on your journey. And, Alexis, remember our training."

She winked, and my mind went completely blank.

"What training?" I asked.

I knew she'd gotten me an ax and that we'd *talked* about

training on our way to the Ley, but... anything and every-thing that had happened in between was either extremely fuzzy or had disappeared completely from my mind. Prob-ably another side effect of the Ley's magical aura—an aura that was now gone.

Instead of answering my question, she reiterated the most important details.

"Swing like you're mining your opponent's body for jewels." She lifted her fists, grabbing nothing but air, and demonstrated how to hold the pretend weapon. "Block by putting your hands on each end of the ax's shaft, and use the handle as a shield."

I grabbed my axe from my belt and copied her move-ments, taking its handle in both of my palms and lifting it up, the left side dipping a bit lower due to the weight of its golden head. She nodded, smiling at my immediate under-standing.

With nothing more to say or do, the guards escorted us out of the palace.

We wandered to the edge of the desert in silence before pausing and waiting on Rob to address the demons. He seemed to be in much less pain, but his teeth still chattered from the cold.

"First of all," he said, raising a single finger, "you can't take those bodies back with you. Leave them here."

One of the stolen bodies rolled their vacant eyes, but as the shadowy demons each stepped from the skin of their vessels and hid behind Rob, the corpses quickly morphed back into disoriented people. They blinked, glancing around as if they had no recollection of where they were or how they'd gotten there.

Cal moved to Rob's left, helping to hide the demons even further with his mountainous frame.

"Thank you for showing us around Erishwar," Ben said,

nodding to the group. "But I'm afraid the heat may have gotten to us a bit. Why don't you head home and rest up? I'm sure we'll all feel better in the morning."

The five of them shared curious glances, then eventually wandered off in, I presumed, the direction of their homes.

I exhaled a sigh of relief I hadn't even realized I'd been holding, and the demons stepped out from behind their Storm-Prince shield.

"Well, this sucks," Larry blurted out.

"Yeah," Sue agreed, crossing his shadowy arms. "I was planning on eating that later."

Rob glanced skyward, his gray eyes rolling. "How many times do I have to tell you?"

"*No eating the humans,*" the demons muttered as one.

It almost made me chuckle. You know, if the very idea of what they were doing wasn't so gods-awful repugnant.

Rob held up another finger. "Second of all, not a single word about the Shifter Prince being alive, understood? No one, and I mean *no one*—especially not the Storm King—can find out that he is alive. If I hear so much as a whisper about Ash's existence, I will personally track down each and every one of you and crush you into dust."

I squeezed Speedy a little tighter as Rob's threat ended.

The demons all nodded quickly, eager to express their 100 percent compliance.

"Yes, Prince Robert," Hugh said reverently. "We would never dream of disobeying you."

"Good." Rob gazed out across the overcast desert, stopping and pointing once he was facing a southwesterly direction. "Home is—"

"That way," Bob interrupted, pointing the exact same way as Rob. "Home is that way, right?"

Rob sighed, raised a brow, and replied in a flat voice, "What gave it away?"

Bob shrugged, looking rather smug at his own cleverness. "Just a gut feeling."

A chuckle passed Rob's lips before he waved them off. "All right, get out of here."

Before they did, they took turns saying goodbye to each of us, making sure to hug me with their flakey, fiery arms. They really were like children in some fucked-up, almost endearing sort of way.

"When will you be coming to Sohsol, Princess Alexis?" Larry asked hopefully.

I glanced at Rob and smiled. "I have no idea. Hopefully someday soon."

"Good," Sue said with a nod. "Look us up. I make a mean brain stew."

My stomach rolled, and I almost gagged.

Rob glanced at me, looking contrite. "I'm sure he's referring to a *boar* brain."

I nodded. I was sure too—sure he was *not* referring to a pig of any sort.

As they disappeared on the horizon, Speedy tumbled from my arms, landing in the sand on his head with an inaudible thud.

"For fuck's sake, Speedy, are you trying to...?" I trailed off and closed my eyes.

Of course, he was trying to kill himself. He was *Ash*, not *Speedy*, and he clearly wanted back in his human form. I couldn't blame him; if I'd been stuck as a sloth for six years, I'd probably hate being back in that particular animal's body too.

I scooped him up and passed him to Cal. "Here you go, neck breaker."

"Neck breaker?" he sputtered out, fumbling to keep from dropping the sloth.

"Yes," I decided. "You're neck breaker and Dan's throat

slitter."

"Dear gods," Cal grumbled in astonishment. But, taking the oh-so-subtle hint, he reached down with his giant hands and snapped Speedy's sweet little neck.

The sound was enough to gut me. Thank the gods that the golden magic quickly turned him back into Asher.

When he was a solid man once more, Ash chuckled and pulled me into his arms. "Aww, Sweets, you're so cute when I die."

I rolled my eyes and jabbed him in the side with my elbow. He didn't even flinch, just laughed as if I'd tickled him or something. I rubbed my arm and glared at his handsome face.

"Next time you shift, turn into something other than a sloth, will you?" I demanded. "*Then* I'll kill you myself."

"I'm going to hold you to it, you know that, right?"

I stuck my tongue out at him, and the other guys chuckled.

"Have fun killing a cute little bunny," Ash teased me. "Or a fluffy little kitten."

My eyes went wide. "You wouldn't..."

But *his* eyes were already alit with the possibilities.

Great. Neck breaker, throat slitter, and kitty killer. Fuck, we were a weird group.

CHAPTER 23

The journey back to Blackwood was almost as terrible as the journey in.

Instead of blazing hot days and extra cold nights, we were drenched to the bone during the day and absolutely frozen at night. If it weren't for the heat we managed to savor by piling up together, we probably would have been icicles.

When we reached Eastern Blackwood, Ben's kingdom, we took a much-needed break.

The six of us sat in a big lounge area on the second story of the Obsidian Palace, relaxing on Ben's plush, white leather furniture and wallowing in self-pity. Sure, we'd saved the chimeras, but the fae were doomed without the magic of the Ley, and we were already too late in giving the Storm King his precious egg.

I tried my best to push Lilah's beautiful little face out of my thoughts, but I knew it was going to haunt me for the rest of my life. I wiped a tear away before the guys could see it.

"We're already fucked," Ben said matter-of-factly. "We may as well pause for a moment and gather our strength and our wits. I need to check on my people and our food supply anyway."

"Can I come with you?" I asked, jumping at the opportunity to take my mind off my guilt and misery. Plus, I wanted to see Essund and see Ben in his element. I wanted to know what he was like as "Prince Benson, Lord of Obsidian Palace."

He smiled and reached his hand out to me. "Sure, Sailor." Then he turned to the guys. "We'll be back in a couple hours. When that time comes, we need to figure some shit out."

They all agreed and decided to take hot showers and a quick nap while we were gone. I couldn't say I didn't want the same things, but I was equally as happy to be hand in hand with Ben.

Being in eastern Blackwood was a lot like being back in Eristan, except there was a homier and more familiar vibe in the air that set me comfortably at ease. The people strolled through the sandy streets wearing dresses and suits made of the same shimmering material I'd seen all throughout Eristan and only once before back in the northern quadrant. Ben had said they were fashioned from the string of desert silkworms, and if that were the case, there must have been an entire silkworm farm somewhere nearby. Either that or the silkworms were ginormous.

The buildings lined the streets, two and three stories high, all clean and pristine with potted plants hanging from their windows and stationed outside their entryways. There was a giant well in the very center of town, big enough to accommodate at least twenty or so people at once, and on each side of that were rows of stalls and vendors selling just about anything you could think of: jewelry, bread, clothing, fresh fruit, trinkets, and so on.

Ben waved pleasantly at everyone he could, stopping to

speak to a few of them at the well as we filled a couple canteens.

"Greetings, Prince Benson!" one of his citizens said. He was dressed a little fancier than everyone else, so I assumed he had more coin. "So glad to have you back after your extended trip to Eristan! I trust everything went well?"

Ben smiled and nodded. "Of course, Mister Resham. How are the silkworms this season?"

Ah, the silk man. No wonder he had a lot of coin.

"Doing excellent, Your Highness. Thank you for asking."

Ben then turned to a woman standing off to our right. "How's the wheat and bread holding out, Mrs. Makhbiz?"

The woman smiled and bowed to him. She was short and slightly wrinkled, with her long, dark hair pulled into a bun at the back of her head. "Fairly well, Your Highness. But as usual, we could always do with more."

Ben's eyes twinkled with warmth as he grinned. "I'll be sure to touch the wheat fields today on my pass through."

"Bless you, Your Highness," she responded with reverence.

We continued on, stopping just outside of the main city in a more rural area that somehow boasted fields of vegetation growing right out of the sand. I stole a glance at Ben from the corner of my eye. I knew it must have been his doing.

He knelt down and touched a vine, extending its reach and doubling its flowers and fruit. Green, striped melons suddenly bloomed all over the place. I smiled, mouth hanging open in awe as I watched. He blinked a few times, shook his head, then took a quick drink of water. The cool liquid instantly paid the price of his magic for him, so he could continue on to another patch of vegetation.

Here, there were long, oval vegetables with skins of yellow, orange, and red. He did the same thing as before, stretching their vines and multiplying their yield.

"You're quiet," he said to me as we made our way toward the wheat fields next.

I glanced up at him, surprised to find worry etched into his features. "I'm sorry. I was just watching you do your thing. It's pretty fascinating."

He smiled back, but it almost looked pained. "I just thought.... We haven't spent much time together since that night in Ravibad, and I was afraid..."

I cocked my head. "Afraid I didn't like the bondage?"

His cheeks flushed a gentle pink. "Sort of. More like..." But he trailed off and didn't finish the sentence.

"More like what?" I asked, taking his hand, eager to set his fears at ease, whatever they may be.

He knelt in front of a patch of wheat and sighed, digging his fingers into the sand. The long, golden stems shot up even taller, and their braided spikes filled with seeds. He quickly took another sip from his canteen and shook his head.

"I've always been afraid that... I'm like *him*."

My stomach dropped, and I shook my head. "No, Ben, you're *nothing* like him."

His smile was wry. "Think about it. He enjoys torture; I enjoy torture—mine's just more of the sexual variety. He restrains people; I restrain people. He likes causing pain; I like causing pain. He's a control freak; I'm a control freak—again, sexually, but still."

I dropped to my knees beside him and took his hand. "No '*but still.*' What you do is not even close to the same thing. Your intentions are totally different."

He shook his head, as if lost in his own thoughts. "I try so hard to be as kind and caring as I can be in real life, but it's just to counterbalance that darkness in me."

I reached out and cupped his cheek with my palm, pulling his brown-eyed gaze onto mine. "You are not dark, Benson

Storm. You are the embodiment of light and goodness. I've never met a person as kind and caring as you, and I don't think that has anything to do with your fear of darkness; I think you're just genuinely *that* amazing."

He took a deep breath and searched my eyes for something—possibly trying to decide if I was being honest or not.

"I know my word isn't as magical and binding as yours," I said, stroking his cheek with my thumb, "but for what it's worth, *you have my word* that I'm telling you the truth."

He leaned in and kissed me so fast, I never even saw it coming. My lips parted automatically, allowing his tongue to slip into my mouth and dominate me. The harder we kissed, the harder it was to breathe, and I was a panting mess before he finally pulled away.

"What's the current score for rule number one?" he asked.

Keep things even. Especially sexually.

I giggled and shook my head as I caught my breath. "I just so happen to owe you one."

"Is that right?" His brows rose and he kissed me again.

I nodded, then slid my tongue across his bottom lip.

He groaned and pulled away, surprising the hell out of me.

"What's wrong?" I asked as my brows knit together.

He spun in a wide circle, dragging his hands through the sand, and suddenly there were trees and tropical plants, bushes, and vines surrounding us from all sides. As I marveled at the sight before me, he chugged the rest of his canteen and tossed it aside.

"I figured we'd need a little privacy," he said, before slowly pulling off his shirt and strolling toward me.

My hands instinctively moved to the muscled ridges of his chest and abs, stroking his tanned skin with greedy fingers. I leaned in and kissed his neck and throat, squeezing his biceps as I made my way up to his lips. Gods, he felt good in my arms, all warm and steadfast—all *mine*.

"We don't have the kind of time we had back in Ravibad," he said against my mouth.

I kissed him again, savoring the taste of his tongue on mine. "I know. We'll have to make it quick."

His grin darkened. "I don't know about *quick*, Sailor." Then he pinned my hands above my head and tied them together with a magical vine, securing the other end to a nearby tree.

I raised a brow, wondering what he had in mind this time. Then he ripped my dress, right down the front. I gasped, shocked by the sudden destruction, but he didn't stop there. He kept tearing the material until it fell completely off my body, lying beneath me like a blanket. Then he did the same to my bra and panties.

I had to admit, his primal caveman-like actions were hot as fuck.

Then his hands were at my eyes, and beautiful pink flowers bloomed in my vision, blocking the world from my sight. All I could smell was honey and peonies, and all I could see were the soft pink petals before me.

"I want to kiss you all over, however I want, without you being able to see or stop me."

That delicious vulnerability washed over me again, and I was grateful once more that I was with a man I trusted completely. I couldn't move, I couldn't see, and I couldn't fucking wait for him to touch me.

His mouth moved down my throat and between my breasts, travelling slowly across the planes of my stomach before trailing down one of my thighs. Then he came back up, moving to the other side of my body as he made his way up to my mouth.

"This body is *mine*," he told me, gliding his hands along

my sides. Then he was back to kissing me, this time sucking on each of my nipples before dipping lower to circle my clit with the tip of his tongue. The soft touch was maddening, making me squirm in pleasure.

He pulled away, and I heard a rustling sound. Excitement filled me as I wondered what I'd feel next.

My skin suddenly tickled as something soft and light was dragged up my arm. It felt like a feathery plant of some sort. It trailed over my breasts, teasing and tantalizing my nipples before snapping down with a sting on my skin. Pain flared, followed quickly by a rush of heat and pleasure.

He mimicked the move again, trailing it over my stomach and lady bits before snapping it down on those as well. Throbbing heat rushed between my legs. I could hardly believe my reaction. I never imagined getting whipped in the crotch would *actually* be pleasurable... yet, there I was, panting like a bitch in heat.

He dragged the plant down my legs and back up again, spreading me open before snapping the inside of my thighs. I couldn't help the moan that escaped my lips.

I jumped slightly as his fingers found my slit, spreading my wetness from top to bottom. I was quickly getting lost in a sea of pleasure, and somehow the pinkish petals in my vision only added to the sensual effect. It was like a dream, a fantasy.

Then the head of his dick was on me, hot and hard, rubbing up and down and driving me insane with need. I lifted my hips, hoping I could coax him inside, but was rewarded with a swift crack on the ass. I hissed in pain, knowing there was probably a pretty, red handprint on my butt cheek, but soon I was so dripping with desire that I didn't even care.

"Fuck, you're so wet," he groaned.

Then his hands were on my hips, pulling me closer to him

as he rammed his cock inside me. I gasped, and my nipples instantly tightened as a wave of goose bumps sailed across my skin.

"Whatever you do, don't come." He thrust into me again, driving his dick like a corkscrew before retreating once more. He continued this pattern for... I didn't even know how long. Long enough for me to go rigid in his grasp; long enough for the pleasure to become overwhelming.

Suddenly my legs were split, one on the ground, one up in the air over his shoulder. He pushed into me, his body pressing my thigh down to my stomach and chest, stretching me in a way I hadn't yet experienced. It somehow allowed his cock to slide in even deeper. He worked his hips, driving in with that same spiraling pattern, the one that so readily hit all the right places.

As the pressure built once more, he paused and peeked under my flowery blindfold. "No coming until I say, okay?"

I bit my bottom lip. "Yes, sir."

His eyes flooded with heat, and he dropped my blinder once more. "Good girl." He made quick work of building me up, before slowing down and whispering, "Not yet."

Then he built me up again, only to slow down and say it again.

"Gods fucking damn it, this is killing me!" I groaned, which of course, earned me another smack on the ass.

"You ready to come?" he demanded. "You can't handle it anymore? Not for another second?"

I didn't know why, but a tear escaped my eye as desperation filled me. "Not another second," I pleaded. "Please."

I was pretty sure my begging set him off. He pounded into me ruthlessly, ratcheting my pleasure to extreme heights before finally allowing me to get off.

"Come for me, sweetheart. *Now*," he growled.

I couldn't help it, it was like his wish was my body's

command, and suddenly I was crying out and clenching down all around him. The orgasm was so intense it was borderline painful, but the pleasure was enough to mask any extreme discomfort. I rode that high until I could barely move, my entire body nothing more than a limp pile of skin and bones puddled in the sand. Ben came not long after me, adding his own fluids to my puddle of bliss.

Suddenly, my wrists were free of the vines, and the flowered blindfold was removed from my eyes. Ben's brown gaze landed on me with so much warmth it could melt the Obsidian sun, and love bubbled up in me, pure and raw.

I loved him. I loved *them*. All of them.

He pulled me to my feet and into his arms, then stroked my skin as he nuzzled his face into my neck.

"We should get back to the palace," he muttered.

I snickered a little humorlessly and gestured to my naked frame. "And how exactly am I going to do that with no dress?"

He sent me a warm grin. "I can control the vegetation, remember?"

He reached over and grabbed a vine, closing his eyes as it quickly braided itself together in midair. The thick, green material wove around and around my body, covering me in a strange dress with peekaboo creases. It was softer than it looked and smelled like summertime.

After using so much magic, Ben crashed to the ground, feeling around as if he couldn't see or hear—and truthfully, he probably couldn't.

I rushed over and tipped my canteen to his lips, allowing the water to trickle in slowly so he didn't choke. He drank and drank until the whole container was empty, and after a few seconds, he blinked and slowly came back to normal.

"Thanks, Sailor," he said with a grateful half smile. "Are

you ready to go wake the guys so we can plan our next move?"

"I am now," I said with a deliberate grin.

Whatever that move actually was, it would have to be *huge*, because the unspoken fact of the matter remained: if chimeras were anti-magic, with the power to incapacitate a god, then there was no way in hades we could hand over a *chimera egg* to their murderous lunatic of a father.

CHAPTER 24

"We are *not* handing you over to the Storm King," Cal growled, scowling at Ash.

"He wouldn't even know it was me!" Ash argued. "I'd be in a damned egg."

This dispute had already been going on for a half hour or so, and we'd basically gotten nowhere.

If we gave the Storm King the real chimera egg, he'd use it to kill us somehow, or at least to control us more thoroughly, there was no doubt about it. But if we gave him a replacement egg, it might buy us some time to come up with a better plan—whatever the hell that might be. Then again, that had the potential to backfire epically when the Storm King found out the truth of our deception.

Ash's plan, unfortunately, made the most sense, but it also came with the highest risk. He wanted to shift into a baby chimera, still in its egg, and spy on the king for as long as he could. If the king smashed the egg right away, Ash would have to hope he could stay in his yolk form long enough to chance turning into a bug and flying away—much like he'd done the last time he escaped the king.

But if the Storm King waited for him to hatch and inadvertently said or did anything in the egg's presence, then that might give us some invaluable insight into the twisted inner-workings of the psycho's mind. And if he took the egg somewhere—say, to a powerful sorcerer—then we'd have *even more* knowledge.

Then came the downside.

What if Ash was found out somehow? The Storm King would torture the hell out of him for, like, *ever*. Or worse, finish what he started all those years ago...

Ash's life was worth way more to us than information. He just didn't see it that way.

"We are not arguing about this any longer, Asher," Cal stated plainly. "It's too dangerous, and we won't risk it. End of story."

Ash glared at him. "Gods, Cal, Alexis is right. I'd forgotten how fucking bossy you are."

Cal almost chuckled, but he quickly put his hard-ass mask back on and sent his brother a glare of his own.

"*Anyway*," Dan said, clearly sensing the tension and trying to diffuse it, "any ideas on how we survived that chimera attack in the first place? Or why we all felt the pain of the blood bond in the woods even though none of us were hurt or in trouble?"

All eyes turned to Ben who looked conflicted. "I have a theory."

"I figured you might," Dan said, grinning.

"Well, spill it, bro," Rob grumbled. "We need to figure this shit out."

Ben looked at each of us, his mind seemingly whirling a mile a minute behind his chocolatey brown eyes. "I think... someone else is included in the bond."

Shut the fuck up.

"*What?*" Rob hissed.

Cal and Dan looked equally as pissed and surprised.

"How could that be possible?" Ash demanded. "It was implausible enough that *I* got included. How the hell could anyone else be involved?"

Ben shook his head as he contemplated all the various possibilities. "You got included because your blood was on Alexis's hand."

Ash shrugged dramatically. "Yeah, so?"

Ben turned to Rob. "You punched Crissen in the nose that night at the ball. It *bled.*"

Rob's eyes narrowed into perilous slits, his plush lips thinning dangerously. "That shouldn't fucking matter. He's not even a Storm!"

Ben shook his head. "But he *is.* His mother gave him the surname even though he was never recognized as an official heir."

A smile crept onto Dan's lips despite the craziness of the situation—or maybe *because* of it. "You have to be fucking kidding me. Rob had Crissen's blood on his hand, and Alexis had Ash's blood on hers, and now there's *seven* of us included in this crazy shit?"

Ben half-shrugged. "It's the most logical explanation I can come up with."

Rob growled and tossed the chair he'd been sitting on across the room, cracking its wooden frame against the wall. "Gods fucking damn it! I hate that guy."

And yet, if you hadn't hated him so much that you punched him in the face, we wouldn't be in this mess. I kept that thought to myself, though. He was already pissed off enough.

"So, what does this mean?" Cal asked, keeping his face carefully neutral. "How do we deal with this?"

Ben chuckled darkly, as if, like Dan, he too couldn't believe our shitty luck. "If it means what I think it does, then this Crissen guy's lifeforce is officially tied to ours. If he's

237

put in mortal peril, he'll continuously suck power from us until he's healed. If we're put in peril, we'll draw strength from him; not much, considering I'm pretty sure he's not a descendant of the gods, but still. It was enough to keep us alive after the chimera attack, so it's at least worth *something*."

Rob nudged Dan's arm until he moved over and made room for him on the couch. When he sat down, he rubbed his temples. "So, basically, we get to babysit a nonmagical dude for the rest of our lives, because if he ever does anything stupid and gets himself hurt, *we're* the ones who are gonna pay for it."

Ben nodded. "Basically, yes."

"But it does go both ways," Cal reminded them, trying to find the diplomatic happy medium.

Dan scoffed. "Barely. There's a chance he can keep us alive for a short time, but it's not like he's really going to benefit us in any way."

"I think *keeping us alive* is a pretty good benefit," I added, vocalizing my opinion for the first time since the subject was brought up. "And by the sounds of things, we're stuck with him. So, we may as well try to find the silver linings through the storm clouds."

Ben sighed and shook his head. "Such a clever little Lexicon, making plays on words."

Cal smirked. "Such a *Peach*."

"While we're on the subject of how clever this peach is," I said, straightening my shoulders and holding my head up high, "I think we should make a fake egg and give it to the Storm King. We can't put Ash in danger like that. Thanks for asking my opinion on the matter, by the way."

"You're welcome to chirp in at any time during these discussions, Jewels," Rob said with a teasing glare. "But speaking of *Ash*, I think we need to clear something up."

Ash and I shared an uneasy glance, each of us having no apparent idea where Rob was going with that statement.

"I've seen the way you act around him," Rob said, "and it's a load of bullshit."

Oh, crap, here comes the pain. Jealousarus attack in *three... two...*

Cal smiled carefully. "We know you love him, Peach."

One...

"So, act like it," Rob finished.

I blinked, not sure I'd heard him correctly. "What?"

He smirked, realizing they'd just played hardball with me. "You love him, so act like it. You don't need to walk around on eggshells around him in front of us. That's not what this bond is about."

I ran a shaky hand through my hair in relief. "I just thought that, since he wasn't originally supposed to be part of the bond, you guys wouldn't appreciate me showing any sort of affection toward him right away."

"It was sweet of you to worry about us like that," Dan said, and I was pretty sure he found it more humorous than touching.

I looked around the lounge at all their handsome faces. "I know I haven't said the word out loud to all of you one-on-one yet, but I want you to know that I love *all* of you. This bond we made out of desperation and longing has quickly turned into something... so much more. For me, at least."

Ben nodded, and Cal said, "It has for us too."

I turned to Dan and Rob, elated to find them nodding as well.

Cal sighed heavily then, and I could tell he was about to lay something heavy on the line. "Speaking of all this love... the Storm King is going to expect us to *make some* when we return. I'd bet every jewel I own on it."

My eyes fell shut. "I don't want to talk about it."

Not necessarily because I detested the idea of fucking in front of everyone while the Storm King sadistically watched —which I most definitely did—but because I didn't want them to know what I was really thinking. How I wasn't going to go through with it. How I was going to hold my ground and make a stand. And if the king got angry and attacked me, then godsdamn it, I was going to fight him right back. I knew it wouldn't be enough to destroy or dethrone him, but it'd be one small step in the right fucking direction.

Cal sighed once more but dropped it. "Well, is there anything else we need to talk about before we go back?"

"What about the fae and the Lunaley?" Ben asked. "The magic is gone. They're going to die if we can't reverse this somehow."

"It'd be easier to reverse it if we knew how it got there in the first place," Rob said, shaking his head. "I wish I would've thought to use my magic. Maybe there was a spirit nearby on the astral plane who could've given us some insight."

"We could always go back," Dan suggested. "*After* we return to Blackwood Palace and speak to our lovely father."

"Maybe," Ben half-assed agreed, pacing around the room. "Or maybe it's already too late. I have no idea how fast their magic will drain now that the doorway is shut."

Sadness crept into me then, along with guilt and regret. I didn't want the fae to die. I didn't want my promise to Bria to mean absolutely nothing.

Cal pinched the bridge of his nose. "This is going to end in war. Not only will Timberlune attack to defend their honor, but Hydratica will back them up."

"Eristan will probably take our side," Ben mumbled.

"Yeah, but this is exactly what we've been trying to avoid," Cal growled, nearly shouting in frustration. "Everything we've done up to this point has been in a futile attempt to prevent war, and for what? We ended up starting one anyway."

"I'm sorry," I muttered as my eyes filled with tears and my face crashed into my palms. "This is all my fault."

If I'd just let Cal marry Bria, then none of this would have happened. He would have ensured the harpies stayed away from the Ley. The god-killing chimeras would have died off —and honestly, that might've been the better option—and there would be no impending war with Hydratica.

"Hey, Peach, no one's blaming—"

"Don't," I said, cutting Cal off. "I don't want your sympathy. I know it's my fault, and I'm going to own it. I just wish there was something I could do to fix it."

But there wasn't. What was done, was done. And if I was going to collapse into a weeping mess of tears and regret, then I damn sure wasn't going to do it in front of them.

I tore from the room like a bolt of lightning, rushing through hallways and corridors I didn't know, flying down staircases I'd never stepped foot on before. I never turned around to make sure I wasn't being followed, but I was pretty sure they knew enough to let me go and cool off.

When I finally discovered a door to the outside, I was pleasantly surprised to find myself in a garden. A stone fence surrounded the place, with green, leafy vines crawling along the cracks in the mortar. Tall trees stood in the middle, lending some much-needed shade to the space, while luscious flowers littered the ground, perfuming the air in a sweet-smelling haze.

I wasn't sure how this garden thrived, considering there didn't appear to be any water source nearby, so I assumed it survived on *Ben*.

Tears continued to roll down my cheeks as I kicked off my shoes and ran barefoot through the sandy grass. The closer I got to the border of the Obsidian Desert, the more the rainy season kicked back in. A slow drizzle formed in the air, dampening my skin, and for some reason, it was almost calming. Maybe because it masked the presence of my own tears and made me feel less vulnerable?

When I came to the end of the garden, I threw myself onto the wall, climbing the vines haphazardly in an attempt to reach the top block, where I sat staring out across the desert as it rained and thundered in the distance.

The mood was fitting.

A tree had grown a little too close to the fence over there, but that made it the perfect candidate for a back rest. I leaned into the smooth bark and let my head fall back, closing my eyes as I listened to the pattering rain. It was peaceful, relaxing. Hopefully it would clear my head enough for me to come up with some sort of plan, some way to stop the damage I'd caused.

A bird chirped nearby, then dove from the air, landing hard in a puff of feathers, its neck bent at a cringeworthy angle.

Son of a bitch. I knew before the magic even started that it was Ash.

Sure enough, one whirlwind of golden magic later, Ash stood at the foot of the fence gazing up at me with soft amber eyes.

"Hey, Sweets," he said, as he climbed the vines to sit beside me on the wall.

I took a deep breath and continued gazing out across the sands, avoiding his gaze. "Hey."

"It's been a long time since it was just you and me," he said.

I stole a quick glance at him from the corner of my eye. He was smiling gently, and I suddenly wondered if he was reminiscing about the past when life was somehow much easier, despite feeling harder.

I nodded my agreement, focusing my gaze back out across the dismal sands.

"Do you think," he asked me thoughtfully, "if you'd never become magical, the Storm King would have still made the guys get the chimera egg?"

I scoffed. I'd never give that fucker the benefit of the doubt.

"Of course he would. That's like the one thing that's all on him and not on me."

Ash nodded slowly, as if caught in a faraway thought. "So even if you and I were safe and sound back in Blackleaf, they guys would have still gone to Eristan and the Lunaley."

I turned to him, unsure of where exactly he was going with this. "Yes. What's your point?"

He shrugged. "Just wondering if they would have discovered the archway on their own and triggered the fae's demise anyway."

He was trying to make me feel less guilty. And believe it or not, the thought was a little welcoming. Maybe it wasn't *all* on me. Maybe some of this would have happened anyway.

I took a deep breath and let it out slowly. "Still, the impending war with Hydratica wouldn't be happening."

"Wouldn't it?" He raised a brow at me. "They've already been amassing a sea of ships. It's like they wanted war, and they were just waiting for the perfect scapegoat to blame it on."

I pursed my lips. Was he right? Had they been playing us? Herding us into war no matter which way we turned?

"Why would they do that, though?" I asked, shaking my head as I thought.

"Come here." He reached his arms out to me, and I curled up between his legs, resting my back and head against his chest. He wrapped his arms around my waist and laid his chin on my shoulder. "It's hard to say why they might've been planning preemptive war. It's not like we're a very well-liked nation, not now that the Storm King is in control. Hydratica is also one of those nations that are quicker to anger and faster to call for drastic measures."

He squeezed me tighter, trying to show that he literally had my back, that he didn't fault me in the slightest.

"I know you, Sweets," he said. "I know you're blaming yourself about Cal and Bria's marriage falling through, but here's the thing—Cal loves you. We all love you. If he'd have gone through with the marriage, then we'd probably be dealing with some sort of divorce and war anyway. And if not, then the fae would still be dying. Cal couldn't have single-handedly saved their entire nation. They had to have known that, even though they clearly didn't care."

As much as I hated to admit it, his words washed over me and cleansed me, rinsing away the guilt and negativity, and left me wide open for a whole new mindset to kick in. It was weird. I'd almost gotten attached to the idea of holding a grudge, of letting it fuel me and consume me until I either got my vengeance or it destroyed me.

But... that wasn't me. I was a "live and let go" kind of person. I didn't dwell on shit for too long, and I'd much rather move forward than look behind me.

"How do we fix this, Ash?" I asked, needing to know there was a way somehow.

He kissed my cheek and snuggled in closer. "We take it one day at a time. It's impossible to know what tomorrow holds until it's here. We'll deal with it as it comes."

I nodded, realizing that was probably as good as I was going to get. Tomorrow we'd travel to Blackwood Palace, and after that... who knew what would happen?

CHAPTER 25

*G*EMMA

I'D HEARD RUMORS THAT ALEXIS AND THE PRINCES WERE DEAD.

It'd been over a month since they left for Eristan and weeks since the Storm King had gotten a single report back on them. I knew, because he took his anger out on me and the harem ladies—including his newest addition, Charity.

Her transition into this lifestyle was not nearly as smooth as mine had been. We were apparently cut from two very different cloths. Like, vibrant, shimmery, rainbow cloth made from silkworms on crack compared to a ripped burlap sack. While I had incessant optimism and a "look on the bright side" mentality, she had a very "all or nothing" one, and once her hopes came crashing down, they crashed *hard*.

Nowadays, she seemed to have a depressed outlook on life in general. She wailed and screamed during her beatings, and she cried herself to sleep every night. We'd tried to comfort and befriend her, but I was pretty sure she hated us by association.

She'd come around.

She had a son named Crissen, which, in hindsight, I realized was the guy the Storm King had questioned me about all those weeks ago. Apparently, he was *actually* curious about Criss because he was the king's bastard son. Another magic wielder. I guess his power was rapid healing or something. I'd heard talk around the servants' quarters that he was a descendant of Asclepius, son of Apollo who was, of course, the son of Zeus. I didn't put much stock into the tales of the gods, but if they were to be believed, then that'd make Criss pretty close to Cal—the only other descendant of Zeus I knew.

I tried my best to stay out of the gossip, but I couldn't help myself. Learning the castle secrets was fascinating to me.

Like the rumor going around about Charity being in love with the Storm King before she found out what a snake-eyed monster he really was. *That* was fascinating. Who the fuck could fall in love with a murderous sociopath? Did that speak of *her* character or *his* cunning? Who knew? See? *Fascinating.*

As far as the rumor about Alexis and the Storms, I refused to believe it. No way had they traveled abroad and just vanished. If the Eristani king had beheaded them or something, we'd have heard about it. I was certain we'd be at war by now too. Well, war with *another* kingdom. We were already declared enemies of Timberlune, probably because Cal married Alexis instead of Princess Bria. But I was a *servant*, not a *soldier*, so details about the war were not readily available for me.

The most logical explanation I could think of for their disappearance was that they planned and executed an escape.

It gave me hope to think they'd been successful—considering Tristan and I were attempting an escape of our own *tonight*.

Ever since I'd uttered the words *"I'll follow you anywhere,"* he'd been planning things down to the finest detail—collecting fur and blood, stray strands of my hair, pieces of ripped-up cloth. He was really creative. My job had been sneaking pieces of food and cutlery from the kitchen and, of course, picking a fight with the king on the night we intended to leave.

Tonight.

Hopefully none of those things made any sort of sense from the outside and couldn't be traced back to us in the slightest.

My hands shook as I sped through the hallway on my way to find the rotten bastard. If I had to guess, he was either in the dungeons beating his prisoners or in the towers beating his wives. He liked variety like that, had to switch it up every so often so the girls didn't get *all* his precious attention. Innocent people who couldn't afford their taxes needed love too, damn it.

I checked the dungeons first, because *optimism*. But he wasn't there, so I made the long trek from the bottom floor up to the tallest tower. Halfway up, I had to pause to catch my breath. Okay, fine, it was a quarter of the way up, and I'd stopped twice. The second time, I accidentally bumped into a suit of armor, rattling its metal appendages with a cringe on my face. Thankfully it didn't crash to the floor, but it did accidentally draw someone's attention.

Crissen's.

He rounded the corner quickly, as if he were about to save somebody from dying, but when he saw it was only me, he just turned around and tried to leave.

"Hey!" I called out. "Hey, you! Criss!"

He stopped, spinning around slowly, reassessing me as if

trying to figure out who I even was. I mean, it wasn't like we'd ever met. Then I realized *who I was* and *who he now was* and how botched that freaking greeting had been.

"I mean—" I dropped into a deep curtsey. "—Your Highness, Prince Crissen."

He sighed and smiled slightly. He looked... defeated and tired. "And you are?"

"Gemma, *Your Highness*. Gemma Darrow."

He waved a dismissive hand in my general direction. "Please don't do that. Just... call me Criss like you did. Was there something you needed?"

"You cut your hair," I blurted out.

He raised a hand to his buzzed-off, brown fuzz and rubbed it curiously, as if he wasn't yet used to it either. "Yeah, I just... had to."

"Storm King make you do it?"

"Sort of."

I nodded. "He's a bit of a control freak."

Crissen's eyes went wide, and he quickly glanced around to make sure no one had heard my blasphemous words.

I let out a nervous chuckle. "No worries, Prince Criss, he's not here. He's up in the towers." I cocked my head and crossed my arms, eager to ferret out some more secrets. "So, how'd you get here?"

"The Storm King fucked my mother," he deadpanned.

"Ha ha. I mean, here, in this palace. How'd he find out you have powers?"

Crissen's jaw tensed, and his lips thinned. He glanced away, like he was thinking something that he had no intention of saying aloud. Eventually, he settled on, "I don't know."

What a buzzkill. No juicy secrets to be squeezed out of *him*.

I nodded. "Right. Well, good talk. Do me a favor though, will you? The next time you see your mom, Charity, tell her that the harem ladies are only trying to help her and that, if she wants to live even a semblance of a normal life, she's going to need their companionship. It gets incredibly lonely in here."

His clear blue eyes darkened suddenly, and he sneered at me. "You have no idea what she's going through. No idea what she's suffered—"

I yanked the long sleeves of my dress up to my elbows and showed him the crisscross of scars scattered all over my skin. I pulled back the collar of my shirt, revealing even more. "I'd show you more, but I have a boyfriend, and he's a brick shithouse, so... Oh, plus, I'm totally moral and shit, and moral girls don't show boys any leg past the ankle, right?"

He stared at my scars, his eyes darting from each shiny white line to the next.

I sighed. "I know *exactly* what your mother is going through, Prince Criss. And I'm telling you right now, from *experience*, she needs to open up to the other harem ladies. They're going to be her lifeline in this fucked-up place."

He nodded, and his eyes lightened to their original shade. "I'm sorry for what you're going through," he said softly.

I laughed. "For this? This isn't your fault. No apologies necessary."

He turned away. "Yeah, but it's the Storm King's fault. And—"

"—And as such, no one else's," I finished, trying to rid him of his guilt. "Just because he's your father doesn't mean his actions reflect on you or who you are as a person. I'm sure the other princes will teach you that."

He scoffed and leaned against the nearest stone wall. "The Storm Princes hate me. They always have."

I cocked my head. "But you just got here. You haven't even met them yet. How could they hate you?"

"We've met before."

"Oh," I said stupidly. "Well, now that you're one of them, I'm sure they'll take you under their wing. They did that with Alexis."

He shot me a flat look. "Alexis is beautiful, and she has a vagina. I'm pretty sure that puts us in two very different categories as far as the Storms are concerned."

I cracked up laughing, accidentally bumping into that stupid suit of armor again. It wobbled on its iron legs, and just before I could catch it, it fell the hell over and crashed to the floor. The sound echoed through the hallway like the Storm King had just murdered a box of cymbals.

"Oh fuck," I muttered.

Well, I'd been looking to start a fight with the king. I had a feeling this would do just fine.

See, that was the last part of the plan. Piss the Storm King off, make him draw blood, then stage our exit in the form of an untimely death via wolf attack. The idea was that my blood would draw the beast in, and it would kill us both in a sort of bloodlust frenzy. I thought it was genius, really. Tris had really outdone himself.

As the sound of footsteps echoed on the stairs behind me, I smiled fleetingly at Crissen and waved. "See ya later, Prince Criss."

He swallowed hard and glanced between me and the mess of armor on the floor. "Would you like some help with that?"

I shook my head and waved him off. "Nah, that's the sound of my servant buddies coming to help clean up. Go ahead. I'll catch you some other time."

He hesitated for a moment then eventually nodded, bowing slightly at me before heading down the hall in the opposite direction.

"Oh, and, Prince Criss?" I called out at the last second. He turned around with a raised brow. "Princes don't bow to servants. They're too good for that."

He scoffed and shook his head. "I'm not too good for anything."

Then he disappeared around the corner.

Poor guy. He was taking his new fate better than his mother was but still not all that well.

As the footsteps drew nearer, I glanced out one of the arched hallway windows, watching as the sun dipped down below the trees. It was almost dark, almost time to leave... forever. Hopefully this beating wouldn't take long.

A hiss left the Storm King's mouth when he found me standing next to the pile of broken armor. "What have you done, you clumsy cunt?"

I spun around, a surprised smile on my face. "Well, hello, Your Majesty. Fancy seeing you here. I was just walking by, minding my own business, when this suit of armor just viciously attacked me."

"It attacked you." It wasn't a question, and he sounded neither surprised nor enthused. His hand found the back of my neck, and he squeezed painfully. "*I'm* about to viciously attack you."

"Over a fallen metal statue?" I hissed, bunching my shoulders up to block some of the sting. "I mean, I expected you to punish me, because that's *your thing*, but viciously? You don't think it's a little much?"

He pinched my neck even harder, momentarily making me see spots. I didn't even realize that was possible.

"No, stupid girl. The vicious part belongs to your lying, smart-ass mouth that has no fucking clue when to shut up. Maybe if we send Alexis your tongue in a package, she'll creep out of hiding and do her godsdamned duty for once!"

"No, no," I begged, feeling genuine fear swim through me. "That's not necessary, Your Majesty. I'll... I'll stop. I won't say another word."

He chuckled darkly. "We'll see about that."

≈

NUMB.

That's how I felt by the time he was done. That's *all* I felt. I knew that pain was searing white-hot across every inch of my skin, but it was *so* hot and *so* painful that it somehow left me feeling cold and numb instead. It was a complicated sensation, one I'd prayed to the gods to take away, but of course, they didn't listen.

I staggered through the palace hallways, dizzy and bleary eyed. I needed to get to the gardens; it's the only thing I could concentrate on. But how the hell was I supposed to travel like this? I honestly didn't know if I'd survive it. Because of that, however, I was more determined than ever to try.

I didn't want to live like this anymore. I almost said *couldn't*, but that wasn't true. The harem ladies were proof of that. Anyone *could* live a life of incessant torture if they had to, but if they didn't have to, why should they? The queens did it in order to keep their sons safe—or at least that's how they felt. But Alexis was not my child, and I knew she would be fine with or without me. As my best friend in the entire world, I also knew she would forgive me and understand why I left... if she knew.

I closed my eyes as a wave of nausea assaulted me.

She *wouldn't* know. She'd believe me to be dead, just like everyone else. I couldn't tell a single soul about mine and Tristan's plan—not even Alexis—or the whole thing might unravel before we could even leave the kingdom.

When I reached the stairs, the dizziness kicked my ass, causing me to tumble to the next floor down. I hissed as sharp pain burned across my skin and the dull ache of bone-deep bruises settled in further.

Get up, Gemma. Get. Up.

I crawled to my feet, using the wall for support, glancing at the blood smeared across the stairs in my wake. When I released the wall, two scarlet handprints remained. I thought about smearing them, trying to erase the evidence of their existence, but what was the point? It'd probably help sell the story anyway.

Stumbling, I hobbled through more hallways until I finally reached the door that led to the gardens. Outside, the moon was nowhere to be found. It was pitch-black, and coupled with my dizzied and disoriented state, that made it nearly impossible to navigate. I crashed to the grassy ground more times than I could count, and every time I stood back up, I was even more confused about where I was going.

This was *so* not part of the plan. If anyone other than Tristan saw me and tried to help, everything would go to shit. We couldn't leave behind witnesses. We'd discussed the necessity of knocking people off if they saw us, but I'd simply resolved to *not* get caught. Problem solved. Now there I was, stumbling through the castle grounds like a newborn calf who was already halfway to becoming a plate of veal.

"Gemma!" a voice hissed into the black. I spun around and tried to think of a solid hiding place because I was terrified of who might've spotted me. I had no idea where the voice had come from and no idea where I was going, but I dropped to the ground on my hands and knees and crawled as fast as I could, trying to get away.

Gods, the pain was excruciating. My limbs shook with every little movement. My skin fevered like a plague. My stomach churned like I might throw up when the voice called out again.

"Gemma, is that you?"

My heart hammered, and I panted wildly, the influx of oxygen intensifying my urge to vomit.

"Gem, it's me, Tristan."

I sucked in a shaky breath and turned in the direction I thought I'd heard his voice coming from.

"Tris?"

"Yeah, Gem, over here." It was dark, but I was pretty sure I could see the vaguest outline of him motioning me over.

I fumbled around on my hands and knees until I somehow, miraculously reached him. He grabbed my arms to help me up, but the pain that the move inflicted was enough to make me gag.

"Please don't touch me," I hissed through clenched teeth.

He removed his hands immediately, staying silent for a moment. "How hurt are you?"

I grimaced and nodded to myself since he probably couldn't see me through the dark. "Not too bad."

"I thought you were only going to pick a small fight with the king?" he asked, seeing right through my little white lie.

I sighed. "I tried, but he's insane."

"Did you pack your medicinal supplies?"

I nodded. "They should already be in the rucksack. You grabbed it, right?"

"Yeah. I just need to scatter the evidence; then we'll be good to go. As soon as we're far enough away, we'll stop and tend those wounds, so they don't get infected. Then we'll keep heading west until we reach the boat."

I swallowed hard, feeling sweat cling to my brow and hairline. The fever was raging hotter. I hoped beyond hope I could make it that far.

Tristan immediately got to work. He sprinkled tufts of fur onto the ground, along with a couple scraps of cloth and a few strands of my long blonde hair. He even situated a fang or two. And after all that, he speckled the area with blood.

Like I said, we were trying to make the whole thing look like a wolf attack. This was my theory: the Storm King didn't want people knowing how sadistic and fucked-up he truly was, so he wouldn't admit to drawing my blood; instead, he'd gratefully cling to blaming the wolf so that he had no part of it; but deep down, he'd believe it happened because of him. With any luck, he'd be too busy feigning his innocence that he wouldn't even consider it was a ploy.

Luck. Right. Exactly what no one in Blackwood seemed to have. Still, I tried to remain optimistic. Even at death's doorstep, I had to stay positive. Otherwise, who the hell even was Gemma Darrow anymore?

"It's done," Tris whispered, taking my hand. "Let's go."

I took a deep breath, gritting my teeth against the all-encompassing pain, and followed him into the woods.

The scene had been set.

Now, all I had to do was *survive*.

CHAPTER 26

ALEXIS

THE SUN HAD ALREADY SET BY THE TIME OUR HORSES cantered into the Blackwood citadel.

Much like the first time we arrived, there appeared to be a large gathering of people at the palace. *Un*like the first time, however, they didn't seem to be waiting on *us*. Thank the gods. There were empty carriages and patient coachmen reading newspapers lined up and down the streets as far as the eye could see, and the sound of elegant music filtered in between the houses, shops, and trees.

I glanced at Cal, and he smiled back in relief. "A ball."

"Yeah," Dan agreed, licking his bottom lip as he thought, "but for *what?*"

"Or for *who?*" Ben specified, as if he already had a suspicion about the recipient's identity.

If that were the case, then he had to have been assuming it was for Crissen. And if the Storm King was throwing a ball on behalf of his bastard son, then he clearly somehow knew about the link he had with us.

"Do you think he knows?" Rob asked, taking the words right out of my mouth.

Ash was nervous. Anyone else would probably think he looked determined or angry, but I could tell he was rattled beneath his thin lips and narrowed brows. "If he knows about Criss, then he probably knows about me."

Ben shook his head. "Not necessarily."

"And we're not going to assume that he does, either," Cal added. "We're going to play it safe, just like we have been, and have you take on your animal form while we're here."

"Don't go anywhere near him," Rob added, glaring at his brother for emphasis as he squeezed his horse's reins. "He's even more of a psycho than you remember."

Ash rolled his amber eyes but nodded. "Fine. I'll stay in bird form, and I'll keep far away from our dickhead father. But you guys have to promise to stay safe. If I feel a tug on the bond, you can bet your asses I'll be there to save you in an instant."

Dan chuckled darkly. "You better feel more than a *tug* before you ride in on your shiny white horse," he teased. "Because I can pretty much assure you there will be *a lot* of pushing and pulling during this cute little visit. There always is. That man drives us to the brink of our very sanity every fucking time."

"It's true," Rob agreed, crossing his tattooed arms in his saddle.

Ash sighed and dismounted with poise. "What are you going to tell the stable boys about the extra horse?"

Cal shrugged. "That I bought my wife a second horse because she loves the beasts so much."

Ash glared at him, as did Rob and Dan, while Ben just looked away.

"You love rubbing that in, don't you?" the Shifter Prince asked.

"What?"

"That she's your *wife*."

"No," Cal defended in an even tone. "It's just true. That's exactly what I'm going to say to the stable boy. You asked. I answered."

This was not a good situation. I could feel the electric tension in the air; there was too much hostility building. I quickly slipped down from my horse's back and got between Cal and the others.

"It's not his fault he was forced to marry me," I explained gently. "Just as it's not *my* fault I was forced to marry *him*. I wish I hadn't been coerced into it, but the Storm King doesn't give any fucks about my wishes, and neither do the gods. I made a promise to you guys, though. I promised that the piece of paper would mean nothing, that it wouldn't change the way I felt about you or how I treated you. I think I've kept my word in that regard.

"But I also promised that if I married *one* of you, I would marry *all* of you. If the Storm King can legally wed more than one person, then so can I. Say the word, and I'll start making good on those promises. I'll marry each of you, one by one. Who wants to be next?"

To my surprise, they didn't just brush my words off as nothing more than hot air. They actually sat there on their horses—or stood there on their feet, as was the case with Asher—and genuinely thought about the question and the consequential answer.

I was sure each of them wanted it to be themselves, but they were trying to be smart and fair about it, and I loved that about them. The selfless way they all contributed to our dynamic was magical in and of itself.

Even though the very idea of the word *marriage* set my

teeth on edge, I had to admit, being married to Cal had changed absolutely nothing. It wasn't as strange or awkward or detrimental as I'd feared it would be to my life or my existence. In fact, I was actually looking forward to going through with it four more times.

Dan took a deep breath and nodded, wordlessly volunteering to speak first. "I think it should be Ben."

"*Me?*" Ben asked in surprise, putting a hand on his chest, exactly mirroring his words and movements from days ago when we stood before the Eristani king.

A cheeky half smile lit up Dan's face. "Yeah, *you*. You're at highest risk right now, thanks to King Solomon taking such a liking to you. If you don't marry Alexis soon, who knows what sort of deal the kings will make behind our backs? You might find yourself promised to Camilla, after all."

Ash groaned. "I know it makes sense to choose Ben, but I've been dying to marry Alexis for *years*. Can we not just give me this one victory without me having to kill myself to earn it first?"

Rob's hardened features softened at his brother's plea. "Let's talk about this more later," he said, gently kicking his horse into a trot. "We need to get this meeting with our father over with so that we can get the fuck out of here."

Cal grabbed the reins of Ash's horse, while Ash helped me back up into my saddle. He grinned, skimming the bare skin of my thigh with his warm hands. "I love that you don't ride sidesaddle."

I scoffed teasingly. "Why would I? I'm awful enough on a horse without having to be *sideways* as a disadvantage. And if you're talking about me spreading my legs in an unladylike manner, well then, we have nothing to discuss. Women should be able to sit however they want without a man feeling entitled to slip between her legs."

"What if *I* was the man who wanted to slip between your legs?" Ash asked in a low and seductive tone.

I glanced up ahead, to where the guys were already moving along, slowly leaving me behind. My gaze slid back over to Asher, and a grin crept onto my lips. "That's different."

He chuckled and gave my horse a quick pat, kicking us into motion. I watched him over my shoulder as he winked and started fading into gold dust.

"I love you, Sweets," he shouted to me when he was already halfway gone.

I took a deep breath, and excitement filled me. I was finally able to say it back. "I love you too, Asher Storm."

He smiled wide, dimples appearing in each one of his cheeks; then they disappeared just as quickly as he finished turning into a bird. He spread his brown wings wide and took to the air, soaring up ahead of me to glide past his brothers on his way toward the palace. He might have agreed to stay away from the Storm King, but I had a feeling he'd at least want to see his mother.

"Son of a fucking bitch!" one of the guys cried out, scaring the living hell out of me.

I thrashed Caramel's reins, and she tore into a gallop, catching up to them rather quickly.

"What?" I shouted, my eyes following everyone else's gaze over to Ben, who sat cringing with his eyes closed, his whole body rigid. "What the fuck is going on? Is he okay?"

Ben's nostrils flared as he took a deep, calming breath. "That fucking bird... shit on me."

Dan immediately burst into a fit of laughter, almost falling off his horse. Even Rob chuckled, but Cal merely grinned and said, "I guess he doesn't like having you as competition for Alexis's hand."

"Oh, it's *on* now," Ben threatened, and considering I'd

never really seen much of a competitive side to him, I was a little turned on by his fire. "He's going down. And so help me gods, if I get Swamp-ass Fever, I am going to rub my blistered ass all over his cheeky face."

"Ooh!" Dan groaned, putting a fist to his mouth as he fought a disgusted chuckle. "That's fucking nasty."

"You bet it is," Ben agreed, narrowing his eyes. "Ash knows how I feel about germs and diseases, and he still crossed that fucking line."

"You know he'll just say it was a bird-like instinct," Rob said, smirking.

"I don't give a fuck. Payback is still going to be a bitch."

When we arrived at the stables, the servants looked genuinely shocked to see us. Their eyes and mouths went wide as they took us in, and they all faltered as if they'd possibly seen a ghost... or five.

Cal spouted off the spiel about purchasing me an extra horse, and as that servant worked on corralling our steeds, he flagged down a different stable hand to run an errand for us.

"Tell the servants inside the palace to have our rooms ready for us. We'll need ballroom attire, a quick bath, and probably a few snacks as we prepare—since we haven't eaten all day. And above all else, *do not* tell our father that we've returned. We want it to be a surprise when we show up at the ball."

The servant smiled and bowed his head. "Yes, Your Highness. Right away." And with that, he ran from the barns.

I turned back to Cal. "How much of a head start do you think he needs?"

He grinned. "Blackwood servants are the best in the land. We can start moving right now, and everything will still be ready for us by the time we reach our bedroom doors."

Both of my brows rose. "Impressive."

As we exited the stables, I scanned the stalls for any servants that might've looked familiar, but I found none.

That's all right. Gemma's not a stable hand. Of course, she wouldn't be here.

By the time we all reached our respective rooms, the doors were open and the requested items were lying on our beds. I glanced inside my room and gasped with glee. "Goodies!"

Tray after tray of cakes, pies, cookies, puddings, crepes, and pastries sat neatly on my silken purple sheets. Beside them rested a gorgeous gown that seemed to be woven out of fine strands of silver and gold. It was thin, possibly even transparent in places, and shimmered like sparkling metal in the candlelight.

"Meet us out here in the hallway in a half hour," Cal said, leaning casually on my doorframe.

I stuffed a cupcake into my mouth and groaned at the delicious vanilla flavor, then nodded my understanding. "I'll be there."

"Don't be late," he pressed.

I crossed my eyes in his general direction. "Don't be bossy."

He grinned and shook his head, patting the bag that hung at his side, the one that held our fake chimera egg. "Moment of truth. Time to see if this plan of ours works or not."

I took a deep breath and swallowed another bite of cupcake. "Don't do that to me. At least allow me to enjoy my sweets before you have my nerves forcing me to puke it all back up."

"Gross," he said with a grin.

"Your fault."

He shook his head and exited my room, shutting the door behind him.

That final half hour was a whirlwind of chaos. One

minute I was splashing rose-scented mineral water all over myself, and the next I was gobbling up crepes. One minute I was attempting to do my hair—rather unsuccessfully, I might add—and the next I was throwing on makeup. One minute I was nibbling on cookies, and the next I was shimmying into my new dress. The shoes that went with it were flats, which I appreciated, but they were absolutely covered in gold and silver beads. Not jewels, I'll admit, but they were still made of a material that I'd mined day in and day out, albeit inadvertently.

The guys were ready and waiting by the time I entered the hall, stunning visions of black and white and gorgeousness. They ranged from blond to brunet, peach to tan, tall to taller, and they all tied in the sexy department. I had a bad feeling I was ogling them all rather inappropriately, so I cleared my throat and smiled brightly. "I'm ready!"

Dan quickly turned to Cal. "Surely the egg can wait?"

Cal sighed and rolled his blue eyes. "No, you cannot have a quickie before the ball. We're already running out of time as it is."

"Damn." Dan shook his head, eyeing me like the icing on a cupcake he very much wanted to lick off.

And fuck if I didn't want to *lick him off* too.

"Speaking of the egg," Ben began, glancing at Cal. "Do you have it?"

Cal patted the messenger bag at his side once more. "Right here and ready to go."

I looked down both sides of the hallway, wondering if I'd find Gemma or my mom roaming the corridors, but I found neither.

"Have you seen anyone I know?" I asked the guys in a nonchalant tone despite the obviousness of my words.

"The queens are probably already at the ball, Jewels," Rob said, trying to reassure me.

"And the servants are no doubt working the kitchens," Ben added. "You'd be surprised the amount of drinks and hors d'oeuvres your guests go through during a ball."

I smiled, but my heart wasn't in it. Something felt... off.

"You ready?" Dan asked me, a little unnecessarily. I mean, I was standing out there, wasn't I? Obviously, I was about as ready as I was ever going to get.

Instead of allowing my nerves to turn me into a smart-ass, I simply nodded and avoided opening my sarcastic mouth.

"All right," Rob said with a devious grin. "Let's do this shit."

Cal smiled sympathetically and offered me his elbow.

I put my hand on his arm, and as we walked to the ball-room, my stomach twisted into knots.

I couldn't put my finger on one particular thing that was bothering me—I mean, pretty much every detail of this hare-brained plan was a risk anyway—but still I knew, in the pits of my soul, that something was about to go terribly wrong.

CHAPTER 27

CRISSEN

A FEW DAYS AGO, I CUT MY HAIR.

My life had changed so abruptly, I now felt like a completely different person. May as well look like a different person too.

I told the dead servant girl with the scars that the Storm King had made me do it, but that was only half true. He didn't tell me to cut it; he didn't hold me down and shave it himself. He just showed me his true colors, and by doing so, altered the very fabric of my being. I could never be the same again after watching him torture my mother in front of me. *Never*. So, I cut my hair—a symbol of who I was now, in stark contrast against the man I was before. It seemed fitting.

I still couldn't believe the girl had died.

He'd beaten her that night when she accidentally knocked the armor down; I was sure of it. I knew in my heart I should have stayed, should have helped her clean up the mess, should have saved her from whatever punishment she had coming by saying it was *me* who ruined the armor... but I didn't. Afterward, she'd wandered out into the gardens, leaving a trail of blood behind her, consequently drawing the keen nose of a wolf. A fucking *wolf*.

The king said it was her own fault for sneaking off to whore around—there'd been two sets of remains found the next day, one of which was a man's—but I knew it was his fault and his alone. If he hadn't hurt her so badly over something so stupid, if he hadn't drawn *blood*, she never would've attracted the wolf in the first place.

I was a guilty fucking mess.

I sat on a throne to the right of *the king*—I refused to call him father anymore, unless he made me—watching the dancing crowd of partygoers with listless eyes. We were at a ball, a ball thrown in *my* honor, to celebrate my newfound status as a prince of Blackwood.

I'd never felt more depressed. More ashamed.

The ballroom was elaborate as ever, all decked out in diamonds that reflected the candlelight, lending a champagne-colored tint to the very air around us. It was beautiful and intoxicating, like something from a fairy tale, but I knew better than to let it sweep me away. I knew what this place really was, and *beauty* had nothing to do with it.

"You should be dancing, Crissen," the king said, a merry smile lighting up his face. He was so good at faking innocence it was sickening. "This is all for you, after all."

I did my best to smile back. "I don't enjoy dancing anymore."

His smile brightened, crinkling the outer corners as if he were happy rather than homicidal. "Allow me to amend that statement. Go dance, *now*, or I'll have no choice but to speak with your mother on the issue of your insubordination."

I stood in an instant, bowing my head to him with a steely glare. "Yes, Your Majesty."

I adjusted the decorative purple jacket I wore, complete with silver tassels and badges, and smoothed down my bright white pants. It still felt foreign to be wearing the royal colors —even more so now that I despised them. I made to smooth down the locks of my hair, then remembered in a listless instant that they were gone, never to return. I paused, midreach, and lowered my fist to my side.

When I was sure I was presentable, I waded out into the crowd and grabbed the first woman I could find—a pretty blonde who practically threw herself in my path.

"Oh my gods," she gushed, clinging to my shoulders tightly. "I can't believe *I* was the first woman you chose to dance with! My friends are going to be so jealous."

"No need to be jealous," I muttered as the music began and we started to sway. I was no one special. But then her smile fell, and I realized she must have taken that the wrong way, that *she* was nothing to be jealous of.

"Shit, sorry. I meant, dancing with me is not that exciting." I glanced down and noticed she was wearing a gaudy pink dress. "You look lovely, by the way."

Her smile returned, almost as if it'd never left. "Thank you! You know, it's not every day a girl gets to stand hand in hand with a prince. I feel so lucky tonight."

I smiled slightly and rolled my eyes. "What about a prince who was raised as a commoner up until a few weeks ago?"

"Beggars mustn't be choosers, Prince Crissen," she said with a sly grin.

If only I'd taken that advice sooner. I could have been tucked peacefully in my bed, awaiting another new day at the forge. Instead, I was keeping my every move in check, hoping I wouldn't somehow sneeze wrong and get my mother flayed.

"You know," she said as we breezed across the dance floor, "I'm in the market for marriage."

I almost tripped over my godsdamned feet.

I tried to swallow, but my mouth was suddenly dry. "Trust me, miss, there's not a woman alive who couldn't do better than a Blackwood prince."

She patted my chest before slipping her hand back onto my shoulder. "So humble, Prince Crissen. But I believe you have that the other way around. No woman *could* do better than a Blackwood prince. You're the top of the food chain now, Your Highness."

I sighed, realizing there was no way to warn her off without getting my mother raked through the coals. Besides, it's not like she stood a chance in hades of ever becoming a princess anyway. This was all just for show, to keep up appearances. I wasn't interested in any of these girls. I was only interested in...

I sighed in frustration and pushed the image of Alexis out of my head.

"Regardless," I said, gazing out at a sea of faces that bled together like watercolors, "none of the princes are all that eligible at the moment."

She giggled as if I'd told a lame joke she was pretending was very funny. "Of course they are! Only Prince Calvin is married. That leaves his three brothers and you wide open. The king has already hinted about the princes taking wives soon, now that they're approaching their thirties."

I blinked. Well, that was news to me. Very bad news.

"We're only twenty-eight," I managed to choke out. "That should give us at least two more years to decide."

As the dance ended, she slipped a piece of paper into the front pocket of my suit. "And when that time comes, you know exactly who will be waiting for you."

I honestly hoped I never saw that woman again. Not because I didn't like her, or she wasn't attractive, but because I wouldn't wish this life on anyone. The people of Blackwood didn't know what horrors lay beyond the palace gates. They didn't know how good their lives truly were. And it needed to stay that way.

As the songs continued, I was forced to deal with more and more ladies, politely turning down their advances after each and every dance. After a few hours, my arms and back were tired from holding my posture, and my legs and feet ached from gliding across the floor in shoes other than boots. Gods, I missed my work boots.

I glanced up at the fancy crystal clock that hung on the side wall above the musicians. It was almost midnight—almost time for this shitshow to finally be over.

My current dance partner and I twirled around the room with a little more pep in our step, but only because I was anxious to get the ball over with. We spun and swayed, making our way from the thrones over to the musicians, to the grand staircase where everyone had originally filtered in from.

And that's when I saw her.

An angelic vision in a thin, gold and silver gown. Her dark hair flowing in some magical breeze that clearly didn't blow by me. I loosened the collar of my dress shirt to try and cool my suddenly heated skin.

As she climbed that final step at the top of the stairs, I gazed from her sandaled feet up to her slim and shapely legs, over her tiny waist and plump breasts, up to her delicate throat and her kissable lips.

Fuck, she was beautiful.

I barely even registered that her husband and the other three Storm Princes were behind her. And for some reason, I didn't even care. I held my current dance partner out at arm's length and let her go, making my way toward Alexis at the top of the stairs.

I bowed to her, having the honor of watching her lips part in surprise and the guys glare fucking daggers my way. Then I turned to Calvin. "You won't mind if I steal a dance with your lovely wife? It is, after all, a ball in my honor."

Calvin's eyes narrowed, taking Alexis's forearm as he scanned the ballroom with suspicion. "And why the hell are we celebrating *you*? Least of all at the palace."

I cocked my head, feigning an arrogance I didn't even feel. "Oh, you haven't heard, *brother*? I'm the newest Prince of Blackwood."

CHAPTER 28

A LEXIS

No fucking way was this actually happening.

My mind went completely numb as Crissen's words played over and over in my head on repeat. *I'm the newest prince of Blackwood.*

Had we read that sneaky servant Frederick's clues all wrong back at Nightshade Castle? When he'd told me the story of the king's sterility and the possibility that the princes were immaculately conceived, I thought that meant the Storm King was onto the fact that the princes weren't really his sons, and neither were any of the bastards. But if the king believed Crissen to be one of his sons, then... maybe we got something backward or confused?

I put my hand in Crissen's and stepped closer.

"It's all right, darling," I said to Cal, trying to sound cool and collected. "It seems to be the final dance of the evening, and I have a few questions for *the new prince* anyway."

Before any of my guys could protest, Crissen was gliding me across the dance floor in a delicate waltz. Our movements were slow and fluid, the tune almost sad.

"How are you, Alexis?" he asked me with a grin.

I was surprised to find three dimples on his face: one in each cheek, and one in the middle of his chin at the base of his broad jaw. It was a strong face, but one that also somehow looked innocent.

"I'm okay," I said, unsure of how to actually address him. *Prince Crissen* just sounded all sorts of wrong, but then, I supposed that's who he was now. The Storm King didn't fuck around with insignificant details. He wouldn't be throwing this ball in Crissen's honor if he wasn't truly an official heir. "And you?"

"Never been better," he said with a smile. The only hint of sarcasm came from his eyes, which visibly darkened when he spoke the words. Plus, I could literally *feel* the malice radiating off him. He was emotionally wounded, and we all knew damn well who to blame.

I nodded. "As a prince of Blackwood, you've no doubt already learned how wonderful it is to be here."

"I dare say, I have."

His words were hollow, and my heart broke for him. No one deserved the torture, the manipulation, and the overwhelming guilt and responsibility that came with being a Blackwood royal. *No one.*

"What did you need to ask me?" he questioned, floating us around the room while the guys glared and made their way closer to the king.

I swallowed hard. "Have you felt anything... strange lately?"

His eyes sharpened on mine, and I knew in an instant that he had. "Why?"

"Was it like..." I continued curiously, "a blood-curdling

pain in your chest, stemming right from your heart? Did it make you feel like you could die at any moment? Or did it *keep you from* dying when you probably should have?"

He'd all but stopped moving, so I had to tug on his muscular arms to keep the dance going. We moved sluggishly as his brain matched my words to the events of the past few weeks, and something like relief washed over him.

"Was that... *you?*" he asked.

I glanced at my Storms as they approached the king. The latter stood up and held out his arms as if he were genuinely pleased to find his sons alive and well.

"It was all of us," I admitted, dragging my eyes back to Crissen. "We forged a bond of blood and magic, and we're pretty sure *you* got included in that."

"Me?" His blue eyes went wide, and for the first time, I realized there was a hint of green and yellow in them. "How could this happen?"

I closed my eyes and shook my head, opening them back up with remorse. "We weren't as careful as we should have been during the ceremony. Your blood... it was on Rob's hand, and..."

His body went suddenly rigid, and his gaze turned hard and cold as stone. "So, you mean to tell me, if I hadn't been punched in the face for no good reason, then I wouldn't have been magically bonded to you guys and none of this shit would have ever happened? I could have been living my life in peace back in Blackhaven?"

I shook my head. "No. The pain we felt coming from your end of the bond a few weeks ago was excruciating. You would be *dead* right now if you hadn't been bonded to us."

His jaw ticked. "And the pain *I* felt coming from *you guys* was equally as terrible. So, I assume it's safe to say we all kept each other alive... thanks to this bond."

I didn't want to admit it for some reason, to give him the

273

satisfaction of knowing he'd saved our lives, but I still felt I owed him the truth. "Yes."

"Stop the dance!" the Storm King shouted above the crowd. Fear liquified in my bones, despite the smile on his face. "My sons have returned! This calls for a toast!"

A row of servants rushed in, passing out small tin goblets of fruity pink wine to the attending guests, while a different servant passed out fancy crystal glasses to us royals. I eyed it carefully, sniffing its contents and wondering if it wasn't poisoned. Then I glanced around the room to all the smiling faces. No, the Storm King wouldn't kill us in front of everyone. He loved being revered during the day and reviled during the night.

I nodded to the brothers, and they nodded in return, silently telling me they figured the same thing—that, at least temporarily, we were safe. I turned to Crissen and held up my glass. He did the same, though to say he looked nervous would be the understatement of the year. The Storm King had apparently done a number on him already.

"To my sons, all *five* of them, and even our dear princess. Long may Storms reign."

"Long may Storms reign!" the crowd echoed back, and as a solid unit, everyone downed their wine.

I took a quick sip and swished the mixture around in my mouth, searching for any hint of a strange taste, but I found none.

Relax, Lex. He's not stupid. He's not going to off you in front of everyone. Just chill.

After giving myself that cheerful little pep talk, I downed the glass in one final gulp and returned it to the servant's tray.

"My lords and ladies," the king began, smiling wide, "commoners and merchants, I appreciate every single one of you for coming to Crissen's inaugural royal ball. It was an important day for us Storms, and we're honored to have shared it with you. I pray you have safe travels back to your manors and villages, and we hope to see you all again very soon. Good night!"

The crowd clapped and cheered, and servants began ushering people down the stairs.

That's when the king's snake-like eyes landed on me. That's when I could practically see the forked tongue and venomous fangs from behind his cunning smirk. That's when I knew I was in for a punishment like I'd never received before. It made my blood run cold, crackling through my veins as if it were chased by ice.

"What's wrong?" Crissen asked, putting a broad hand on my shoulder to steady me.

I shook my head. "Nothing. I just... have a bad feeling about our time here."

He nodded. "I feel that way every single day of my life."

I glanced at him and forced a smile. "I'm really sorry, Criss, for dragging you into this. I just have to believe it happened for a reason. If not, you'd be dead."

His brows rose, and for a moment, I was pretty sure he was going to say death would be the better option, but he didn't.

"I don't know what the Storm King might've tasked you with doing," I began hesitantly, "but you're going to have to stick with us from now on."

He blinked, and I could feel his jealousy and incredulity leaking into the air. "No, thank you. I'd hate to be a... *sixth* wheel? I don't even know..."

I cocked my head and put a hand on my hip, the silver and gold tassels of my gown shimmering in the chandelier light. "Are you magical?"

"What kind of question is that?"

I rolled my eyes. "Yes or no."

He sighed heavily, but instead of answering, he simply shook his head.

"That's what I thought. And that means you're going to need our protection. And yes, it will be mutually beneficial. We have ulterior motives, such as keeping you alive so that you don't accidentally drain us all of life somehow."

His blue eyes hardened. "I'm not a child, Alexis. I have no need to be babysat. I've done quite well at staying alive thus far in my life, and I certainly don't need your help now."

With that, he walked away, but before he could leave the room, the Storm King stopped him.

"Crissen!" he called, waving him over. Then he turned to me. "Alexis, you too. It's time for the real party to begin."

Cal and I shared a hopeless, knowing glance.

This was it. The moment of truth. The moment in which I stood up to Zacharias motherfucking Storm and refused to let him manipulate me in such a vile way ever again.

"What's this about?" Crissen asked me quietly as we joined the others.

I could barely even breathe, let alone speak. "You'll see soon enough."

"Calvin, Alexis," the king said, calling us to the front. When we reached his side, my hands were shaking uncontrollably. He led our group through the passageways to the outdated section of the castle where that dreadful red bed would be waiting with an audience of kidnapped queens held at knifepoint. "I trust you were able to secure the chimera egg?" he muttered in a deep whisper.

My heart raced as I nodded, and Cal opened the messenger bag at his side. A large, white egg covered in big, brown spots peeked from the shadows within, and the Storm King's eyes filled with sparkling fire.

"Excellent."

Hopefully that meant he wouldn't be able to tell our fake egg from the real thing.

We passed through the ancient hallway with the mounted animal heads and antique paintings, and the dread I felt this time around was ten times worse than before. Maybe I should have felt better now that I knew what lay before me, but I could only feel trepidation. It filled me to the brim, spilling over me in waves.

Like last time, once we entered the room, the king's guards grabbed the guys, pushed them onto their knees, and held a blade to their throats.

"What the fuck is going on?" Crissen demanded, thrashing violently in his guard's grasp.

He hadn't been there last time, so it was no surprise to me that he was the only one flailing about and trying to break free. Even though it was *my* doom about to play out, I couldn't help but feel bad for him. This couldn't be much easier to watch than it was to experience.

"Silence!" the Storm King shouted, his malevolence echoing off the stone walls of the circular chamber. Now that his citizens were gone, he clearly felt no need for benevolence.

Crissen's mouth snapped shut in an instant, and his bluish-hazel eyes scanned the room with suspicious shock.

I followed suit, glancing from Caroline to Delilah, from Bibi to Rosemary, from Ashlynn to Francesca, then over to a woman I didn't recognize, one I assumed must've been Crissen's mother. She was pretty, but it was clear her life hadn't been easy. Her features were hard, rough, and worn out despite the sad and horrified look in her hazel eyes. Her dark hair didn't shine; her tanned skin didn't glow; her off-white teeth didn't sparkle.

But that was all who I saw—the queens.

No Gemma. No little Lilah or her mother. Their absences

terrified me. Each passing second was like another heavy stone being added to my pile of fears and worries.

I spun around and faced the king, who seemed to be waiting on my upcoming question. "Where is Gemma? Where's my cousin and her mother?"

His smile stretched, crinkling the corners of his eyes with warm madness.

"You had one month to return with the egg," he said easily. "When you failed to uphold your end of the deal, I was forced to uphold mine."

No!

My heart shattered like glass, and my mind crashed to a halt in an instant. The whole room narrowed into a darkened tunnel as my vision distorted and my breathing shallowed. My limbs shook like branches in a storm, and I was suddenly freezing cold all the way to the bones.

My throat was wound so tight I thought my vocal cords might snap from the strain.

"You killed... *a baby?*"

CHAPTER 29

*M*y question was barely more than a whisper of pain, and his cruel response was a metaphorical slap to the face.

"No, Alexis, *you* killed a baby, and her mother, because you were careless and irresponsible. You didn't take your duty as Princess of Blackwood seriously, and despite the fact that you knew the price, you refused to cooperate anyway. It's a travesty."

A scalding hot tear dripped from my eye, landing on my cheek with an inaudible hiss.

"And Gemma?"

As soon as the bastard's smile broadened, I knew he would say she was gone.

I had no chance in hades of stopping the sobs that wrecked me. My knees gave out, and I crumpled to the floor in a boneless heap of misery and despair. Cal quickly dropped to a knee to help me, but I couldn't even feel his touch. I was so numb.

"Gemma had a rather unfortunate run-in with a wolf," the Storm King informed me.

"You're the wolf!" I screamed, hatred and anger burning through every cell in my body. "You're the hideous beast with vicious claws and venomous teeth! You're the sadistic bastard who makes his son fuck in front of his mothers and brothers, the sick asshole who kills children for fun, the tyrant who rules with a silver tongue of lies and an iron fist of injustice—"

As I spouted off the last word, his fist connected with my cheek hard enough to split my skin. I crashed to the ground, seeing colorful spots dotting in and out of my vision.

Cal rushed to protect me, daring to challenge his father for the first time in years, but despite his strength and mountainous size, the Storm King took him down in an instant. He hit the ground with a sickening crack, the back of his head connecting violently with the stone floor. My eyes went wide with terror, but as I scrambled over to him, I was relieved to find he was still conscious.

No way in hell was this normal or even possible... without magic. But the Storm King wasn't *supposed* to have magic. Something was seriously not right here.

"Do not ever say such vile things about your king again," Zacharias threatened me, rubbing his knuckles before shaking them out. Mine and Cal's blood coated his skin, and it somehow made me feel violated. "As for the servant, Gemma, she really was eaten by a wolf, you can ask anyone. Crissen?"

I turned to him, staring through the one eye that hadn't begun sealing itself shut. Raw emotion poured from his eyes, reaching for me in a way I couldn't understand. Then he nodded.

"Ladies?" the king asked his wives. One by one, after carefully waiting for the blades at their throats to lower, they too nodded.

It was strange, not knowing what to believe. *I* sure as hell wouldn't defy that psycho if I had a blade to my neck, and yet, there was something so painfully honest swirling in the depths of their eyes that I was terrified it was actually true.

Gemma was... gone?

My very best friend, the girl who was there for me when no one else was, the girl who made me laugh no matter how dark our circumstances seemed, the girl who made me feel at home and at ease no matter where we were as long as we were together... was gone?

Her image pervaded my mind. A beautiful girl with bouncy blonde curls and cheerful blue eyes, a smile bright as the sun, and a soul full of wisdom well beyond her optimistic years. I could practically hear her laughter echoing against my skull, haunting me—a sound that I'd never hear again.

"Get up," the king commanded Cal and me, "and get in the bed. We don't have all night."

The two of us slowly stood, but as Cal removed his shirt, my fists tightened at my side. "No."

The Storm King smiled—an actual fucking smile, as if he'd been hoping and waiting for me to defy him this whole time. "Oh?"

Cal grabbed my bicep and tried to yank me back to my senses. "Alexis, please. Let's just get this over with. We survived it once; we can survive it again."

But I held firm, my gaze locked onto the king. "Who will you kill this time if I refuse?"

The king sighed and removed a scroll from the inside pocket of his robes. The parchment unrolled and stretched out across the floor a few feet. My heart clenched. The son of a bitch had clearly done more research since I first arrived.

"It would appear you have another aunt left on your mother's side—Marianne. She has a husband, three daughters, and one son. I think they'll do nicely."

The children in question ranged in age from three to ten.

How could he be so disgustingly cruel? As the gods-awful images of murdered children passed through my mind, I was slammed with a tide of guilt and nausea. I bent over, squeezed my knees, and puked on the stone floor.

If I was ever going to survive this man, I was going to need a stronger stomach.

The king tsked disapprovingly. "That's unfortunate for you, eh, Calvin? Now you get to smell and taste vomit while you sully her."

Cal growled from my side, and I could tell he was thinking about having another go at his father, despite the fact that he was clearly magically endowed at the moment. "It's not like that, and you know it. I would never do anything to hurt Alexis. She's my *wife*. That means something to me that it never meant to you."

"All that means is that you are weak."

"He's not," I said calmly, rising back up to my full height. My composure was eerie, even to me. "None of your sons are weak, and neither am I. You'll not be controlling us like this anymore, or ever again."

His smile broadened as his dark eyes narrowed. "Are you refusing to bear Storm heirs?"

I swallowed hard. "No. But I'm refusing to do it *this* way. I am not an object for you to manipulate, and I am certainly not your monthly sexual entertainment."

The Storm King sniggered. "Trust me, *Princess*, I've seen better sexual entertainment from the squirrels in the woods. Don't flatter yourself. But, regardless to whatever you may or may not be thinking or feeling, I am still, in fact, the King of Blackwood. You will listen to me, no matter how ridiculous or appalling the request, and you will do it however I see fit. So if I order you to strip...."

He suddenly turned violent and enraged, clawing at my gown and tearing it down the front.

"Then you will strip!" His face reddened, and an angry vein bulged in the center of his forehead. "And if I tell you to fuck my son while the queens watch, then you damn well better fuck him!"

Shocked, I tried to cover myself, but he grabbed my arm and threw me toward the bed. I half landed on the silky red sheets, but I quickly slipped off and crashed to the floor. Cal lost his shit and attacked savagely, throwing a punch at his father's head, but the Storm King dodged it with unbelievable ease. While Cal recovered his balance from his missed swing, Zacharias ducked down and jabbed his son in the side, probably hard enough to crack a rib.

As they fought, the other Storms struggled to escape the guards. In addition to the knives at their throats, their hands had also been tied behind their backs, so it was no easy feat. But they seemed to be making headway, so I directed my attention back to Cal and Zacharias.

A snarl escaped my mouth, and my lips curled furiously.

"Fire!" I cried, but was horrified to find *no* curly peach flames erupting from my palm.

The Storm King threw his head back and laughed, a belly-shaking thing that rattled me to the bone. He'd somehow stemmed my power.

That motherfucking wine! It must've been laced with something—not *deadly*, but something equally as dangerous. A touch of chimera venom, perhaps? A potion from his insidious sorcerer? Some other plant or animal or mineral I'd yet to discover? Nothing off limits anymore, nor would anything surprise me.

"Try again, Alexis," he taunted as he wiped the laughter tears from his eyes. "The look on your face was absolutely priceless."

Rob was the first to break free from his guard, headbutting the man hard enough to send him crumpling to the floor in a boneless heap. He quickly turned to his father and closed his eyes, searching the astral plane—or so I assumed—for any sort of spirit he might be able to manipulate in our favor. But when his eyes snapped open and fury radiated through the stormy gray depths, I knew he too had been unsuccessful in using his power.

He quickly changed tactics, spinning on his heel and helping Dan break away from his own guard. Once Dan was free, they helped untie Ben. And after him, they loosened the bonds of the queens and even Crissen.

Rob rushed to help Cal fight his father, while Ben and Dan tried to clear the rest of the room.

"Run!" Dan shouted at them.

The queens didn't hesitate to flee, scampering from the room in a delicate, single-file line. But Crissen lagged behind, staring at us as if he wanted to join the fight.

"Go!" Dan shouted, jabbing a finger toward the exit.

"You're going to need my help," Criss protested, his chest puffing out a bit as honor seemed to fill him.

Ben put a hand on his shoulder and made meaningful eye contact. "The best help you can give us is by *staying alive*."

That's when Ben's words seemed to dawn on him. The likelihood that we would be slaughtered was surprisingly quite high, given the circumstances, and the only hope we had of survival was sharing any drop of life Crissen could spare us.

"Go to your room and lie down," Ben instructed him. "I have a feeling it's going to be a rough couple of weeks."

With that, Crissen nodded and darted from the room.

By the time I turned back around, Cal and Rob were both on the floor, struggling to get up.

Ben and Dan acknowledged that as their cue to take over the fight, and they both attacked at the same time. It was an absolutely bizarre sight, watching that tussle. While their fists and knees and elbows *did* make contact with the Storm King's body, there wasn't any bodily reaction from him. It was as if his very skin was made of steel, unbreakable, unfeeling, and untouchable. Or perhaps there was some magical aura surrounding and protecting him?

Either way, every last one of the guys were down a few minutes later, and then it was just me. I squared my shoulders and widened my stance, waiting for *him* to attack *me*. It seemed smarter than rushing to my death; though in hindsight, maybe it would have been better to just get it over with.

The king circled me, like a snake about to squeeze and suffocate his prey, and I twitched like a cornered mouse unsure if trying to run would somehow kill me faster.

"You never should have said those vile things about me," he chastised coldly.

I held my ground and watched him for any signs of attack. "Maybe you shouldn't *be* those vile things if you don't want to be associated with them?"

His eyes narrowed, and his fingers twitched, rotating the rings on his hands so they'd inflict maximum damage once they connected with my skin and bone.

"My rule would be ineffective if no one obeyed my commands," he explained, slowly revolving around me. "I cannot allow anyone to defy me, not even my sons—especially not them. And definitely not you."

I held my chin up high, trying to watch his movements while still appearing unaffected. "You could rule in a just way, and people would obey you because they respected you, rather than feared you."

He chuckled and made his way behind my back. I didn't trust him, not one freaking bit, but for some reason I felt the need to be brave. I stared straight ahead, exhaling a massive, weighted breath when he reappeared on my other side and I was still unharmed.

"I tried that once—a few times, actually—in my youth." When he reached the front of me, he finally stopped circling, planting his feet and staring intently, unnervingly, into my eyes. "If it had worked, obviously, we wouldn't be having this conversation right now. *Fear* is a more effective tactic than *respect*. It's been proven true time and time again."

His arm was around my throat in an instant, his inner elbow blocking my windpipe.

Damn me for letting my guard down for even a second!

I reared back and smashed my head into his nose, but nothing happened—no crack, no blood, no shouting. Nothing. He squeezed even tighter. I could feel my face turning red as the pressure built in my veins. Attempting another tactic, I elbowed him in the ribs. Again, nothing. I punched backward into his crotch, but his junk was solid as iron.

This was it. I was going to syphon the life out of every Storm alive and then finally die myself, effectively killing us all in one moment of stupidity and weakness.

Anger fumed and boiled beneath my skin as the darkness of oblivion crept closer. I hated him. I needed to end him. *Kill the king.* Rory's words... or perhaps now they were mine? The phrase echoed in my head like a mantra. *Kill the king. Kill the king.* Kill that motherfucking bastard once and for all.

All at once, the pressure exploded. I sucked in a deep, ragged breath as curly peach flames broke out across my flesh, singeing the king's arm and chest. He cursed and jumped backward, eyes wide when I turned around and glared at him.

Then his gaze lost focus as something seemingly dawned on him. "You puked."

"So, there *was* something laced in the wine." It wasn't a question. I didn't expect him to admit to anything.

"You really shouldn't have done that."

He lashed out at me, but now that my strength was back, I dodged him quickly. That's when I saw a strange weapon gripped in his fist. It was white and curved, wide at the base and deadly sharp at the tip.

I didn't have a weapon. I didn't have a shield. I'd left my ax back in my room along with my rucksack and dirty traveling clothes. So basically, I didn't have a chance. Still, I fought like hell as long as I could. I shot him with fire over and over, but it seemed his exterior defenses had somehow been refortified. Like before, it was as if his skin were impenetrable—even against fire.

All I did was turn a disgusting situation into something horrific. The more I used my power, the more the side effects kicked in. The guys were a heap of painful moans and unconsciousness on the floor, which really only left the fucking Storm King to target.

No! I screamed internally as revulsion and abhorrence filled me. *Don't you dare single in on him!*

But, unfortunately, I couldn't control that particular aspect.

I forced myself into defense, blocking his white tooth-like weapon with my bare forearms, because I knew I couldn't afford to use my power any more than I already had. If I ended up fucking the Storm King tonight, I'd never be able to live with myself. I'd rather drink chimera blood and plunge from the top of the Dryroot Canyons.

He readjusted his grip on the white weapon, his forearms flexing where his robes had crept up his arm. The way his muscles moved momentarily distracted me, making me wonder what it'd feel like to rake my fingers up his body.

Gods damn it, this was repulsive!

It was almost a relief when he finally stabbed the damn thing into my chest, causing me to crash to the floor in an instant, surrounded by an ever-growing puddle of blood. My eyes blurred, slipping in and out of focus. I glanced right and somehow managed to noticed that none of my guys were moving anymore.

No...

My internal plea was weak. I was barely able to concentrate on it—or anything else for that matter—as I quickly drifted closer to the blackness of unconsciousness.

The last thing I remembered was the Storm King carefully slinging the bag with the chimera egg over his shoulder and leaving us to die.

CHAPTER 30

$\mathscr{CB}$

$\mathcal{A}$SHER

ONE HOUR EARLIER...

AFTER I FLITTED AWAY FROM THE GROUP IN BIRD FORM, leaving them to deposit their horses and make their way into the palace, I scanned the rooms in search of Cal's.

One servant was already in there hurrying to lay out his clothes, and not long after, a second servant entered carrying a tray of meats and chocolates.

I waited anxiously for them both to leave, and as soon as they did, I swooped into the room and crashed into the wall with enough force to shatter my skull. The pain was short-lived, though, and soon I was back in my human form, scrambling to find a hiding place. I lurched under the bed, tugging on the sheet skirts to hide me a little better when I heard voices out in the hall.

If those fucking servants hadn't dawdled so long, I wouldn't be cutting it this damned close.

The voices carried on for a few moments, their tones low and muffled so I couldn't make out what they were saying. Eventually, Cal walked in and shut the door, depositing the messenger bag at his feet—directly beside the godsforsaken bed.

I couldn't believe my luck.

His clothes hit the floor, and he quickly padded over to the shower and turned on the water.

This was it. I reached out and stole the fake egg, tucking it into the mattress above my head, where—hopefully—Cal would never think to look. Then I called on my magic and focused on the bag. In a rush of adrenaline, my body dematerialized and floated through the air, swirling like a cyclone of golden dust... and I landed—in egg form—half in and half out of the sack.

Shit!

It wasn't how Cal had left it. He was going to notice the change right away and call me out on my bullshit. He'd probably kick my ass too, then forbid me from doing anything so stupid ever again.

Basically, he was going to ruin everything.

I pushed at the inside of my shell, surprised to find that it tipped slightly.

Yes!

I pushed again and got my egg a bit further into the bag.

Then Cal turned off the water.

No!

I pushed harder, putting all my pathetic baby strength into rolling that massive eggshell over, and while I *did* make progress, it still wasn't enough. I was only about three-quarters of the way in now.

Cal dried off and dropped the towel on the floor. I couldn't see anything through the shell, but I could hear and smell everything plain as day. The shuffling of clothing, the spicy scent of the meats on the tray, a spray of cologne, a deep sigh of nervousness.

Yeah, you and me both, bro.

I heard his footsteps drawing nearer, felt the vibrations of them echoing on the stone floor. I closed my eyes, waiting for him to realize what I'd done... but he didn't. He gently rolled my egg the rest of the way into the bag and shouldered it.

I cracked open an eye. Holy fucking shit! My plan was going to work after all! He must've just assumed the egg had rolled out a bit when he dropped the bag on the floor. I could hardly breathe through my enormous relief.

From there, I listened as Cal met Alexis and the rest of our brothers in the hallway. I swayed back and forth as he carried the bag down the corridors and stairways and then up the grand staircase that led into the ballroom.

Everything was louder there, but despite the buzzing noise of voices, I could hear the melody of a beautiful tune playing in the background and the laughter of some nearby party guests.

It was calming, swaying at Cal's side as he walked, while the melody twinkled all around us, enveloping me like a blanket of warmth and comfort. Soon my chimera eyes were drooping shut.

Son of a bitch, no!

But I couldn't help it. It was difficult to fight the natural instincts of the animals I became, and babies especially.

Before I knew it, I was fast asleep.

~

OVERWHELMING PAIN AWOKE ME FROM MY PEACEFUL DREAMS. It gripped my heart like a vice, squeezing until I thought it might burst.

The blood bond.

Oh shit.

I scrambled to crack a small hole in my shell, but it took a ridiculous amount of work; I was a baby, after all. I hacked and hacked at the damned thing with my claws for I didn't even know how long, listening in terror to the sounds of fighting in the background.

When I finally knocked out a chunk of shell just big enough to see through, that's when I saw Alexis crash to the stone floor in a barely conscious heap. It took every ounce of willpower I possessed to keep from bursting from my egg in a fit of rage. My protective instincts were soaring high, urging me to avenge my fallen lover and my brothers, but I knew that as long as *I* survived, *they* would survive. Plus, we really needed this plan to work if we ever hoped to defeat the Storm King.

So, I forced myself to stay still.

The king strutted over to me and scooped up the bag that held my egg. He stared down at me with far too much interest and excitement, then shut the flap and started moving.

Everything was shadowed, and I couldn't see anything aside from the inside of the bag. I closed my eyes and listened instead, hearing the loud thump of his boots on the marble floors of the palace.

Several servants muttered, "Good evening, Your Majesty," probably while kissing their damn toes in a bow so low, but the Storm King didn't reply; he just kept on walking.

A few minutes later, he paused, and I heard the faint squeak of a door opening followed by a fresh breeze. His footsteps were quieter then, possibly crossing the lawn, but to where? The barns? The woods? Into a carriage? Into town?

He kept walking until his steps grew louder as twigs and dry leaves crackled under his feet.

Okay, so woods it is then.

I had no idea how far he'd walked, but it was long enough for the dim light in the messenger bag to fade into the inky blackness of night. Insects chirped peacefully all around. Nocturnal birds cooed from their perches in the trees. There was absolutely nothing I could do to keep my drowsy, baby chimera ass from falling asleep.

Again.

~

SOMETIME LATER, I AWOKE WITH A *THUD*.

The Storm King had dropped the bag—with me in it—and suddenly, I could see again. Not much, considering it was still dark as fuck, but at least the material of the bag had slipped enough for me to *attempt* squinting through the darkness.

There was a tall stone arch standing in the middle of a forest, but beyond that there was... nothing. It wasn't attached to anything that I could see—no walls, no columns, not even a tree. It just stood there, silent and alone. It looked like any other ruin to me, but since the Storm King apparently thought it was important, I knew better than to dismiss it at face value.

He stepped forward and rapped his knuckles on the stones, as if knocking on a door. He waited, but nothing happened. So, he knocked again, crossing his arms and tapping his foot. Suddenly, the stones illuminated, and a door appeared, opening slowly.

A man stood on the other side with mussed-up dark hair

and groggy eyes. He rubbed at his temples as he tried to focus on my father. "What do you want?"

The Storm King cleared his throat and tried to make himself look taller. "I've brought the chimera egg you requested."

"No shit?" The man squinted, as if trying to see clearly through bleary eyes. Then he turned around and called into the space beyond. "Dion! The king is back with the egg!"

"Dude," a muffled voice called back, "I'm trying to sleep. What time is it?"

"Early," the dark-haired man replied. Then he brought his attention back to my father. "I didn't think you had it in you."

The Storm King scoffed. "Of course I did."

Yeah. Right. He was a pussy-ass bitch who'd sent his own kids to their doom on his pathetic behalf. And for what? That's what I needed to know.

Another man appeared in the doorway—Dion, most likely—ruffling the tight ombre curls piled atop his head. The bottom half of his head was shaved short, giving him a chill yet sophisticated air. "Let's see this egg, then."

Suddenly, I was floating through the air on my way to the Dion guy. He took me in his smooth, brown hands and spun me around. I watched the forest swirl by through the crack in my shell, then I stopped in front of his face as he scrutinized me. "It's real."

The dark-haired man chuckled. "You did good, Zachy-boy."

I glanced at my father, grinning as he visibly bristled at their casual nickname. Whoever these guys were, they clearly had much more power and authority than he did. He'd never have let them speak to him in such a way otherwise. He wouldn't have been on a mission for them either. It was kind of odd though, because they didn't look any older than me and my brothers.

"I suppose you want your potion now," the dark-haired man mused.

The Storm King bowed slightly. "I would, very much, yes."

He passed the king a tiny teardrop-shaped vial with a cork in the top.

"You know the rules," the dark-haired man said. "It'll only last a month. If you want another vial, you'll have to complete another task."

The king nodded curtly. "What might the next task be?"

The man rubbed his chin theatrically. "How about the Eye of the Sea."

The Storm King's brows furrowed. "The Eye of the Sea? What's that?"

Dion held up his hand. "No hints. That's cheating. Now go."

Without another word, my father scurried off into the night like a reprimanded child. It was incredible. I'd only ever seen him as an unbreakable monster, so it was fucking delightful to see him so frail and pathetic.

Dion sighed and passed the other man my egg. "Why the fuck did you want a chimera egg again?"

The man sniggered. "I don't know. It'd make a pretty badass pet, don't you think?"

Dion stared flatly. "A deadly pet that could kill you at any second maybe."

"Oh, that's the fun of it," the other man insisted. "What's life without a little danger and risk?"

Dion sniffed out a laugh. "You're fucked up, Ares, you know that?"

"Yeah, but you love it."

Dion shook his head, sending his spiraled curls springing. "I *tolerate* it because you're the only one who parties as hard as I do, and I need a solid wingman."

Ares patted Dion on the back and shut the door behind

us, escorting me into another world entirely, another dimension.

"You know Hydratica has the Eye of the Sea at the moment, right?" Dion asked blandly.

Ares chuckled and set my egg down on a random stand. "Of course I do. Why do you think I chose it?"

"Honestly?" Dion asked, trudging through a sea of passed-out bodies and overturned bottles of alcohol. "I thought you wanted it as a fish tank decoration."

"Oh, now there's a good idea."

I watched in awe as Dion clapped his hands and the mess just magically vanished—including their sleeping guests.

"But I also just want to fuck with that dude," Ares continued, as if his friend hadn't just enacted the most badass magic I'd ever seen. "He's so hell-bent on ruling that world; it's going to be epic to pull the rug out from under his feet. Plus, it's been a while since they've had a good war there, and my previous attempts have all fallen through."

Dion smirked. "Those demigods are giving you a run for your money."

Ares glared, and I'd swear I saw literal fire blazing behind his darkened eyes. "Why don't you go fuck yourself, Dionysus?"

Dion merely chuckled, completely unfazed by the War God's anger, then clapped his hands once more.

Suddenly, all new décor appeared: flashing purple lights, trays of fresh alcohol, new leather furniture, and even a different set of scantily dressed partygoers. Music filled the air in deep, vibrating waves, rattling small chunks of shell right off of me, and I couldn't help the wide-eyed sense of wonder that overcame me.

Whatever this crazy place was, I knew one thing for sure:

The Greek gods were not as fucking *gone* as we'd once thought.

THE END of book two

∾

Continue the hot and heavy adventure with Alexis and her Storm Princes in Storm Chaser!

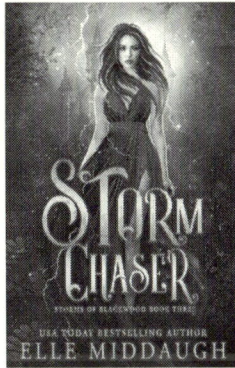

AFTERWORD

I hope you're enjoying this crazy-sexy journey, because I sure as hell am! Alexis and the Storm Princes are seriously my new favorite characters! Xoxo. I can't wait for you to see what they get up to in book 3 – *Storm Chaser*!

If you liked this book, I hope you'll consider leaving a review. Pretty please with a cherry on top? :)

To stay updated on new releases and everything bookish, feel free to join: *Elle Middaugh — Reader Group*!

ACKNOWLEDGMENTS

A huge HUGE thank you to these amazing people: Michelle, Jess, and Brittany—alpha readers extraordinaire! Lori—the best cover designer ever! lol Virginia (and the staff of Hot Tree Editing)—as always, you ladies are amazing!

Thank you to my family for being so supportive as I write my ass off lately.

And finally, eternal thanks to my fans... without you guys, and your love of Alexis and the Storms, none of this would be possible.

Xoxo

ALSO BY ELLE MIDDAUGH

Storms of Blackwood Series

Taken by Storm

Stormy Nights

Storm Chaser

Snow Storms holiday novella

Perfect Storms

The Mage Shifter War Duet

Fae Captive

Fae Unchained

Cruel Fae Court

Heartless Liar (coming soon)

Callous Prince (coming soon)

Depraved King (coming soon)

Fierce Queen (coming soon)

Enchanted Royals Series

A Crown of Blood and Ashes

Trials of Enchantment

Queen Witch

The Essential Elements

Elemental Secrets

Elemental Lies

Elemental Betrayal

Standalones

Siren Awakened

IF YOU LIKED STORMS OF
BLACKWOOD BECAUSE...

— It was a Reverse Harem

Then you might want to try **the Mage Shifter War Duet** that I wrote with the insanely talented Ann Denton!

— It was Steamy

Then you might want to try **A Crown of Blood and Ashes**! It's a sexy, (loose) fairytale retelling of Tristan and Isolde!

— It was Humorous

Then you might want to check out **Queen Witch**! There's a cat familiar in there that's pretty snarky and hilarious lol

CONNECT WITH ELLE

Website:
www.ellemiddaugh.com

Newsletter:
www.ellemiddaugh.com/newsletter

Facebook Group:
www.facebook.com/groups/ellemiddaugh

ABOUT THE AUTHOR

Elle Middaugh is a USA Today bestselling author living in the Pennsylvania Allegheny Mountains with her wonderful husband and three beautiful children. She spends most of her time raising kids, writing stories, playing video games, reading, and attempting to keep a clean house.

She's a proud Navy wife, a frazzle-brained mother, a fan of health and fitness, a lover of tea and red wine, and a believer in happily-ever-afters.

Sassy. Seductive. Spellbinding.
www.ellemiddaugh.com

facebook.com/ellemiddaugh
twitter.com/ellemiddaugh
instagram.com/Ellemiddaugh

67161473R00189